Secrets at the House by the Creek

BOOKS BY ELIZABETH BROMKE

Elizabeth
BROMKE
Secrets at the
House by
the Creek

Bookouture

Published by Bookouture in 2022

An imprint of Storyfire Ltd.
Carmelite House
50 Victoria Embankment
London EC4Y 0DZ

www.bookouture.com

ISBN: 978-1-80314-651-5
eBook ISBN: 978-1-80314-650-8

For Rory "Story" Engelhard

PROLOGUE

PRESENT DAY

Morgan Jo

Morgan Jo Coyle let a sip of white wine trickle over her tongue like a fresh creek.

Her nostrils flared at the tartness, and she pouted her full, pink lips as she let the fluid spill around her mouth before swallowing it. Once she did, she took a deep breath through her nose and shook her long, chestnut waves back.

"Okay," Morgan said, closing her eyes and mentally groping for the right words to describe what she'd experienced.

Only recently had Morgan learned how to *taste* wine, as if it weren't a natural thing but a skill that came after practice. She needed a lot more practice.

Across the farmhouse table sat Morgan's fiancé, Emmett Dawson. Although they'd only been engaged a short couple of months, Morgan and Emmett had loved each other since they were sun-kissed kids running wild at Moonshine Creek together. It didn't escape Morgan that she had her cousin, Geddy, to thank for that. He might be a rascal, but at least Geddy was a good enough person to have attracted a buddy like

Emmett and keep that friendship alive long enough for Morgan to wind her way back home.

Broad-shouldered and blond with eyes the color of the sea, Emmett could have stepped out of a fairy tale. Instead, he'd just stepped out of the barn at Moonshine Creek.

In a year's time, the family farm had opened up like a newly bloomed buttercup. Though it was never a closed-off place, the previous years had seen the Nelson–Coyle property go cold with disuse and age. Farms weren't like wine. They couldn't just set and improve. They needed constant attention.

When Morgan had returned the summer before, when her Memaw Essie had taken a turn for the worse, she'd found the rambling grounds had fallen apart. Even with Morgan's mom, CarlaMay, at the helm of the place, the grass had grown over, the crops were weedy or rotted out. The outbuildings consumed in rust and cobwebs, dirt and dust.

Of course, the big house itself was every bit the same as it had been when she was a young woman—when she'd still lived there. Unlike the grounds, which were the shell of the property, the house was its soul. Everlasting. Even in her later years, Memaw Essie had kept up with maintenance, putting Morgan's cousins to work whenever a household issue arose. CarlaMay cleaned weekly and waxed the wooden floors as if she were tending to a museum. Which the big house *was*. It was one of Brambleberry Creek's oldest homes. It had seen the birth of the small town, the changes, and it had lived on to welcome home its granddaughter, Morgan Jo Coyle.

Presently, Morgan and Emmett sat together in the big house at the long wooden farmhouse table. Situated just off the kitchen where the table stretched was neither a dining room nor a breakfast nook. Instead, it was its own space, sun-drenched thanks to a bank of picture windows and easily accessible from the stove and oven, fridge and cutting board. Memaw had always believed that mealtimes weren't about one person serving the others, but about everybody working, eating, laughing, and crying, *together*.

Closing her eyes, Morgan tried her best to tune into the sensation of her sip. She opened her eyes and looked at Emmett. "Notes of..." she tried, squinting and biting her lower lip as she gave it one more think. "Peach?" Hope lifted her mouth into a weak smile.

Emmett referred to his laminated sheet. "If you're tasting *fruit*, then it must be..."

Morgan groaned and squeezed her eyes shut. She felt like she was taking the SAT again, but as a thirty-one-year-old whose future relied not on her ability to compute algebra but on her skill at distinguishing Malbec from Riesling. "Moscato," she said at last. Of all the wines their little operation had made so far, Moscato was Morgan's favorite. It reminded her of summers on the farm—the easy, sweet days that stretched on endlessly. Their Moscato was perhaps going to be the bestseller, once things got rolling both with the vineyard *and* the winery and tasting services.

"Ding, ding, ding," Emmett squeezed her hand atop the table. "Notes of peach. What else?"

The test wasn't over.

"I'd say it's definitely *sweet*. Lower acid? But it *is* crisp."

He nodded, encouragingly.

Morgan went on. "The mouthfeel is more like sweet tea than whole milk. So it's light-bodied."

"Can you be more specific?"

"Yes." Morgan plucked the stem of her glass and lifted it first to her nose, again, then to her lips. She took a longer sip this time. Again, she let the liquid coat her tongue and slip behind her teeth before it slid down her throat. Her eyes remained closed. After several seconds, she said, "Crisp but delicate. Sweet with a light body and a smooth if short finish." She opened her eyes and smiled brighter at Emmett.

He studied her soberly.

"What?" Morgan's face started to fall.

"You *know* this. You're doing great." Emmett laid the card down and picked up the glass Morgan had tasted from, sipping it too. "And so is this."

It was a miracle. After just two weeks, Morgan and Emmett, together with help from Amber, Julia, Geddy, and Uncle Garold, had fashioned a decent wine sampling from their very own supply of heritage fruit.

What's more, Morgan could *identify* it.

Everything related to the family business was shaping up nicely. Thanks to the heritage vines out at Uncle Gary's, they had the fruit. Thanks to Grandad's notes and Geddy's knowledge, they had the recipes.

In fact, all of the batches of wine planned for the gala were mixed and ready. Some, like the one they were testing from now, were already fermented well enough to sample. No, the wine wasn't aged—that could only come with time, and it was a part of their vineyard and winery that Morgan knew needed to be established up front. Customers and guests would have to know that this business was only just emerging. The wine was, well, *fresh*. Not ideal, but it was genuine. It was a *start*.

Now that everything was set and fermenting, all Morgan and her team could do was wait. Well, wait and pray. And *plan*. There was always more planning to be done.

Morgan pulled a notepad and pen in front of her as Emmett finished the wine.

"Okay, so we're looking at October eighth for a soft opening."

"Soft opening," Emmett echoed. "What exactly does that mean?"

"It means a limited opening. Limited hours. Perhaps we only open for, like, two to four hours, for example."

"Okay. Who comes?" he asked.

"Again, it's *limited*."

"Limited as in we cap attendance, or—?"

"I don't know." Thoughtfully, she looked up at him. "How do you limit who can come?"

"You make tickets?" he asked.

"That's maybe tacky." She fell quiet and pensive a moment. "But yeah. Something like tickets." Her face lit up. "Invitations!"

He smiled. "There you go. It's all about *branding*, right?" His smile was wry, and she gave him a playful scowl.

"It *is* about branding. Especially in this day and age." She started her list on her pad as she recounted what they had so far. "Limited time. Limited attendance. Maybe extra fancy, too. But not as fancy as a *grand* opening. More like an intimate affair."

"Intimate," Emmett purred. "I like the sound of that."

She smiled but ignored him. "Hors d'oeuvres. Soft music. Oh!" She scratched something out on her pad then flashed her eyes back up to Emmett. "The invitation list should include a few key players. For like... a preview. We could even call it a preview. Where local bloggers or foodie types come and get a sneak peek. Right?"

"Right." He was just playing along now, but Morgan didn't mind. Emmett's face pulled down. "What about friends and family?"

"What about them?"

"Do we invite them, too?" he asked.

"Obviously," Morgan answered, dismissively. In her mind, the event was as much for friends and family as it was for anyone. With friends and family, she could ensure the atmosphere was convivial and warm. Photographs would reflect that, and—"We'll have to hire a photographer."

"What'll you wear?" Emmett asked.

After she added that note to her pad, she looked at him and

saw humor twirling in his eyes. Morgan frowned. "I guess that's important, too."

"Maybe I'll rent a tux." Emmett finished the last of the wine and pinned his stare on Morgan.

"A tux?"

He pulled her left hand across the table and examined her engagement ring. It was an heirloom from Morgan's late grandmother, Essie. She followed Emmett's stare, admiring the pretty gem and feeling the powers of her past like the ring was magic.

Emmett dipped his face to her hand and pressed his lips against it. When he came back up, his eyes danced with enchantment.

"A *tux*?" she repeated.

"Limited time frame," he began, dragging his words out tantalizingly. He held out a thumb as if he was counting. Then he unfurled his index finger. "Limited attendance. Soft music. Refreshments. A *photographer*."

"I'm listening." Filled with the humming sensation of delicious anticipation, Morgan smirked and lowered her pen to the notebook.

"It sounds an awful lot like..."

Morgan bit her lower lip and slipped her fingers through his, interlocking their hands together. Then she finished his sentence for him. "A *wedding*?"

CHAPTER ONE

PRESENT DAY

Amber

Amber Lee Taylor woke up feeling different than she had the last month or so.

A good different. Gone was the consistent first-thing-in-the-morning headache. Her appetite rushed in, as did the craving for coffee.

All signs pointed to happiness, Amber knew. Finally, months after cutting her toxic ex-fiancé, Grant Maycomb, out of her life, Amber was free. Free not only of the stress that he brought about, but also free of the feeling that without him, she was somehow less.

Amber sat up, took in a deep breath, let it out, and smiled.

Today was going to be a very good day.

As such, she needed to *look* very good.

Setting about her morning routine, Amber gave extra-careful thought to every step.

First, a shower. The long kind that included a shampoo, cream rinse, body exfoliation, shave, the works.

After, she towel-dried her hair, applied sunscreen—her aunt

CarlaMay (Morgan Jo's mother) had taught her about the necessity of sunscreen—and smoothed lotion over her skin.

Once that set, she went to her closet. A boxy space in the crook of her basement bedroom, the closet had a slanting ceiling that led around the corner to the crawl space that once fed beneath the house. When Amber—and Grant—had moved into the basement of the big house, Grant put up a sheet of plywood to cordon off their garments from the earthen storage area. Amber had painted it cream to match the rest of the room, and *voila*. A real closet.

She slid a hand between each piece—beginning with her Sunday sundresses on the far left and moving across until she'd come to the slacks she'd slung over velvet-covered hangers. It was a modest wardrobe, but it was neat, clean, and each piece served a purpose.

After the first go-through, Amber went back. A dress would be too formal. It wouldn't do.

Same went for silk blouses.

Amber didn't look great in T-shirts, so she flipped back to the blouses. There was one cotton blouse with billowing shoulders and a drapey neckline. Pale yellow with nearly imperceptible white polka dots. She pulled it.

Then, she flipped back to slacks, landing at the very end, where she kept a single pair of white jeans. Being that it was after Memorial Day—and being that Amber couldn't be sure that rule applied anyway—she plucked the hanger with the jeans and got dressed. The shirt lay nicely, and the jeans weren't too tight—but that was only because they'd once been too big for her. At least they fit, she figured.

Once dressed, Amber stood in front of her full-length mirror. It revealed a top-heavy girly-girl with limp wet hair.

Amber took to the bathroom and blew out her hair, skipping curls and opting for a great big round bush. Volume was the goal, and today it came quickly. She didn't even pull many hairs out of the brush once her mane was dried and set in big, soft waves. In fact, Amber was quite sure her hair had never looked better.

It was a sign.

She moved on to the next step: accessories.

A belt was a must—what with hips that were narrower than her torso, pants had a tendency to slip right down. But, when Amber looped her white belt through her jeans and went to fasten it, she saw it was a no-go. Normally, Amber was already on the last hole of the belt. Now, if she tried to pull the leather strap into position, she created an aggravated muffin top. It was one thing to deal with a muffin top—after all, her shirt would hide it. But it was another to get a stomachache on account of the belt.

Disappointed in herself for gaining weight and disappointed in her belt for not keeping up, Amber whipped it out and tossed it on the bed. She'd have to do without. But it'd be fine. The jeans weren't bagging yet, and they seemed to stay in position there, right at her hip line. Thank God for small miracles.

After the belt, she slipped into her tan espadrilles, only to realize they'd look foolish. This wasn't a date. Not technically. Not even close.

Flats were best. Casual flats, at that. She opted for leather slides. Comfortable and flattering. It occurred to Amber that only pudgy girls had to worry about flattering shoes. Oh well.

Jewelry would be trying too hard, so Amber simply wore her smartwatch. A gift from Grant that she didn't mind keeping around. After all, it was something she'd flat-out asked for. Not like he'd had the wherewithal to pick it out himself. She'd even told him what make, model, and color to get. Hah.

Last, but not least—makeup. After applying a dab of well-matched BB cream, she ran a light sweep of blush on each cheek, then coated her lashes thickly in mascara and filled in her pale eyebrows. Finally, Amber applied gloss to her lips.

She stood back.

It was too much. Not any one piece—her shirt was cotton and summery. Fine. Her jeans were casual and comfortable. Good. Her hair was uncurled, just... *full*-looking. *Nice*-looking. And her makeup was, well, *evident*.

Something needed to go.

Without the benefit of jewelry or even a belt, Coco Chanel's adage about removing one piece was useless.

When in doubt, Amber relied upon her professional knowledge in times like these.

She could easily change her hair. And when you changed your hair, you changed your entire look.

A cute ponytail. Of course, one didn't normally think *ponytail* when she thought about a *first date*. But Amber also knew there was a hidden magic to pulling one's hair back. Your neck showed, and according to a Ted Talk Amber once watched on human sexuality, the nape of the neck was the number-one erogenous zone on a woman's body, according to women. Of course, whether *men* knew this was another question. Of course, it wasn't like Amber's neck was going to see any action. It wasn't actually a date. It was a... a meeting. That's it.

Still, Amber raked her short, dark blonde tresses back and secured it with a pretty soft-yellow headband. Then she tugged loose some strands of her hair, pulling them around her face in easy, framing slivers.

She stood back again.

Perfection.

A knock came from upstairs, at the interior door to the big house. Amber unplugged her hair dryer, stowed it, killed the lights, and climbed the stairs.

She opened the door. Her cousin, Morgan Jo, stood there. A gleeful grin playing over her face.

"Hey," Morgan Jo cooed. "Coffee's on. I figured you could use a little fortification before heading out."

Amber stepped through the door and closed it behind her, following Morgan Jo into the kitchen where a full breakfast awaited her.

"Oh, my." Amber sucked in a breath. Eggs, bacon, toast, fresh fruit cut up. And, naturally, Emmett. "You two have been busy."

"Yes. We have." Morgan Jo's eyes twinkled. "We've got a wedding venue."

"And a date!" Emmett added.

Amber squealed in delight and grabbed Morgan Jo into a tight hug. Then she held Morgan Jo back and stared at her, hopelessly romantic on her cousin's behalf. "Oh, yay!" She turned to Emmett. "Congrats you-all! When? Where? Tell me everything. Like, right now!"

"Here. October the eighth."

"But that's—" Amber eyed Morgan Jo, and she felt a great burst of excitement zing up her spine. "That's—"

They grabbed hands and started jumping up and down, squealing together this time. They sang out in tandem. "The gala!"

Once they came down and Amber gave her cousin's hands one last squeeze, she added, "You're going to share your wedding with the soft gala?"

"Emmett had the idea to match the two things together." Morgan Jo said this coyly.

Emmett held up his hands. "Hey, now—"

"No, in a good way! It's brilliant. Seriously."

"It *is* brilliant," Amber agreed readily.

"It takes the pressure off a little," Morgan Jo added. "Weddings scare me." She laughed nervously.

Emmett looped his arm around Morgan Jo's waist. "And vineyard openings scare *me*."

Amber gave them her best smile. "I think we'd have more to fear if you two *weren't* getting hitched."

Morgan Jo blushed like a little girl, and Emmett squeezed her closer, kissing her head. Amber beamed at the sweet thing she'd managed to say, but deep down, Amber knew she was projecting on them. Ever since Amber had dumped Grant—cheater that he was—she was scared. Very scared. Scared that she'd somehow made the wrong choice. Scared to be alone.

Scared, mostly, that she may never have another shot at walking down the aisle.

CHAPTER TWO

APRIL 1991

CarlaMay

I once asked my mother why Catholics have to confess their sins to a priest. Why not take your sins directly to God?

Being a good Catholic and a smart woman, she answered me fast. It's a way for the sinner to unburden herself, my mama told me.

Back then, it was easy enough for me to do it, too. It's easy for a girl to admit to cheating on her diet or fibbing to her daddy about getting all the peaches from the peach tree. Maybe there were one or two left at the top, but they'd fall to the ground and the bugs would eat 'em up, anyway. So what?

Those were easy sins.

Some sins aren't so easy.

I suppose that's why I'm taking to writing in this old thing now. Because the sin I've done is so big that I can't ever confess it. I can't ever confess it to anyone. And yet, Mama was right about sinners and their burdens. This weight on my shoulders is so heavy I have to unload it somewhere.

So, here it goes. My first ever diary entry.

．　．　．

I remember distinctly that first day he arrived, with only minimal pomp and circumstance.

I stared at him from the front row.

The front row.

Who was I kidding? I'm not front row material.

What college girl is?

Anyway, they introduced him as the newbie, and that word struck me as embarrassing. Maybe because he really did look new. And maybe because it was the same way I felt.

He walked up from the back with the usual suspects.

A golden rush of hair swooped forward and back, maddeningly stylish, and he had no right to be stylish. No right to a great, thick swatch of golden hair.

It was his expression, however, that gave me the jolt. Not quite a smile—God forbid anyone smile in there—but not a smirk, either. Rather, it was a delectable mix of unbridled elation and inner calm.

Dashing but unassuming, like he was happy to be there but still couldn't believe that this was his. This room. These people.

This life.

His brown eyes were flecked mischievously with green, and on the whole, he looked like he felt lucky.

I wanted to feel lucky.

Once in front of us, he opened his big leather-bound book, all soft covers and gold-tipped pages. He cleared his throat into the microphone and all eyes were on him, but I think mine were the only set to really bore a hole through the invisible line of us and him.

He was tall and... not thin, but. But. Sinewy. Yes. I saw that word once somewhere and it reminded me of an adolescent juniper oak that shot up high into the sky but not without about a hundred arms twisting around its trunk, fortifying its rapid, untimely growth.

I watched him, my own book in my lap and my heart racing beneath my silk blouse.

He commanded the room with confidence but not without error, tripping up over a hard word early on and sending us all into a spatter of eyelash batting and polite giggles at the foible. The mistake didn't detract from his presence. It didn't lessen him. It added something to him.

Not only was this newbie tall and sinewy, dashing and unassuming, golden-haired and lucky.

He was human, too.

And positively untouchable.

I suspected it was this final truth that made me want him most of all. That I couldn't have him.

It would be a sin if I did.

CHAPTER THREE

PRESENT DAY

Morgan Jo

After Amber left, Emmett kissed Morgan on the head. "I have to go, too. Brunch with Mom up in Louisville, remember?"

Morgan nodded. Emmett's mother, Padgett Dawson, was everything you could want in a future mother-in-law. Smart and sassy, stylish, funny. All together, Padgett put the *fire* in *fire-cracker*.

As such, though, she had a heavy pull on Emmett. Pasting a smile onto her mouth, Morgan lifted her face up to Emmett. "Tell her hi for me?"

"Of course. In fact," he added, walking backward toward the front door, "she wants to talk about planning your bridal shower."

Dread filled Morgan at the very phrase. She winced at Emmett, then said, in a squeaky question, "I wasn't going to have one?"

He brushed her off. "Don't be silly. My mama'll handle everything!" Emmett was at the door now, but he hesitated. "*If* you want her to, that is."

Morgan chewed the insides of her cheeks. The attention of a wedding was more than enough to handle. Throwing in a shower added a layer of anxiety.

Morgan's mom, CarlaMay, appeared from the short hallway to her bedroom. "Did I hear bridal shower?"

Grimacing, Morgan waved Emmett off and grumbled, "Yes," as she turned back to the kitchen to fetch the woman her favorite coffee mug.

CarlaMay took the mug and moved to the coffeemaker, filling it and tweaking the drink with creamer and sugar before joining Morgan back at the table. "Let me guess, Emmett's mom has big plans?"

Something about the question irked Morgan. "Well, I don't know if she has *plans*, but I guess she's interested in the whole thing." She took a pull of her water and plucked up her pen, doodling aimlessly on a blank sheet of paper. Then Morgan glanced up at her mother, whose face affixed itself to her phone screen. Morgan frowned. "Were you thinking about a bridal shower?"

A small smile curled over CarlaMay's lips, but her eyes remained on the screen. She didn't answer.

"Mom," Morgan prompted.

CarlaMay glanced up, and her smile fell away. "Yes, baby?"

"Never mind. I don't want one."

"Oh, a shower. Honey, of course we'll have a shower. Does Mrs. Dawson have ideas? She gon' host it?"

"I don't know— I—" Morgan lost her mother's attention again as CarlaMay's gaze slid back to her phone. Emboldened by her annoyance, Morgan grabbed for the dang device. "Who're you talking to anyway?"

CarlaMay was faster, pulling her phone into her chest and glaring at her daughter like a truculent teenager. "None 'a yer beeswax." She pushed her lips into a pout, but it quickly evaporated. "Just my, um—well, *you* know. The man I've been dating."

"Ah, yes. The mystery man. You gonna tell me his name or make me guess?"

CarlaMay seemed to think up a reply and tapped her finger against her lips. "Honey, it's complicated."

Morgan burst out with a laugh. "His name is complicated?"

"No—*no*. Well, *yes*." She squinted and rounded her mouth to the side. "I'm not ready to talk about him."

Morgan held up her hands in surrender. "Okay. I'm not one to pry." And in truth, Morgan had little interest in her mother's dating life. That the woman was dating at all felt... weird. Normally, it was CarlaMay who rooted around for details of *Morgan's* love connections.

CarlaMay slid her phone down the table and cupped her hands around her coffee. "Let's talk wedding."

CHAPTER FOUR

PRESENT DAY

Amber

Amber parked her car in front of a meter across from the Dewdrop Diner. She drank in the warm morning air with a great big gulp, her face lifted to the sky, then she let out the breath and steadied her gaze down the street. There was a chance he was already there. Her *date*. Okay, *no*, he wasn't her date. Today was not a *date*. It was a meeting. A chance for Amber to unlock her past with the help of an AV whiz.

And yet hope lived in her heart like a fresh spring clover, emerging pale yellow from the soil and reaching for the sun, waiting to turn ripe with color. With life.

He would still be on the clock, but that was okay. He'd gotten the go-ahead to invite her into Olde Towne Video's back room where they would test out the archaic video tapes Amber had uncovered. He'd told her to text him when she was close and he'd take a quick break. They could meet at the diner, he'd said. He'd probably want a Coke, anyway.

Amber had easily agreed. After all, it'd be good to have

something to do with her hands. Otherwise, her nerves might overtake her entire body. Plus, getting a drink or a snack made the whole thing feel less like business and more like, well, *pleasure.* Or something close.

She locked her car and adjusted her glasses higher up on her nose, regretting that she didn't prefer contacts.

Before mounting the sidewalk to enter the diner, Amber tugged her blouse down. Though it was a flattering outfit, she couldn't help but feel like a pincushion in the white jeans. Too late to change now.

In her hand, her phone rang. It didn't ding. It rang. "Run For The Roses" never ceased to melt her heart a little. It had been her ringtone forever, but right in this moment, it carried a new meaning. Her chest tightened as the song turned over to the chorus. Amber's pulse quickened when she saw the name on the screen.

It was *him.*

She swiped the call to life.

"Hello?" Her voice measured, she tamed any excitement that might peek through it.

"Hey! I'm in the diner. You on your way?"

Hope leapt in her chest. "Actually, I just got here." She hazarded a glance through the pane glass of the diner, but the freshly painted lettering blocked her view. *Now offering fresh baked pies!*

"*Here* here?" His voice over the phone was deep and calm, and it tossed up her nerves like they were nothin' more than a crisp Caesar salad.

"In front of the diner. Like, out front, I mean. I'm, well, yeah. *Here* here."

Before she could smooth out her rambling sentence into something coherent, the diner door jangled open.

Holding a cherry-topped vanilla milkshake, to go, in each

hand, there he was, grinning from ear to ear. "Hey, Amber." He was cuter than ever.

Amber smiled back. "Hi, Callum."

CHAPTER FIVE

1991

CarlaMay

A week after I first laid eyes on the new man, God remembered to change the weather.

The skies cleared and the gusting winds settled to a light, occasional breeze.

I talked to him.

It was the afternoon at the end-of-semester barbecue out there on the lawn that spread down from the hall.

I was just standing in line to collect my burger and condiments and a cola from the cooler. When I rose up, my hand dripping melted ice water, there he was.

Foolishly, perhaps, I wore a sundress one size too small. It was all I had for such an event, though. Mama had made me the dress for my Confirmation at St. Mark's, which was two years before. I still don't have much in the way of a figure, but my junior year of high school I was nothin' more than a stick, really. And so the dress hung simply and chastely down my skinny body. Soft yellow with white checks running every which way. I felt a little like Dorothy from The Wizard of Oz *in that dress.*

Anyway.

The problem with the dress wasn't so much the dress itself, rather it was my body. In just the two years since my mom had measured me and sewed the dress together, parts of me had finally come in. Namely, my hips. But also, humiliatingly, my boobs.

Back at the dorm, when I'd pulled the dress on, I hadn't really noticed how it made me feel to wear something that fit so tight.

But at the barbecue, all I could do was feel the cotton fabric hugging my newly hewn curves.

So, there I was—unbending from the cooler, with a cola dripping from my hands. I guess it was the lady in me, but I remember lifting that sweaty can to my chest as if to shield him from it. Or to protect me from him. Who could tell? My stomach roiled and twisted and I had that funny feeling that I'd had when I first got my period. The feeling that my body was doing things that might draw attention, and I didn't want it. A terrible uncomfortable feeling like I wanted to crawl out of my skin and into a big burlap sack and go live in a cave somewhere.

He didn't seem to notice—not the cola can or my chest or the dress snug on my body. Instead, he pierced me straight in the eyes.

I lowered the can and rolled my shoulders back.

"Hi." He smiled, and I saw how straight and white his teeth were. Maybe he'd had braces as a kid. I never did.

I offered a closed-lip smile before peeping, "Hi."

Once the can was down and my chest stuck out and I'd found my voice, he seemed to lose his.

That was the first time in my life I wondered if that terrible uncomfortable feeling was actually a good feeling in disguise.

At least, in that moment it was as though my body prickled to life, and my senses took in a whole slew of new things.

The warmth of the air and the gentle lift of the breeze. Where the cotton hem of my dress hit an inch above my knee, kissing my thighs. How heavy my plate of food felt—and that was all gonna go into my stomach? I looked around for a trash can, but of course I wouldn't throw it away.

Waste not, want not, and all.

After giving up the search, my gaze landed back on him, and I noticed new things there, too.

He was dressed in just a T-shirt and jeans. It always strikes me as funny when I see someone out of their usual get-up. Like when I catch a glimpse of my daddy in his nightgown, rather than workin' clothes. Or that one time I saw Mr. Denham, the postman, in a white tank top and loose-fitting trousers as opposed to his baby-blue collared shirt and fitted black shorts. He'd come to the farm for some of daddy's wine, and I'd hardly recognized him.

I tried to shake loose the thought of this man, this stranger who'd come to lord over me in such a powerful, important position, wearing street clothes like he himself was a student at the college.

When I dared to glance his way again, he lifted a burger to his own mouth and sank his teeth into it. I could see his jaw muscles work like gears.

The sight of it turned on my own mouth, and I sucked the insides of my cheeks between my teeth. Then I bit down on my lower lip and eyed my food again. Any appetite I'd had was long gone now.

Other partygoers drifted around us like ghosts, and I found myself hugging nearer to him, forced by the cramped space into a corner made by the buffet table and an umbrella that spread overhead, keeping out the sun.

It didn't keep out fresh air, though, and that sweet Kentucky breeze lifted my wispy chestnut hair across my face.

Clumsily, I looped a finger from the cola can and tucked the hair behind my ear.

It occurred to me then that we'd formed something of a pair. Like we'd become barbecue partners, being together to eat our food and make pleasant chit-chat.

I hadn't yet had to make much chit-chat in my life. The curse of having several siblings was that you were always insulated by their company. When it came to greeting new people in our life—which was a rarity—all I'd ever had to do was give a little wave and say, "Good to meet you, ma'am, sir."

The very existence of the burger on my plate was turning my stomach. I set it down on the edge of the buffet table and cracked open the cola, taking a ladylike sip as my eyes searched for someone else I might know. Someone to whom I could point and say, oh, there's my friend. I'd better go see her.

I didn't really have many friends, though. Not yet, anyway. Plus, I didn't actually want to leave his side.

He swallowed his bite and pushed a crumpled napkin over his mouth before asking, "You're CarlaMay?"

I almost dropped the cola.

Recovering and pressing it against the flesh of my chest, I felt goosebumps zing across my skin like I'd been dunked in the cooler.

A better-socialized girl might have nodded and given him a neat fact about her life. But I was just a farm girl from down south, and it made no sense to me that this man, a stranger and a leader and the one in charge of the lot of us, knew me. "You know my name?" I probably sounded harsh. Harsh or dumb.

His smile had turned up bigger, though. "It's my job to know everyone's name," he answered.

"Oh." I blinked. "But, how do you know my name?"

At this, he laughed, but something told me he wasn't exactly laughing at me, so I laughed, too.

"Wow, you've got a great smile."

I stopped smiling. On the outside, at least.

On the inside, though, my body was lit up like the Fourth of

July.

CHAPTER SIX

PRESENT DAY

Amber

"Hope you're not a chocolate person." Callum said this so seriously that Amber burst out in laughter.

She took the shake and thanked him before adding, "I like vanilla and chocolate."

"Both together?" He threw her a suspicious glance.

"Separate, together, any which way."

"Ah, so you're easy going."

"I guess." Amber took a sip of her shake, savoring the thick sweetness. She really shouldn't be drinking a milkshake because of the calories, but it tasted so dang good. And being with him *felt* so dang good and easy, too. Amber Lee Taylor wasn't one to turn away goodness.

"I consider myself easy going, too. But I'm generally an organized person, and that's not necessarily a trait of someone laidback, now, is it?"

"I think you can be both."

"Separately? Or together?"

Amber made a face, and it was Callum's turn to laugh. "Sorry. I'm... *awkward*," he said.

Inside, Amber felt about a million times as awkward as Callum, and that's probably why they quickly found a rhythm together.

The pair strolled leisurely down Main Street, their lips puckered around white-and-red striped straws as they passed neatly trimmed dogwoods. At the base of the trees, freshly planted annuals in reds, whites, and blues hedged the sidewalk.

Amber had kept her focus on her feet, though—forsaking her usual joy of window shopping. She worried if she didn't watch where she was going, she'd trip and fall. Her body was abuzz with nerves the whole walk, and even more so now that they were huddled in the video store. Callum was just cute enough to make Amber feel off-kilter.

"Here we go," he announced as they came upon Olde Towne Video, where he unlocked the door and flipped the sign over from *We'll be right back!* to *Open!*

Soon enough, they settled in the back room, their shakes sweating together on a neat side table while Callum selected a black VHS tape from a short stack on that same table.

"Strawberry wine," Callum declared to Amber, reading the label on the tape.

Wordlessly, she joined him in front of a medium-sized television screen on a media cart. The rig looked like it was set up especially for Amber. On the shallow shelf beneath the top where the TV sat was a wide, complicated-looking VCR with more than one tape deck, about a bazillion buttons, and probably two bazillion cords choking out the back and slithering up to the TV.

Callum pushed the black cassette into the left-hand-side tape deck. It rolled in, and clicked into place. Amber gave Callum a grateful smile, and he winked at her.

It was the wink to end all winks, and even though Amber

knew it was just meant for encouragement, that it was just meant to say *we can do this!*, well, she grabbed it with her heart and stowed it away for later. She never once remembered Grant winking at her. Heck, she couldn't recall any man ever winking at her in her life.

Amber had met Callum just a couple of weeks back, when she'd brought the haul of Grandad's ancient VHS tapes into the archaic storefront to see if there was any saving them.

If it was possible to recover what was on the tapes, Amber and Morgan were hopeful that what they found would correspond to each tape's careful label: a type of homemade wine, complete with the full recipe and a step-by-step process showing the cousins how to make Grandad's famous drink. Emulating the age-old family method would anchor their product and their vision for the business.

There had been other things mixed in too: a few blank cassettes, or, at least, cassettes without labels. And two with ambiguous labels. Dates. Winter 1992 and Summer 1993, specifically.

Before Callum had agreed to help Amber restore the tapes, he had to have permission from his boss, the owner of the shop. None other than Hank Taylor himself. Amber's estranged dad.

This had presented a briefly awkward sequence of events. Not awkward for Amber, who felt confident that her father—though he may be deadbeat or runaway or however you wanted to describe him—should gladly grant permission. It was awkward for Callum, who had to call Hank and explain that his long-lost, local daughter had requested the shop's help in uncovering her own history.

In the end, Hank had agreed. Amber figured he had no cause not to agree—she was a paying customer, after all. Anyway, the tapes had nothing to do with Hank and all to do with Bill Coyle. Hank could safely know that Amber would get her hands on those old recipes and be on her merry way.

"Strawberry wine," Amber repeated now, settling into a metal chair Callum had readied for her.

He followed her lead, and lifted a remote, pointing it at the television screen. Amber was grateful she didn't have to re-explain that she was scavenging for wine-making information for her family business. Callum seemed to keep up on things just fine. If he was dying to see what was on the tapes, too, it didn't show. Mostly, he seemed blandly interested in the tape while stealing regular, quick glances at her. With each of these glances, Amber could feel herself flush. His nervous attention distracted her from her mission.

In a good way.

The fuzzy screen folded into a black slit which spread in its place.

Then, the very first of Grandad's dusty old wine tapes scratched to life.

As soon as Grandad's face came on the screen, Amber's heart sank. She shouldn't be watching this alone with a cute shop clerk.

She should be watching it with her cousins. Her mother. Her brother and sister. Her *family*.

As Grandad stood central to the frame, Amber became transfixed.

On the one hand, he was nothing like she remembered him. On the other hand, he was everything like she remembered him. His stoop and his familiar, soft-looking flannel, tucked down into too-big pants held up by weathered black suspenders. But his hair was less white and more pepper in the video.

Amber sat next to Callum in silence, watching Grandad, in his cranky way, introducing the process of harvesting and fermenting wine.

After Grandad gave a quick, uncomfortable primer, the scene moved from the barn, out over the green sloping hill, and off toward the fence that bordered the property.

Just as Grandad turned to face the camera and presumably pick back up where he left off, the TV screen flickered to static. Callum clicked his tongue and shook his head. "I'm sorry, I thought I fixed it. Let me take a look."

He fiddled at the VCR, and Amber couldn't help but to watch his sinewy arms. Callum's fingers worked dexterously at the old-fashioned machine, popping out the VHS at last and studying the tape with an expert eye. It was enchanting, in a way, watching a man with an aptitude. Amber had never given much thought to how there was something attractive about a man with a skill. Then again, maybe it wasn't that Callum was skillful with the tape so much as his fingers moved with such care and gentleness.

A shiver coursed up her spine. Amber swallowed and blinked, ejecting herself from the fleeting trance.

She offered sweetly, "It's okay. I don't have anywhere to be. I mean, if you're up to working on it now?"

Callum turned to her and gave a meek shrug. "I mean, restoring old VHS tapes can be hit or miss. Half of these might come out just fine. And the other half, well, we may never get them to work." He studied the one in his hands and frowned deeply. "But *this* one, I could have sworn—" His voice fell away and he stuck his pinky into the white wheel on the back of the tape, twisting it.

Amber noticed that Callum didn't wear the Brambleberry uniform of Wranglers, a button-down flannel, dusty boots, and a deep tan on his neck. Neither did he wear any semblance of an Olde Towne Video uniform. Instead, he was dressed in straight black jeans and a blue, threadbare T-shirt with the age-old Blockbuster logo splashed in yellow across his chest. Amber figured if anyone could get away with wearing an old Blockbuster T-shirt, it had to be Callum Dockerty.

Amber's heart thumped beneath her blouse. Her skin

tingled. "Is there anything I can do to help?" Rising from her metal chair, she indicated the tape and neared him.

Callum looked up from the tape. His brown eyes crinkled at the edges. "Really? You don't, like, have to go do somebody's *hair?*" He chewed his bottom lip, and those brown eyes glimmered with mischief.

Amber's heart skipped a beat. "You know I do hair?" It was a question more than a statement, but Callum didn't answer her.

Instead, he grinned, and a pair of dimples appeared.

Amber had never before known the meaning of the phrase *weak in the knees*. Until this very moment. "Well, then. What else do you know?"

He tapped a finger to his lips. "Let's see. I know you come from the Nelson family."

"Everybody knows that. Everybody local, anyhow."

"Something more personal, then?" His smile slipped and his finger traced down his lower lip and fell back to the cassette tape which he still held. He tapped a quick pattern on the black plastic.

The idea that a cute new shop clerk knew things about Amber—*personal* things—well, it gave her a thrill. A zing up in her spine, turning her skin all into goosebumps and making her wonder if she should have gone with a cute sundress after all.

She leveled her chin at Callum. "Let's see what you got."

"All right, then." He sheathed the cassette tape in its original box and shut off the TV, then moved to the box with the remaining tapes, set on a table. Callum gripped both sides of the box and leaned it for her to see inside. "These tapes? They're of your grandpa."

"You know that from what you just watched with me," Amber smirked.

Callum returned the box to its place and folded his arms over his chest. Amber noticed—it was hard not to—that he was flexing his forearms. Or, at least, the muscles along his forearms rippled like Moonshine Creek after a storm. Images of the property and Grandad out on the creek at his old moonshine still filled up Amber's brain.

"Fair enough. But I also know he goes all through how to make his special homemade wine. Out there on the Nelson farm, what do locals call it?"

"Moonshine Creek," Amber whispered. It was like he could read her mind. She cleared her throat. "None of that is altogether personal."

"I know you and your daddy aren't on speaking terms." A shadow crossed Callum's features, and Amber's joy turned to smoke.

She looked down at her feet.

"Sorry. That was—too far?" He'd dropped his chin to his chest and now looked up at her from beneath his eyelashes.

Callum had dark, thick eyelashes that any one of Amber's clients would be jealous of. They were gorgeous, just like the rest of him.

How could she stay joyless when she had this cutie staring up at her with those brown, puppy dog eyes? Her heart filled back up and floated to the tip-top of her chest again. She had to let out a deep breath to assure him, "No. That's just one more thing locals know about me. That my daddy left years and years ago." She wanted to keep her tone flat and lifeless, like it didn't matter to her that her father was out of the picture. But she couldn't help that a fraction of an ounce of hurt crept into her voice.

"I don't know my dad, either," Callum confessed, his posture normal again and his face cocked to the side just barely.

"But you know my dad," she said, furrowing her brows and thinking about the great ironies of the world. Like the fact that Callum wore an old Blockbuster shirt and that she'd had to get her own dad's permission to fix up her grandfather's artifacts.

Well, maybe none of that was *irony*. Amber wasn't exactly sure what *irony* meant anyway. But it was all funny business, that was for sure.

Amber just smiled.

Callum patted the box of tapes once more. "So, why are you hell-bent on getting all these to work? Are they like, what d'ya call it—*keepsakes*? If I had a video of my grandpa, I'd want to watch it. It's cool."

"Keepsakes, yeah. Plus—the wine recipes. We have Grandad's recipe book, but it's incomplete at best. We're trying to plug the holes with knowledge from my uncle. You don't know him, probably. Garold Taylor? He lives out in Widow Holler. His son is Geddy? Geddy Taylor?"

"Geddy." Callum squinted. "I swear I know that name from somewhere."

"Probaby the market. He works there. Just got promoted to manager, I guess."

"Right—he's running a little campaign to reinvigorate things. Like, a farmers' market. I might ask him if he wants to consign some of my merch."

"Your merch?" Amber lifted an eyebrow.

Callum pinched his T-shirt and gave her a half-grin. "Vintage apparel." His slow nod did something to her insides. After nodding her comprehension, she tried to refocus the conversation.

"Anyway, Geddy and Uncle Gary are helping us perfect the recipe. We—that's my cousin, Morgan Jo and me—hope to find more information from the tapes. That way we can preserve our Grandad's process and recipes."

"Well, why not just ask Mr. Taylor?" Callum said, like it was the easiest answer in the world.

"You mean my *dad*?" she withdrew a step. "Why would I ask him?"

Callum seemed unfazed. "I mean, I'm sure he remembers

some of it, right?"

"Some of it?" Amber narrowed her eyes further.

Callum scratched the back of his head and shrugged. "Yeah, sure. He was telling me about how Old Man Coyle made his own wine."

It hadn't occurred to Amber that her own daddy had known that Grandad had a little wine operation going on in the barn at Moonshine. For all Amber ever figured, her daddy hadn't really known Grandad at all.

Amber folded her arms over her front. A light, edgy laugh bubbled up from her throat. "Sorry, but—what did he tell you?"

Callum chewed his bottom lip again and glanced down at the floor before a stitch pulled his brows in and he returned his gaze to Amber's.

"Mr. Hank Taylor's the one who filmed these."

"My dad?" Amber frowned deeper. "What, exactly, did he film?"

Callum patted the box. "The tapes you brought in?"

"What are you talking about?" Her insides twisted up, and her chest tightened as a premature understanding formed.

"Yeah." Callum shoved his hands into his pockets and lifted his shoulders up. "You see, when I called Mr. Taylor and asked him if I could fix up his daughter's VHS tapes, well, he asked me about them. I told him you'd brought in a box of old tapes. He came on down just after you were here, in fact, and he took a look at the tapes. He said sure we can fix them up. And he figured they'd still be in good shape even, because they were *his*."

"His?" A sick-like feeling pooled in Amber's stomach.

Amber swallowed the lump that formed in her throat. "As in, he watched them here? With you—or something?"

Callum's voice fell low, and he dropped his chin, but his gaze remained heavy on Amber. "Amber, your dad is the one who filmed your grandad."

CHAPTER SEVEN

PRESENT DAY

Morgan Jo

The month of June drained away like a perfectly sweet lemonade.

Morgan knew her window to prepare not only for the soft opening of the vineyard but for her own wedding was slipping away with every sip.

It was time to call a meeting of the family business, and Morgan did just that, planning a fish fry for Friday evening.

The plan was to cook up something Geddy and Trav caught that morning on their fishing trip out in Widow Holler. While they cooked and ate, Morgan figured they'd talk about all things vineyard, winery, business name and then a rollout plan for October the eighth. Since Julia got off work by about four and Emmett by five, Morgan fixed it for six. From there, she was just waiting on Amber to confirm that she had no hair appointments for the evening, which she shouldn't.

But come Friday at four, Amber had appeared in the kitchen of the big house with a weak smile and a bad excuse.

Morgan was in there brewing sweet iced tea while Julia stood at the island, mixing up batter for the fish.

"Morgan Jo," Amber started, her voice high and sharp.

Morgan turned to see she was dressed to the nines in a flowing, buttery-yellow sundress, her makeup and hair impeccably fixed.

"Hey, Amber." She frowned. "You look pretty." The frown turned to a suspicious smirk. "*Why?*"

Julia elbowed Morgan. "Maybe she invited that cute boy from Main Street."

"Cute boy from Main Street?" Morgan arched a brow. What had she missed? "Who?"

Amber's rosy cheeks turned crimson. "Um." She glanced at Julia. "You know about Callum?"

Julia shrugged her shoulders and returned to the batter and fish. "Geddy mentioned it. I guess he saw the guy in the store and invited him along to fish."

Amber asked, a shade too eagerly, "Did Callum go with Geddy and Trav? Fishing, I mean?"

"Or maybe it was Travis who told me about him. When I went back to the bunkhouses to get the fish, Geddy mentioned that they'd made a new friend. Callum. Works at the video place."

Morgan added, "Oh, right. You've been getting the tapes recovered, still. Amber, honey—it's not—"

But Julia cut her off. "Geddy says Callum likes Amber."

The air went still.

"Wait—so he *is* coming here? For our meeting?" Morgan considered the idea of it. It might be good to have an objective third party listen in on some of their ideas. She opened her mouth to approve the idea, but Amber shook her head and swiped her hands through the air.

"No, no. He's not coming here," she said emphatically, then

looked again at Julia, her cheeks returning to their regular blush-pink shade. "He likes me? Like, as a friend? What exactly did Geddy say?"

Julia gave Morgan a knowing look. Morgan cocked her head. Her eyes grew wide. "Oh, my. Amber—" she gushed, a smile spilling over her mouth. "You've got a crush! And... he likes you back!"

Amber broke a shy smile, but again she shook her head. "Morgan Jo, I'm *so* sorry. It's just... something came up."

"What?" Morgan made a face. "A hair appointment or something? At the last minute?" Frustration cranked her muscles. "Amber Lee, you knew about this meeting. And you scheduled a hair appointment?"

Amber stammered, "It's not a hair appointment, Morgan Jo."

Morgan said, "Well, what is it, then?"

"It's related to the business," Amber replied, but her face had grown red again.

"Amber, our meeting is related to the business. What could you possibly be doing?" Morgan sighed.

"It's the tapes. Callum, um, he worked them up again, and they should be ready to watch now. You could come, Morgan Jo—"

"Come? Are you crazy? We're having a fish fry, Amber. We have to cover a lot, and you're going off to watch those tapes."

"You don't want to see them?"

"I do, of course I do—but we have Uncle Gary now. And Geddy with the heritage fruits. We don't need the tapes. Not for information, at least. Why don't you pick the tapes up and invite Callum to join us? He can come eat and listen in on our ideas." Morgan brightened back up.

"It's not just Callum I'm going to see right now, Morgan Jo." Amber twisted her hands together in a knot on top of her belly.

Morgan and Julia exchanged a look. Morgan asked Amber, "Who are you going to see?"

Amber looked down at her hands on top of her stomach, then she smoothed her dress and sucked her stomach in. "My daddy."

CHAPTER EIGHT

1991

CarlaMay

Four weeks after the barbecue, Barb stayed with me at the dorm. I begged her. Usually, she goes out on the weekends with her boyfriend-of-the-month. That weekend, however, her most recent boyfriend had dumped her.

Now, I'm no barfly. Not like Barb is. But I don't mind a beer here or there, and the few times I've been to parties, I've had my fun. All that to say, it wasn't hard to convince me to get out.

After a light supper at the cafeteria, we followed the Saturday-night college crowd as they wound their way in and out of bars along 4th Street.

After an hour wandering through darkened, noisy joints, we stumbled to the tucked-away entrance of a little hole-in-the-wall called The Holler.

It became clear just as soon as we stepped through the door that this place wasn't the usual coed haunt. A little bit tavern and a little bit honky-tonk, the feeling of the place was older.

Sure enough, a lone man wearing sunglasses and sporting a long white beard sat on a stool in the corner opposite the bar.

There, he strummed a banjo expertly, but no one much bothered to watch him or show they were listening. In fact, the seating in there was so limited that the bar looked as much like a corral as anything.

Barb turned to me with a glittering smile on her peach-painted lips. I know Barb, and I know she had one goal tonight: to get drunk.

Okay, maybe two goals: to get drunk and smooch on a cute boy.

The thing is, Barb knows how to do both these things on a budget, and I realized that's exactly why she dragged me away from the pricey, trendy bars into this shack.

I kind of hate to sit at the actual bar, because it really shines a light on you, but there wasn't another place to sit and even if there were, Barb wouldn't stand for it.

We hauled ourselves up onto the cracked vinyl-top stools smack dab in the center of the grimy, waxen top.

On either side of us, old cowboys hunched over amber drinks, their hats pulled down over their eyes as they sipped the thick liquor and garbled to one another about topics surprisingly familiar to me and to Barb. Farming work, business exchanges, livestock auctions. None of this is a strange topic from some other world, and it made me realize we fit in better than I figured.

After a few moments of me sliding my gaze around, taking everything in, and Barb twisting to watch the banjo player, I asked my sister, "Are we ordering something or not?"

"Of course. Just give it a li'l time. 'Kay?" She winked at me then looked past me to the far side of the bar where a pair of men who didn't wear cowboy hats sat.

I looked their way to see them staring at us, then I looked back at Barb.

She pouted her lips, elbowed me, then lifted a hand for the bartender.

A gruff, cranky-looking guy, the bartender laid a cracked, crimped hand in front of Barb. "What'll it be, ma'am?"

"Two shots of tequila."

He lifted a bottle of Patron, but she made a face. "Cheaper."

The bartender fussed under his breath and reached toward the bottom shelf before filling two shot glasses and sliding them our way.

"To you," Barb held up her glass for a toast.

"To me?" I was bewildered. Barb wasn't like herself when she was out at the bars. Or maybe she was, and I had everything backward.

"You're finishing your first semester of college, aren't you? I say that calls for a toast. A celebration, even."

I agreed, but only silently. After all, Mom and Dad back home need us more than I need an education. And I don't even know what I want to do with my life anyway. Maybe be a teacher? I don't know. My being at college is irrelevant to the rest of my life. More like a vacation than a serious thing. That's how I see it, anyway. It's most definitely how my family sees it.

We slugged back the shots. It stung my throat so bad I about choked it all back up.

Barb laughed at me, and the old crusty cowboy on my right growled something I couldn't quite make out.

The banjo player stopped, and I wondered if the whole bar could hear me sputtering and choking. But just as soon as he was done with his set, music came on a real live jukebox from the corner.

"I'm So Lonesome I Could Cry" started playing, and I managed to stop coughing.

Barb asked the bartender for a pair of waters, then pointed to the small area where the banjo player had been moments before. He was gone and in his place two couples slowly two-stepped as Hank Williams crooned his troubles.

"See? This place isn't so bad."

I couldn't exactly see that. The one shot was already making me feel a little gooey, though, so I greedily drank down my water as we watched the dancers in their high-waist, rhinestone-studded blue jeans and dusty boots kick up their private romances on the narrow dance floor.

"Ladies."

Barb and I whipped around, and the bartender was presenting us with a second set of shots.

"Oh, no—" I frowned at Barb.

The bartender didn't have time for rejection, though. He simply tossed his head to the coupla younger guys at the far side of the bar. "Courtesy of your admir'rs," the crusty old man added.

Barb's face lit up, but I was in no mood for wooing from a pair of drunks slumming in a joint like that.

"You never turn down a free drink, CarlaMay." Barb said this as she gripped my forearm, gave a sumptuous smile and little wave to the boys. Then, I watched her mouth thank you to them. "Your turn," she said to me from the corner of her mouth.

When I looked at the pair, I saw they surely weren't cowboys, and they weren't frat boys either. In fact, they looked like nerds. Like they didn't quite belong on the college scene, so they hid out in the safest—and cheapest—bar they could find.

Lucky for them, Barb and I had effectively done the same.

I had little choice but to play along, and soon enough we were four shots in and crowded on the dance floor, smooshed up against the boys as the jukebox twanged on and my vision got blurrier and blurrier.

"What are y'all's names?" the taller one with whom Barb danced asked us above the din.

"I'm Barb! This is my little sister, CarlaMay."

The guy spinning me around in choppy circles mumbled out his name, which I am embarrassed to say I promptly forgot.

We turned in time for me to hear Barb's partner holler his name.

"I'm Hank!" He was grinning at Barb, and she was grinning at him.

Another song down, and I was ready to go home. I grabbed Barb by the hand and gave it a sharp tug. "You about ready?"

"Are you crazy?" she hollered back.

"The night is young," my dance partner added. He leered at me with a greasy grin.

I felt drunk, sloppy, and sick. I was done. "Barb, I'm going back to the dorm." Once I made my mind on something, it stuck.

"You can't go without me," Barb protested. Then she gave me a serious look. "I like this guy."

She meant Hank. He seemed nice enough, sure. But I couldn't hardly stand up, and it was liable to get worse.

The last thing I wanted was for the no-name greaseball to try any funny business, so I realized I needed to stick it out or find a safe way to split.

I looked around the darkened tavern, searching for an answer. Something to help me escape.

Nothing appeared.

I spun back and tugged Barb's hand, pulling her away from Hank and the dance floor. "Barb, come on. It's late. I'm tired. I wanna go home."

As if the tequila had turned to venom in her veins, she scowled and glared at me. "I'm not leaving. 'Least, not with you and not now," she spat.

I tried to see it through her eyes. Hank was handsome and tall. I could tell why she wanted to stay, pressed up against him, their mouths inches apart.

But Barb wasn't thinking about things through my eyes. I wanted to leave. We were at an impasse.

I looked beyond her toward Hank, my eyes pleading.

He left the dance floor and joined us at the corner of the bar, where he held up a hand. "Waters, please," he told the bartender.

Hope leapt in my chest. Maybe we could all just sober up and go home.

"CarlaMay, right?" Hank asked.

I nodded, sullenly.

"You don't like Whit, do you?" he asked.

Whit. That was his name. I looked around, but my dance partner had disappeared. "No."

Hank leaned closer to me. "I don't know him well. He just works at the video store with me."

"Video store?"

"In Brambleberry. That's where I live. I work at Olde Towne Video down there."

Barb and I looked at each other. He was from Brambleberry, too? And they didn't know him? Wasn't like they ever went to the video store, or maybe he only just moved there.

The coincidence could not be ignored. Even I realized how important it was that Barb spend more time with this man. Maybe they were soul mates. How could I possibly interfere with my sister finding everlasting love?

I smiled, and Barb smiled back at me. It was settled. Barb could stay.

"Don't be out too late," I warned her.

"Be safe walking back," she warned me.

Whit came up behind me right then. "I'll walk you," he offered. In the light of my new circumstances—my determination to go home and also my support of Barb staying—Whit didn't seem so bad.

Still, I looked from him to Barb. Unease coated my stomach. But Barb was already turned back to Hank.

I turned to Whit and nodded. "Okay," I said, defeated for myself but excited for my sister. "Let's go."

CHAPTER NINE

PRESENT DAY

Amber

Amber showed up to Olde Towne Video at five on the dot. She smoothed her dress for the umpteenth time, worried her shapewear wasn't quite cutting it. As much as she wanted to look trim and pretty for Callum, it was important to Amber that she make her father proud. After all, this would be the very first time she'd seen him since he'd left her family.

Before she'd left the farm, Amber had shot a group text to her mom, her sister, Tiffany, and her brother, Travis. Did they want to come along and see Dad?

The answer from all three was *no*.

Oh, well. Amber knew that families could be fickle, but all it took was one person to make the first move. Amber would be that one person. She'd keep at it, inviting them to pull back together with Hank.

After that, hopefully a reconciliation would take shape. Fortunately, it hadn't rested solely on Amber's shoulders to make that first move. According to Callum, Hank Taylor also wanted to patch things up between him and his family, and he was happy to meet with Amber and chat. About what—well, that was simple enough. They'd catch up on their lives, for starters. And then? With any luck, he'd walk her through how it was that he came to film Grandad making wine and what he'd learned in the process.

She closed the door to her car and moved across the parking lot and to the front door of the shop.

The parking lot was full, which was to be expected of a Friday night. Squeezing in between vehicles reminded Amber of how she hadn't exactly lost the weight she'd wanted to lose. It had been a week since she'd last seen Callum and since he'd promised her he'd get at least one full tape working. One week since she'd promised *herself* to cut back on the calories, walk more, help in the vineyard more... all in the hopes of shedding at least a pound or two and looking slightly leaner by the time she was due to meet him and her father again.

Shapewear could only carry her so far at this point, and now it was simply up to two men to see her for who she was: a simple small-town girl on a mission.

To bring her daddy back into the fold and maybe, just *maybe*, strike something up with Callum that was more than a clerk–customer relationship.

"Amber, hey."

From midstride on the sidewalk, Amber looked up. Callum stood in the doorway to the shop, his face masked by a look of concern.

"Hi, Callum." Her heart leapt up in her chest at the very sight of him. She tucked a strand of her hair behind her ear and rolled her shoulders back. Then, Amber offered a bright smile. "How've you been doin'?"

Was it just Amber's imagination or did he *wince* at the question? "Good, *real* good. Got the tapes ready. I've got two working like perfect. The others—" He held up a flat hand and wobbled it.

Amber just brushed the worry away. "You know something? My cousin, Morgan Jo, says we don't even really need those dang tapes, anyhow. At this point, it's mostly for fun." She smiled again and felt her stomach flutter to life. "So, is my daddy here yet?"

"Ah." Callum looked behind him into the shop and then let the door slowly shut. "Amber, I'm so sorry. He just called—something came up."

"Something came up?"

He winced again. "He isn't coming."

Without any warning—without any forecast of a potential disappointment—tears sprang up in Amber's eyes. And they didn't stop. In just a moment, Amber was all-out crying, complete with body-wracking heaves and choking sobs.

She perceived Callum coming to her side and patting her back, but it wasn't until she felt his arm slip around her shoulders that the sobbing subsided.

"I'm *so* sorry," she managed through final hiccups. Awkwardly, she lifted her face to Callum, who remained at her side.

"It's okay," he said softly. "I figured you'd be upset. I would be, too, honestly."

Amber sniffled and a small laugh escaped. "Yeah, but—I mean, it's not like I even know him. Why should I *care*?" Her last word came out on a choke, and she dropped her head to her chest.

"He left *you*, right?"

Amber frowned and looked up at Callum. "Well..." Her eyebrows involuntarily crimped together, a miniature spasm. "Yes, he left me. He left us all."

"I know this isn't my business, Amber," Callum said, his voice soft and warm like honey. "Why *do* you still care about him?" The honey turned to acid.

"It's... it's complicated." She blew out a breath and lifted her chin to the video shop door, out of which a small family emerged. A mother and father and between them, clutching their hands, a young boy—a son. The boy, his mop of dark curls jiggling as he giggled, suddenly lifted up his feet and launched his head back. His face opened up to the sunset-washed sky. It was as confusing a sight as any—he should have flailed and fallen. But he didn't. His parents predicted his leap. He lifted his arms and instead of letting him fall, they helped him soar.

CHAPTER TEN

PRESENT DAY

Morgan Jo

"Let's start with layout." Morgan was positioned at the head of the picnic table. Her plastic tumbler of strawberry wine sat at the corner of her notebook. Behind her, Emmett and Geddy worked the grill. Seated along the bench of the table was Julia, who compulsively applied Chapstick and threw stares toward the boys. Her wine—a citrus variety they were experimenting with—was long gone.

Morgan snapped her fingers in front of Julia's face. "Hello? Earth to Jules?"

Julia managed to tear her gaze from the barbecue long enough to nod. "Yes. Layout."

"What's going on? Is it Geddy? Are you serious right now? You know you're acting like a fifteen-year-old." Even if she was annoyed, Morgan still couldn't hold back a smile. Julia had never in her life shown much of an interest in dating. She'd put her education then her career first, accepting dates from locals only to complain that no good men existed in Nelson County.

Her obvious crush on Geddy was a departure, and Morgan

would be a terrible best friend not to confront it. "Geddy Coyle. Think about this, Jules." She gave it a beat during which Julia again looked over toward the guys. Morgan let out a sigh. "It's *Geddy*, Jules. Geddy. He's not exactly—"

Julia snapped her head back to Morgan. "What? He's not Emmett?" A snort escaped her mouth. "News flash, MoJo, I don't want an Emmett. I want a..."

Morgan drawled heavily, "A shop clerk with a penchant for chewin' baccy?"

But it was no deterrent to Julia, who flashed a huge grin. "Admit it. Emmett might have success, but Geddy has *potential*."

Morgan rolled her eyes. "What*ever*. Let's talk layout, *please*." Morgan splayed her hands across the blank notebook page, then picked up her pencil and scratched out a quick map of the property, including only the barn, hangar, fence, and orchards beyond. There was no need to think of the other structures, not for a wedding or an opening.

Then, Morgan labeled the barn *Winery*. "We'll continue fermentation and bottling operations in the barn. It's working well there. We can make improvements as they become necessary."

Julia nodded.

Morgan moved right on the page to the fence that cut the page in half. "We'll funnel traffic through here for the ceremony. I mean the beginning, right?"

Julia studied the page and frowned. "So you're thinking of exchanging vows back in the orchard?"

Morgan lifted her voice to Emmett. "Honey, will you come here?"

He joined them, but Geddy stayed back and manned the grill. "What do you think? Saying vows in the orchard?"

Emmett pointed the long throat of his beer bottle toward the page. "Everyone invited is coming to the ceremony, right?"

"Right. That's the point of a soft, intimate opening, after all."

"And how many are we inviting?"

"How many are we inviting?" Morgan blinked and looked at Julia, who just shrugged.

"I mean—"

Julia lifted her phone to her face and tapped around for a moment. "Here we go," she said at last. "Invitation List." She ran through the names of family, close friends, a handful of prominent community members, and the short list of nearby vineyard owners and professionals. Meanwhile, Morgan kept a tally on a fresh sheet of paper.

When Julia was done, Morgan counted her sets of five. "That's twenty-five, but it's not including plus-ones."

"Plus-ones?" Emmett scratched the back of his head. "That could come to over fifty people."

"It's small for an event. And very small for a wedding," Morgan pointed out.

"But the orchard can't hold seats for that many."

"What about out past the orchard? Beyond the row of peach trees where there's a meadow before the creek?" Morgan made her eyes twinkle with supplication at her fiancé.

He gave a half-grin. "That'd work." Then kissed the top of her head and returned to the grill. "Dinner in ten," he called behind him.

"Fifty people max. In the meadow beyond the orchard. That'll push everyone through the vineyards—we can really show off."

"Assuming there's fruit to show off."

"We'll be harvested by the wedding, probably. It's not about showing off the fruit. Anyway, we won't hide that we are bringing in outside product from Widow's Holler."

"So what are you showing off by having folks walk half a mile to the ceremony location?"

Morgan eyed her friend. Julia was being unnecessarily diffi-
cult, and it was starting to piss Morgan off. "The alternative is
people parking forty yards away from the altar. We can show
everyone the space of our vineyard, our vines, our trees, bushes,
flowers. We can show them our *potential*."

"Potential," Julia echoed, a coy smile rippling over her lips.

CHAPTER ELEVEN

1991

CarlaMay

We left the hole-in-the-wall bar. Barb and Hank remained behind, cozying up to a Dolly hit and probably falling in love so hard I'd never see her again.

I forced myself to focus on Whit, the greasy guy who'd offered to walk me. Though I didn't care for him, it was clear enough Whit was harmless. And skinny, to boot.

I followed him out of The Holler and up 4th Street toward the quad on a straight path back to my dorm. He walked ahead of me, talking into the air, mostly about himself.

As we got to the edge of the street, ready to cross into campus, he turned.

"You're real pretty, Mary," he said.

"My name isn't Mary," I answered, confused and still bleary from all that damn tequila.

He laughed and turned his whole body toward me, blocking my path from the crosswalk. There wasn't any traffic coming or going—it was late. We could have crossed right away, but he stood as firm as an oak tree.

"You're real pretty," he said again.

I got irritated, so I moved to the side to pass by him and push ahead, but he mirrored my movement, blocking me again.

Laughter spilled out behind us. I turned to see a rowdy bunch of frat boys trip over themselves and head down the opposite way.

Across the street, adjacent to where we stood at the other end of the strip of bars, a pair of men stood talking and smoking. Maybe cigars, though. They didn't look my age. Maybe a little older. Taller. Handsome. Like they didn't quite fit. Nothing was fitting right that night. From The Holler to Hank and Whit bein' in there, to the sights and sounds outside that night. Like a shattered mirror of a normal night out.

I shivered hard.

I looked back up at Whit and wrapped my arms around myself. "Come on. Let's go," I urged him.

But he wasn't smiling anymore, and his sloppiness seemed to slide away. His face went cold and stony. He reached a hand toward me.

I slapped at it.

"Hey, now." His voice was like syrup—the phony kind you buy generic from the A&P. Too sweet and plasticky. "Come on, baby. I know why you left."

"I want to go to bed." I moved right and again tried to dart around him, but before my foot even hit the asphalt, he grabbed my right hand with his left and slid two fingers into the waist of my jeans. My skin went so cold, the breath froze in my chest. I'd never been in a position like that—something so damn scary.

I pulled back, and contorted my face angrily. "You'll knock that off right now," I hissed, and met his gaze with as sharp a one of my own as I could muster under the circumstances.

Whit let go of my jeans but not my hand. "You're a rowdy one." He sneered at me.

I was at that moment of run or fight. The one when a normal

person has the good sense to sock somebody square in the face or to dash away lickety-split. But my body didn't seem to know to do either one of those things. Or maybe it was my mind. Both failed me. I was a statue of nerves, buzzing with fear.

Whit sneered deeper and drew nearer, and all I could manage to do was stammer a few words. "I'm—I'm going home. Please—"

"CarlaMay?"

The voice broke Whit's trance, and he turned. I managed to unfreeze myself enough to move my gaze past Whit and to the man who'd come up to where we were. When I saw the lanky, tall build and dark hair, my body melted.

It was him. My savior.

CHAPTER TWELVE

PRESENT DAY

Morgan Jo

The sun dipped lower, casting long shadows from the big house and the barn. "We might just need a bit more light out here," Morgan remarked, setting her pen alongside her notebook as Julia rose, too.

"Well, I need to go in and check the potatoes. They've been boiling for too long, probably." Julia left, and Morgan watched Geddy watch her go. She held back a sigh. After all, there was something to be said for *potential*. If Julia and Geddy were developing a mutual crush, then so be it. They were single consenting adults, after all. What did it matter if they nurtured a summer fling? So long as Morgan's best friend in the world didn't get hurt.

Morgan got up and eyed the woods past the fence line of the property. She propped her hands on her hips then spun and looked back at the iron-framed firepit that sat near their picnic spot.

Emmett lifted his voice to her. "What you thinkin' on, MoJo?"

"Oh. Just that it's too dark to see what I'm writing. Maybe a little fire will help."

"I can go grab the floods from the barn," Geddy offered.

Morgan wrapped her arms around herself. "A fire would be nice anyway. It's cooling down enough." Morgan was actually feeling a little on edge. A fire wouldn't give her good enough light to finish their rough-hewn event plan. All it would do was give her an excuse to escape for a minute. Maybe five minutes.

Ten.

An hour...

How long could she get away? How long *should* she get away? It was like that urge to run had crawled down inside of her and fought its way back. Only now, Morgan was moored to Brambleberry. She was starting a business.

She was *engaged*, for goodness' sake. Did she really think she could run from all that?

And even if she did, *why*? Why was Morgan running?

What was she running from?

Without so much as a grunt that she'd be back, Morgan set off toward the far back of the property.

The idea was to gather up a good armful of kindling and firewood. If nothing else, the little errand would give her mind a reprieve from planning the event. A reprieve from her sudden urge to *run*. Not away from Emmett, but away from the growing pressures around her.

Julia and Morgan had gotten quite a lot done in a short amount of time. They'd scribbled down a working guest list, sketched out an arrangement for the ceremony, and traced a procession path. The event would have professionally made signage that began out on the main road and led the guests to park along Brambleberry Road on up to the gravel lot that spread from the drive to the right of the property. The sliver of that gravel way had normally been reserved as parking for the family. The far right of it was just empty gravel lot, perfect for a parking situation.

The guests would park there and move to stepping stones that Trav promised to pour and set. The stones led from the edge of the gravel lot to the grass, where Morgan intended to demarcate a pathway over the gentle green slope, past the barn and to the gap in the fence. There, they'd have an initial archway, a cedar piece to match the one made expressly for the arch beneath which Morgan and Emmett would stand.

All the woodwork would be handled by the boys, and they were supposed to begin those projects soon. Tomorrow, maybe. Always *tomorrow, maybe.*

From the gap in the fence, a path through the brambles, the vines, and finally the orchards would be demarcated, too. Morgan had the idea to plant fresh flowers along the route, but Julia wondered how much upkeep they'd take.

Not much, Morgan thought, but that was the thing about sharing a business with a friend—you had to give in to their bad ideas as often as they had to give in to yours.

It was the cost of sharing an enterprise with someone you loved. An affordable cost, though.

As such, Morgan agreed to consider Julia's idea about adding crafty wooden arrows, instead. Anyway, it *would* help keep all foliage focus on the fruit.

Once at the crest of where the pond careened off into the backwoods, Morgan squinted into the dwindling sunlight. Trees as old as her ancestors shot up from the earth and into the pink sky, darkening Morgan's entrance into the one-hundred-acre thatch of tree'd beauty that belonged to Morgan. Morgan and her family, that was.

At one point, Morgan had asked Grandad to walk her through the woods so she could learn about the varieties and the responsibilities associated with living within what was officially named Moonshine Creek Forest. The US Forestry had deemed it an agricultural site of interest and required that the soil be maintained between crops—but that was years back. Now, the forest had grown in over what used to include other crops than just the tobacco.

In here were pine trees and cedar, oak, too. A bit of everything, really.

The forest floor was littered with old wood among damp leaves and poison oak and ivy. Morgan took care to select pieces that lay in a rough path once shorn into the woods that—although it had long grown over—still existed like a ghost. The grass shorter. The dirt more visible.

She stood from plucking a perfect specimen from the center of the old path to hear the crack of branches behind her.

Morgan swiveled around, not *scared*, but... surprised? "Hello?"

No answer came.

Woodland critters were nothing new to Morgan, and she easily shrugged off the sound. Another several steps down the unkempt path, she found a scattering of good kindling and bent to pick it up.

A low whistle shrilled behind her.

Morgan swiveled as she bent, attempting a graceful, swooping defensive maneuver, but her hip screamed out in pain, and she fell into it, clutching her side and letting the collected stack of wood tumble to the forest floor.

The source of the whistle was irrelevant with the zinging old ache—or perhaps somewhere deep down, Morgan knew not to be afraid.

She knew all along, probably, it was Emmett.

Sure enough, she lifted her head to make out the sight of him jogging her way in the descending darkness. Concern streaked his features. "I'm the worst," he bemoaned, falling to his knees in front of her. "Here, let me." By then, Emmett knew how Morgan's body worked. At least, insomuch as he possibly could. She straightened, but again the zing shot up her thigh and deep into the heart of her injury, beneath the skin and where screws and pins held her shattered hip into some semblance of its original position.

Emmett pressed one palm directly onto the plastic veneer that lay just beneath her flesh. With his other hand, he held her lower back, squeezing her body like a sandwich.

The pain ebbed. Morgan straightened. "Why does it still hurt?" she murmured. A rhetorical question if ever there was one.

After some moments, Emmett gradually eased his pressure, and by the time he stood with her, the zing was only a memory. A cruel one. "Better?" he asked, dipping his face to hers and brushing her forehead with his lips.

"Better."

"Let me help with that firewood." He got busy recollecting the small logs that had rolled from her arms, and soon enough they were on their way back through the woods and toward their fish fry. "Food's all ready. Fish is *perfect*, if I do say so myself. Julia says the potatoes are soupy, but you know what? I *like* soupy potatoes." He rambled on like that until they rounded the pond that separated the woods from the back of the fence line. Before stepping through, Morgan stopped.

Behind her, Emmett made a whinnying sound almost like horse. "What is it?" She felt him peer around her, maybe looking for fallen barbed wire. Or a big ol' black spider with red splashing its belly.

Morgan turned to him and looked up, her face pinched and a headache coming on. "It's hurting again." It did that, her injury. Flared up. With stress or weight gain. Weight loss. Almost as if the scar tissue that formed inside of her pelvis was less a part of her loins and more a part of her heart.

Emmett's face remained open, devoid of worry. He was

good at that—playing it cool. "Take your time. We can ask Julia to stretch you out when we get back."

Morgan shook her head. "I'm just gon' need a minute." She gripped her hip and took deep, slow breaths.

Emmett rounded her and lowered the bundle of firewood to the ground before wrapping her up in his arms and pulling her in, rocking Morgan against him like a mother rocks a sick child. Then he whispered, "I hope you won't be mad about this—" he started, and flags of panic perked up in her mind.

She leaned away and eyed him. The pain turned again to that niggling memory. "Mad about what?"

Emmett pressed his mouth in a line and moved his arms from her waist to her elbows, holding her in place—maybe so that she wouldn't run. "I mentioned your fits to my mama."

"My *fits*?"

"Your bouts. The *pain*, Morgan. It worries me."

Her eyes must have widened into greater panic yet because he backtracked fast.

"Not—it doesn't worry me seriously. I mean, it worries me that you have to face any discomfort at all. That's it, MoJo. And you know my mama was a nurse, and she has a good sense of these things."

Mrs. Dawson was a nurse, that was true. In fact, in Morgan's whole world of people, she didn't know one medical professional outside of Julia. To Morgan, Julia, a board-certified physical therapist, was the beginning and the end of medical knowledge. She was competent and practical, and that suited Morgan well. She wanted to have someone in her court who could tell her to push harder or take a day off, but come back and stretch further the next day. She needed someone to brush aside the drama of a limp or the commotion of a sharp stabbing pain. She needed someone to tell her that it was all in her head.

Because if it was all in Morgan's head, then the pain wasn't real. It wasn't something she had to deal with.

CHAPTER THIRTEEN

PRESENT DAY

Morgan Jo

Emmett explained that his mother knew an internist who could help Morgan. They'd examine her inside and out and see what they could do about the ongoing fits of pain.

"I'm not taking pain medication, if that's what you mean," she retorted. "Those days are long over. This is just... aftershocks."

"No, no. Not pain management. He'll do scans to see about the scar tissue and check on healing. Maybe there's more can be done."

"What kind of a doctor is an internist, anyway?" she didn't mean to be suspicious, but she also knew her own history. She'd been to plenty of doctors. None could do much more to help her. Julia was the best so far. The therapy had offered the greatest strides toward healing. Morgan hardly limped at all anymore. And after a few years of limping, that was nothing short of a miracle.

"I think he's sort of a general doctor who can look at your insides and help." Emmett bent to get the firewood. With an effortless sweep, he had the bundle tucked beneath one arm. "If you don't want to, you don't have to. We just want to help."

It wasn't that she didn't want to that was nagging on Morgan. It was that Emmett was talking to his mama about her. Behind her back. It wasn't like him. Morgan couldn't bat away the silly feeling of suspicion as they moved through the gap in the fence and passed the hangar.

She eyed the old structure, wondering what in the world they would do with it. And *when*. A spell of overwhelm was quickly descending. "Who brought it up?" she asked Emmett.

"Brought what up?"

"My pains. I mean, did you tell your mom or something?"

He stopped walking. Morgan turned. "I mean, how did it come up? Why were you talking about me?"

Emmett looked crestfallen. "Morgan, why am I *ever* talking about you?" A smile tinted his features. "Because I'm crazy for you, girl."

It was enough. She agreed to see Mrs. Dawson's friend the internist. Once it was settled, they ambled along back to the barbecue.

"Look who made it!" Julia called out as they neared.

Morgan peered through the dusky evening sky until two shapes formed at the picnic table, alongside Julia and Geddy.

"Amber?" Morgan picked up her pace. "You came after all."

The pair hugged and Morgan noticed Amber had brought Callum, too. His hands were deep in his pockets and though he smiled, his face hung down toward the ground. When Morgan lifted her hand for a small wave, he grabbed his bucket hat from his head and pulled it down, first. An act of deference, maybe. "Hey Callum."

He looked up from beneath a mop of dark curls. She couldn't tell if he was younger than Amber—maybe closer to twenty-five?—or simply shy. "Good to see you, Miss Morgan Jo."

"And this here is Morgan Jo's fiancé, Emmett Dawson," Amber introduced them.

Emmett lowered the firewood skillfully to the picnic seat and offered his hand to Callum. "Hi there, Callum. Glad you could make it." Emmett gave a winning grin and nodded to Geddy. "Did this guy get you a beer yet?"

Callum shook his head, and off they went, like old friends. Everyone sat. Julia forced Grace on the group, thanking Lord Jesus for the food and company. Once tucked into the fish and taters, Morgan asked Amber and Callum together, "You-all find anything good on the tapes? Think we'll be able to watch 'em soon?"

Amber answered, "We didn't get a chance."

"Oh, my word." Julia clamped a hand over mouth, all drama and apologies. "Amber Lee—you were gon' meet your daddy! Well?"

Morgan about spat her beer over the table. "Oh, hell. Amber, I can't believe I didn't ask." She shared a look with Jules. "*Well?*"

But Amber didn't meet their gaze. Instead, she pushed food around her plate, a curious thing for Amber to do. She gave a quick shake of her head but kept her gaze on her uneaten fried catfish.

"What happened?" Morgan frowned at Callum, who winced.

"He couldn't come. Her dad, I mean. Hank. He, um—he just couldn't come."

Morgan reached across the table and patted the spot between Amber and Callum. "Hey, Amber. *Amber*, it's okay. Another time, right?"

Geddy snorted, but Morgan shot him a quick glare.

Amber lifted her face and smiled weakly. "It's fine. Really. I don't think I was ready to see him. Not yet. I felt like I was going to barf." A little laugh slipped through her mouth and she set her fork down then hooked a thumb back to the house. "I'm gon' go get a tea. Anyone else?"

The rest of the table held up beers, except Morgan. "I'll join you."

As they walked, Morgan turned giddy. "He's cute, you know."

"Who?" Amber shot back.

"Callum. Who else?"

Color bloomed in Amber's cheeks. She looked up at Morgan. "You think?"

"He likes you. I can tell."

"I like him, too. Which is really freakin' weird, Morgan Jo."

"Why? You're a red-blooded woman. It's an eventuality that you'll find a handsome man, well, handsome. And plus, I think Callum is *objectively* attractive."

"It's weird because I was literally engaged like, *months* ago. And I don't know him. He's a video clerk. He works for my dad. He's the opposite of Grant in every way, just about."

"That's a good thing, I promise you." Morgan gave her cousin a squeeze and in through the back door, they entered the big house.

Inside the kitchen, they met with CarlaMay, who was dressed to the nines. "Somebody's got a hot date," Amber teased. Morgan set about the tea, unamused and even uneasy as a cloud of her mother's perfume enveloped them.

CarlaMay greedily drank from a tall, iced water when she stifled laughter at Amber's remark. "Amber Lee, you're bad." She shook her head and her soft brown waves lifted around her face. It was a haircut that would age any other fifty-something woman. Not CarlaMay, though. The close-cropped 'do, when curled, gave her an elegant, timeless look. Like an actress from the 1940s. Vivien Leigh, maybe.

"Are you going out with the same guy?" Morgan tried to keep the accusatory tone out of her voice but failed.

"Is that okay?" CarlaMay's tone was just as clipped. She wasn't asking permission. She was warning her daughter. She was dating a man. No secret about it. No creeping around in the shadows. This was real.

"It's fine, Mom."

Morgan set her jaw and focused on steeping tea bags in the kettle. Then she turned. "Who is he? What's his name, anyway? Do we know him?" The questions tumbled out, a wagon rolling down a wet, slick, grassy hill.

CarlaMay's shoulders rolled forward. The oomph from just a moment before left her like air whistling out, like a tired balloon with a fresh puncture. "Yes."

"Yes, *what?*"

"Yes, you know him."

CHAPTER FOURTEEN

PRESENT DAY

Amber

CarlaMay had left them with *no* other information. Just the bombshell that whoever her man of mystery was, well, he was *known* to them.

"Wow." Amber clicked her tongue and shook her head, accepting the fresh-brewed tea from Morgan and following her shell-shocked cousin out the back door. "Do you have any clue who it could be?"

Morgan turned and gave Amber a thoughtful look. "I'm not sure I even want to guess."

"What are we guessin' about?" Geddy appeared and took the pitcher of tea from Morgan, his face turned red from drink and the warmth of the fire Emmett had gotten going.

"Guessin' who Aunt CarlaMay is seeing behind all our backs, that's what." If there was one thing that could distract Amber from being stood up by her dad, it was somebody else's drama.

Amber caught Emmett's expression. A look of warning crossed his features. He reached out a hand to Morgan and helped her down onto her seat along the picnic table. "Everything okay?" Though he spoke low, Amber picked up the message. *Tread lightly*. Something was amiss, perhaps.

But to Amber's surprise, Morgan broke out a mischievous smile. "I think my mom is seeing someone from out of town. That's what I think."

"Who do you know from out of town?" Amber lowered her chin and smirked, hungry for girl talk.

Morgan started into the fields as Amber filled Callum in on the unfolding family dynamic.

He nodded as if he understood, and the six of them were pleasantly off to the races, naming every random Joe they could think of and laughing at the very idea of Amber's prim-and-proper aunt letting her hair down and gallivanting out into the night like a teenager.

Once they'd run through the options, they accepted that even their own family—or especially their own family—kept secrets.

They all finished supper, and the boys rounded up chairs to set around the fire. Amber went in to get s'mores fixin's and when she came back, she found the conversation had shifted.

"I have a question," Geddy chimed in as he took the tray from Amber and put together a little s'mores station. He started poking marshmallows through skewers and passing them out. "What if Aunt Carla brings this lover guy to the weddin'?"

"To *our* wedding? Emmett's and mine?" Morgan pursed her lips and stared over at the fire.

Amber followed her stare and got lost in the flickering orange flames.

Morgan murmured an answer to her own question. "I can't imagine she'd do that."

Geddy guffawed. "Why not? You're gonna need someone to walk you down the aisle, Mo."

As if ice descended over the fire, their chatter froze. All that could be heard was the crackle of the flames eating through logs.

Amber shifted her weight to the edge of her chair and grabbed a skewer from Geddy. "Morgan Jo doesn't need anyone to walk her down the aisle. That's a silly tradition, anyway." But when Amber turned to see Morgan's reaction, there was nothing there. Just a blank face, and dull, dark eyes, as if the heat of the fire—of Geddy's idiocy—had charred her from the inside out.

The get-together broke up just as soon as Geddy made his gaffe. First with Emmett standing and sharply admonishing Geddy, then with Morgan leaving, zombie-like, toward the big house. After that, Julia went after Morgan and it was just Geddy, Callum, and Amber left at the camp.

Callum didn't say anything, but instead he stood and moved to the table where he deftly swept paper plates into a plastic bag that had been tied off of the side. Geddy muttered some choice words and went to the grill, where he took up a brush with steel bristles and furiously scrubbed at the grates along the quickly cooling metal.

Amber felt antsy, as though her discontent over her dad was rounding back. She twisted her fingers together and worried her lower lip between her teeth. Callum stuck his hands down his jeans pockets and wandered toward Amber, who stood at the far side of the picnic table.

Callum lifted his chin off toward the dark vastness of the rest of the property. "You got a barn?"

Following his gaze, Amber peered at the nearest outbuilding. "Yep. We're converting right now, though." Callum took a tentative step forward and looked back at her. Amber smiled. "Want a twilight tour?"

CHAPTER FIFTEEN

1991

CarlaMay

Whit, angered and alarmed, backed away from us, his hands in the air. Then, he turned and headed back onto 4th Street. Maybe he'd look for another victim or maybe he'd hail a cab and go sleep it off.

I really hoped it would be the latter, but watching him go, I really thought his anger wasn't tempered. Rather, he seemed emboldened. Unbridled, even. Like a wild horse who refused to be broken.

"You okay, CarlaMay?"

I looked up at my savior—that's how I decided I'd think of him now. His light eyes glowed with concern. I nodded.

"I'll walk you home. Okay?"

I looked past him to the other man he was with.

He turned to follow my gaze, then lifted a hand to his friend. "I'll catch up later. Gonna walk Miss CarlaMay back to her dorm." Then he looked at me. "If you want me to, that is."

My heartbeat hadn't slowed, but it was quieter now, like a gentle thrum inside of a frantic rattle. I nodded.

We walked through the night without speaking a word to one another. They were there, though—the words. A million bits of confetti down my throat and piling up in my chest. I wanted to say so many things. What I thought of him in his professional role. What I thought of him as a person—a human. And I promise I just knew he was holding back that same burst down inside. It was like we were walking with a sheet of electricity buzzing in between us. Our silence did nothing but add to it.

It's like, if things between us were normal, *we'd talk, right? We'd talk about the weather or what a jerk Whit was. I'd tell him my sister was back at the bar and maybe we should go get her. He'd ask me what I thought of his talk from this past week. I'd tell him it was good. That I learned a lot. He'd ask what I was studying, and I'd tell him I was only at school because I got a grant that paid for it and it gave me a break from the farm.*

He'd tell me why he decided to do what he does, and I'd learn that we were more alike than I guessed. Two people wandering through life and goin' along to get along. That's just what we both are, I think.

Anyway, we got closer to my dorm, and that's when my insides started feeling weird. A heavy weight in my loins that made my legs antsy—I knew what it was, that feeling. It's the devil doin' his work on me in the face of temptation.

My chest rose up high and sank shallow and as my heart thrummed my breaths came in and out short. It felt like I was losing control of my body. My nostrils flared with each exhale. I sucked my cheeks in between my teeth, and my lips just parted without my sayin' so.

We stood at the back entrance to the dorm, him and me, both staring up. I could tell from the edge of my vision that he was working up to say something, like the confetti was gon' spill right out his mouth, but something was in the way. Maybe it was the short breath and the thrumming of his heart. Heat emanated between us—or maybe it was just from me, from my loins and my shallow breaths.

I took a slight turn toward him. He turned more fully to me. I lifted my face up, and a streetlamp glowed over his face. Maybe mine, too. I could tell he could see my face because he had the same look on his that I had on my heart, like he knew what was in my soul in that moment.

What happened next, I'll never tell anyone. But that's the thing, you see. It can't live inside of me. It can't hang on my shoulders like sandbags. It has to come out.

So, here it goes.

CHAPTER SIXTEEN

PRESENT DAY

Morgan Jo

Once inside the big house, Morgan Jo stopped at the kitchen. Dishes from food prep were piled high in the sink. Normally, she was irritated to find a mess so late in the evening.

Now, she needed the distraction of work.

Before she got so far as to run hot water, Julia and Emmett were behind her.

"Mo," Julia said. "Geddy wasn't thinking."

"He's an idiot," Emmett added.

Morgan could all but feel Julia give Emmett a sharp look. Julia was falling in love with Geddy. Julia could get married to Geddy one day. Safe in the knowledge that she didn't have scar tissue, pins, and plastic holding up half her body. Safe in the knowledge she had a regular chance to have babies one day.

Safe in the knowledge that her daddy was around to walk her down the aisle when it was time for the unlikely pair to say I do.

"I don't want to talk about it," Morgan said, more to herself than to her two shadows.

Hushed words were exchanged behind her, and once the sink was filled with hot, sudsy water and the scent of acrid dish soap, Morgan lifted her chin over her shoulder.

Julia was gone.

Emmett leaned into the kitchen island, a thoughtful expression over his face. "You okay?"

Morgan sniffed and returned to the dishes, dunking her hands into the water, scalding the skin hot pink. "I'm fine. Geddy isn't an idiot. He's just—"

"He shouldn't have said that. It was dumb of him, at best. Rude at worst."

"He, of all people, should understand what it's like." Geddy's dad wasn't around for most all his life. And his own mother had bounced around apartments and farmhouses so often it was a wonder Geddy was as successful as he was—not that he was very successful. Morgan was just waiting for him to quit his job at the market and turn up asking to work at the winery one day.

"Maybe that's why he said it?"

Morgan felt Emmett's hands rest on her shoulders. She didn't shake him away. "Are you sure you want to marry into this mess?"

He let out a short chuckle and moved next to her, edging her gently over with his hip and taking on the dishes with slow care. "I can handle dirty pots and pans."

"No." The tip of a sob formed a bulge in her throat. She swallowed it down hard. "I mean my family. We're—" She squeezed her eyes shut and when she opened them again, they fell on that old familiar wooden sign that hung over the sink. *Remember, as far as anyone knows, we're a nice, normal family.* "Dysfunctional," she finished her thought half-heartedly.

"What family isn't?" Emmett rinsed a pan and passed it to Morgan to dry.

"Yours. Your folks are together. You don't have orphan cousins. Everyone seems to know who their daddy is."

"Just because a married couple stays together, doesn't mean they're entirely functional." He said this without irony.

Morgan snorted. "That's true. Even my family members who stayed married were train wrecks."

He snapped the faucet shut and grabbed the towel from Morgan. "I didn't mean that. I didn't mean your grandfolks, MoJo. I meant *my* parents. My dad can't stand my mom. My mom can't stand her own life. And it's... well, on the outside, anyway, it's as perfect as perfect can get."

Morgan frowned. "She seems happy to me."

He shook his head. "Why do you think she's nosing into our business? Planning your wedding shower and setting up your doctor's appointments?"

"Because she cares," Morgan answered like it was a no-brainer.

"Because she's bored." He let a beat pass. "Nobody is perfect. No *marriage* is perfect. No parents are perfect."

"And yet you still want to get married to me? What if—"

"What if it's hard?" His face pulled, and his eyes searched Morgan's.

"Yeah," she whispered, the sob slipping down her throat and settling on top of her heart.

He reached up and tucked a loose lock of hair behind her ear. "What if it's easy?"

"What if I go to the doctor and he says I can't have kids?"

"What if I go to the doctor and he says the same thing?" Emmett's voice was devoid of humor. He was being serious. Sincere. Breathlessly sincere. "What if the world ends tomorrow?"

She didn't laugh.

Emmett gripped her face gently between his hands and

pressed his forehead into hers. He whispered, "We can 'what if' until the end of time, MoJo. But it won't change what's meant to be."

CHAPTER SEVENTEEN

PRESENT DAY

Amber

Together, Amber and Callum slipped into the twilit night.

Amber had forgotten how much she loved late-summer evenings on the farm. The heat of the day burned off, and in its place settled a balmy warmth. Crickets, hidden from view, chirped out creaking backwoods melodies. Lightning bugs sparked to life in swirling flashes.

"When we were little, we were obsessed with catching lightnin' bugs," she confessed. "But now, it seems cruel."

They walked along slowly. Callum asked, "Cruel?"

"Well, sure. To capture them in mason jars and treat 'em like our own personal lanterns."

"It's part of childhood, I think."

"You did it, too?" She slid her gaze his way.

He shrugged. "My sisters did. I was more interested in taking apart my dad's AV equipment."

"You didn't play outside?"

He seemed to consider this for a moment. "Sometimes I took apart his radios on the back porch."

Amber couldn't help but laugh. "You're not what I'm used to, you know?"

"Really?" Genuine surprise filled his voice.

"I'm used to boys who blow up bullfrogs and get their four-wheelers stuck in the mud down by the pond."

"That's not what I heard." His voice was so quiet, Amber couldn't be sure she heard him right. They came to a stop just outside of the barn.

"Pardon me?"

He cleared his throat. "Sorry. I didn't mean to be rude—"

"No, no. What did you *hear*?" She wasn't mad. She was curious.

"I know Grant Maycomb. A little."

Amber's blood came to a stop in her veins. She blinked. "You know I was engaged?"

"It's a small town."

"I thought you just moved here."

"I did."

"How do you know him?"

"He came in for video games."

Amber nodded and indicated the barn. "Here's where we're making the wine."

"Cool."

Their eyes met. Amber ran her tongue over her lips. "From what I can tell, you're not a lick like my ex."

As if he'd been holding a great big breath, he pushed air through his mouth, and his body sagged forward a little. "Thank God."

Amber giggled. "Thank God?"

"I don't mean to use the Lord's name in vain, but yeah. I can't stand that guy."

"No one can."

"Plus..." He scratched the back of his neck. "I don't want you to think I'm like him."

"You don't?" Amber's breath caught in her chest.

Callum shook his head and opened his body to her. "I mean... is that weird to say?"

She smiled. "No."

He grinned back, and the air seemed to grow wet around them, as if a rainstorm might be comin' on.

If Amber wasn't imagining things, Callum was swaying closer to her, and she closer to him. But before their bodies met, a lightning bug lit up smack dab between them.

"Oh!" Amber cried in nervous delight. Laughter spilled out of her mouth. Callum's gaze left her and narrowed on the space between them.

Amber spotted the unpredictable bug and held a palm beneath it. A miniature glowing orb, the little guy hovered there, blinking on and off and sucking away the time and Amber's words. Finally, it blinked a last time and flit away. Amber looked up at Callum and then past him toward the barn. "Want to go inside?"

After a brief visit of the barn, they left, and Amber closed it up. She didn't want the night to be over.

Maybe Callum didn't either. He pointed north. "What's that?"

Peering into the night, she answered, "The hangar."

"Hangar? Oh—for the tobacco!" His voice crept up in excitement. "It's like visiting a museum being here. You hear all about it, and then you come here and—" He held up his hands like he was framing a scene for a movie shoot. "*Boom.*"

"Boom." Amber giggled. "I never realized the farm was famous."

"So, is it operable?" He started that way, and Amber followed him, sashaying her hips to the rhythm of the night sounds. Crickets. The soft padding of their feet on the damp grass below.

Behind them, back near the big house, Geddy had since disappeared with the others. Amber wondered what would become of him next. If he was in as much trouble with Julia as he was with Emmett and Morgan Jo. A gentle breeze carried the scent of campfire on it, and the very smell rejuvenated her. "The hangar has been closed up for years. Nothing happens in there. In fact, our Memaw wanted us to tear it down."

"So why don't you?"

Amber had never been with a guy who was so chatty and curious. Callum was refreshing. "That's as good a question as any. It's a long story." She pulled to a stop just outside the doors. A rusty padlock dangled, open, at the latch.

Callum bent over at the waist, examining the lock. He angled his thumb at it. "I've got time."

Amber glanced toward the big house then back at him. Mint and Julep, her precious pair of cats, would be expecting her soon. They'd start swatting knickknacks off of her dresser if she was gone much longer.

Callum stood up fast and shoved his hands back down his pockets. "Another time, maybe. It's late."

"It's not that late." Amber eyed him, her heart torn between her cats and Callum. It was silly that she felt she had to choose. She looked at her wristwatch. In fact, it wasn't all that late. "I have an idea," she said, feeling emboldened by the warm night air. "I'll show you round the hangar, then I can show you where I live?"

He grinned wide. "I'd like that."

As Callum tugged open the wide wooden door of the hangar, they were hit with a hot, wet, musty smell.

"Woo-*wee*!" Callum cried. "Smells like my Great-Aunt

Edna's basement up in the city."

Amber likened it to her childhood. She smiled. "Smells like fall." And it did, too. Of course, there were no tobacco leaves left, but their scent had grown into the wood siding, the metal roof. Heck, even the nails probably smelled a little bit like baccy, as Grandad used to call it.

It wasn't just the age-old tobacco leaves that they smelled, though. It was the damp hay that coated the elevated coves. It was the dirt floor—dirt that had seen seeping rain and snow run-off (when they'd had snow). It was the long copper-top work-bench that bore the welts of hammers and mallets. The rusted-over mini backhoe that had long-ago died in the back left corner.

It was every harvest season of Amber's life. Of Grandad chewing and hockin' baccy in an old spittoon. Of freshly rolled bales of hay. Of Aunt Carla's candied apples for Halloween. And Memaw's Spicy Holler Roasts for All Saints' Day. Pumpkin pie just because it was in season and the canned pumpkin was buy-one-get-one free.

It was the best days of Amber's life in that there hangar.

Amber wrapped herself in the memories with a slow twirl as Callum inspected the space like it could be the perfect set for his next film production.

She was studying a brittle wooden pipe when he called over to her from the back right corner. "Hey, look at this."

Amber glanced Callum's way, made clearer by the beam of his phone's flashlight app. The narrow ray lit up a sliver of what was once a twisted family tragedy. Amber frowned but joined him along the splintered plywood nailed over a haunted history.

Innocent as a newborn babe, Callum asked, "What's in there?" He gave the wood a light knock.

Amber grimaced. "Remember that long story I mentioned?"

He nodded.

She pressed her hand along the wood. "That's what's in there."

CHAPTER EIGHTEEN

1991

CarlaMay

It took just the look. Just that one look, and as though we were already inside one another—already a part of one another—I fell into him.

I'd kissed boys before, sure I had. Bumpkins from Brambleberry all the way up to Bardstown. I let boys put their hands up my shirt. I let them grab my behind and try to push me into doing something I didn't want to do.

But I wanted this.

Our mouths, his and mine, worked together like the surf and the shore. And our bodies did, too. Soon enough, we stumbled together, locked at the lips, in through the back door—I withdrew my key and gave it to him and he let us in. The hallways lit just by emergency exits, we didn't care about gettin' caught or anything. We kept on, the key stowed back in my purse, his hands framing my face, his body stooped down and mine pushed up on the balls of my feet, we staggered and tripped down the hall until we came to my room, which I shared with a girl who'd dropped out, leaving me alone in there, miserably and wonderfully alone.

He went for the doorknob behind his back, and we laughed, because I'd put my key away. Silly. Frantic and hungry and thirsty and every sort of feeling that demanded I consume, I groped in my bag and came up with the keys and unlocked the door myself this time, ripping the key from the lock as we crashed into the room.

Somehow or another the door closed.

Once inside, things decelerated, almost like those videos that people submit to television producers who then edit the clips and show someone falling in slow motion. In the show, the result is funny.

In my room, it wasn't funny at all. But it wasn't serious either.

I didn't turn on the lights. The moon spilled in through lace drapes my mama helped me make—sheer pink cotton fabric with lace trim. They didn't belong in a college dorm room.

Neither did I.

And neither did he.

CHAPTER NINETEEN

PRESENT DAY

Morgan Jo

Once Emmett left to go home, Morgan returned to the site of their ill-fated barbecue. Her notepad remained on the far side of the picnic table, its pen tucked neatly into the seam. The night was warm, but a heavy wetness hung in the air.

She looked out toward their vineyard and orchards. Sometimes, it took a little imagining to put things in perspective. Morgan now imagined another hailstorm crackling down on the farm. Another ruining of what they had. One worse than the last—one so bad that it not only damaged their trees and vines but also their vehicles. The barn. The house. She then imagined a tornado sweeping through the property.

Morgan imagined herself as her grandmother, Essie, standing out in the ominous calm before such a storm.

She imagined her grandmother wondering what the weather could and would do to their very livelihood. How they'd save the livestock. How they'd save the windows on the big house. Boards. All the while she'd mostly wonder how in the world they'd sell a whole crop's worth of ruined tobacco that wasn't fit to hang and dry. How would they feed the kids?

And Morgan felt worse and better.

Worse because she had no right to worry.

Better because she didn't have to worry anyway. Not thanks to Uncle Gary and his heritage plants. Praise be.

Morgan sat at the picnic table and stared at the notes she had for her own wedding. Her business opening. A two-for-one deal, her mom would probably call it. A great way to save a buck, Grandad might say.

A risk that needed takin'.

Morgan took up her pencil and pressed it down on a fresh sheet of paper.

Then, like a hailstorm, she rained down every last crazy idea she had.

CHAPTER TWENTY

PRESENT DAY

Amber

Amber and Callum stood in quiet contemplation at the boarded-up corner of the hangar.

It occurred to her she wasn't entirely certain if what happened in that wooden box was supposed to be a family secret. The family had lots of those, Amber knew. And even she herself was lately implicated in such a secret. The secret of Grant Maycomb cheating on her.

When Amber thought about what happened with the Grant secret, she remembered that the only thing that made it better—that relieved the pain—was popping the secret like a boil. That's how Amber saw her failed relationship with Grant Maycomb. Like a boil. A festering blister. A zit, even. If she could just clear it away and come clean, then maybe she'd feel better.

Maybe it helped that Callum either didn't seem interested or wasn't one to pressure her. "It's sort of a bad story," she confessed after several silent beats.

"I gathered that."

"Right." She twisted her fingers and spied a corner of the bottom sheet of plywood that had warped outward. Its nail was loose and dangling, tempting her to grab the splintered edge and pry it free. See what the big deal was. Then her eyes fell along the seam that spread down from that corner, where the plywood met the back wall of the barn. There were five nails in total, and every single one looked loose. As if it had been plucked loose with the split end of a hammer, then pushed back into the wood like a thumbtack.

"Amber?" She blinked and looked up. Concern pulled on Callum's features. "You okay?"

A quick nod. "Yeah. I can tell you the story. I don't think it's, like, private or anything. I mean, actually it even made the news."

"The news?"

She dared a glance toward the gaping barn door. "I really need to check on my girls. Would you—would you want to come back to my place? I'll tell you the story."

Once nestled down in Amber's basement apartment, she set about boiling milk for hot cocoa. Summer or not, who didn't enjoy a hot chocolate on a pretty evening?

Callum made himself at home on the sofa, and Mint and Julep inspected him carefully, each one nosing either side as he sat still, his palms up, an offer of safety to them. "Gorgeous cats," he remarked.

Amber's heart skipped a beat. "They're good girls, usually. Can't trust them not to dart outside, though."

"You don't let them out?"

She brought two mugs to the coffee table and lowered herself to the opposite end of the sofa, one full cushion away from him. She didn't want Callum to feel her weight. It seemed important to preserve some degree of mystery in that regard.

"No. They were brought up indoors, and I wouldn't want a critter to mess with them." Mint heard her and padded over the middle cushion to rub her head against Amber's thigh. Then the silly cat pushed herself all the way to Amber's belly, where she cuddled up tight.

"Makes sense." Callum took a sip. "This is the best hot chocolate I've ever had in my life."

"The secret is cinnamon." *Secret.* "Speaking of which. The boarded-up... *room*, I guess you could call it?"

He cocked his head. "Sure. Does it maybe have to do with the tapes?"

"The tapes?" Amber frowned. "Oh. The VHS tapes? No." A quick shake of the head drew the attention of Julep, who crept to Amber, sniffed her knee, then returned to Callum, whose lap she snuggled into. "Oh my. She doesn't usually like men."

"Men?"

"I think when they were kittens, they weren't treated all too great. By the guy, I mean. The husband of the wife who gave them away."

"I don't understand people who aren't kind to animals." Callum shifted and settled his hand on Julep's back, petting in long, slow strokes until Julep purred contentedly.

"The tapes were filmed in the barn, from what I saw. I mean—maybe some took place in the hangar, but it doesn't seem like they'd have a reason to be in there."

"Oh." Callum didn't press her. This gave Amber permission to confess. Not that what happened in the boarded-up corner was her sin to confess. Or even a sin at all. Although the Pope might disagree.

"Anyway. This farm has been in my Memaw's family since forever. She had a lot of brothers and sisters, my Memaw."

"Lots of families used to."

Amber didn't want to change the conversation, but she felt a strange compulsion to break the subject. "Do you want kids?"

He didn't flinch. "Definitely. I could have ten. I've got one little brother and one little sister, and they're the best. When we were growing up, I babysat. Some people think that's weird, for a boy to be a babysitter."

"But you were their brother."

"Exactly. Anyway, we're still close. I've got two nieces. My brother's girls. They live up in the city. I visit lots. Hoping to get them down here to Brambleberry."

"You live in town?"

"I rent a room from Miss Delcey. You know her?"

Amber nodded. "She goes to our church. Not that I'm ever there." Miss Delcey was a spinster straight out of an old-timey Victorian movie, complete with a little mean dog who raced the white picket fence that framed the front of her property. Nobody knew if Miss Delcey had old money or no money or what. She was as much a mystery as the Catholic faith itself.

"Are any of your Memaw's siblings still alive?"

Amber shook her head. "They were all older, except for one." Talking about the story of Aunt Dottie was like pressing play on a tape recording. All Amber had to do was tap a button and the story came to life, a complete-if-tinny record of events Amber hadn't personally witnessed but rather had committed so precisely to her memory that she could spit facts on the subject.

"Her name was Dorothy, but she went by Dottie. She was my Memaw's twin sister. Anyhow, they played in the hangar, which I guess wasn't altogether allowed. One day, Dottie wanted to play Cops and Robbers or something like that. She took a gun up there. A pistol. They had a fight, Memaw—Essie —and Dottie. The gun went off." Amber delivered the tale with cold detachment, but deep down inside a sadness about it burned like fire. Almost as though tragedy was imprinted on her. A fact of her heritage. A part of her DNA. A sliver of her heart.

Callum let out a low whistle. "I'm really sorry."

"I didn't know her."

"How old were they? Your Memaw and Dottie?"

Julep mewed in his lap, reminding Callum not to forget about her.

"They were just ten years old."

"It must have changed the course of your Memaw's life."

Amber liked the way he put that. "Yeah. It was... one of those moments."

"Moments," Callum echoed the word. "Where you think everything is business as usual, then a tractor runs you down, flattens you out? You think your life is over."

"Dottie's was."

"How did your Memaw get over it?"

Amber thought about it for a beat. "I don't think she ever did."

CHAPTER TWENTY-ONE

1991

CarlaMay

In my room, where none of us belonged—not the farmhouse curtains, not me, not him. In there that night, he stared at me in a way I had never seen a man stare at a woman. It was fear. It was want. It was everything bad and good and holy and sinful.

My chest rose and fell. My heart pounded hard in my chest, and I was certain I was going to have a heart attack just like my Grandad Coyle had. I was going to crumple onto the floor, dead as a doornail.

But the heart attack didn't come as a medical emergency. It came as another thing entirely. Instead of crumpling on the floor and dying, I lived.

I moved to him, one small step at a time, savoring the moment and dreading it. Like the dread I used to have when I had to go to the orchards and fill a basket of peaches, but I was worried there wouldn't be any to pick, and I'd come home empty-handed and get a scolding like mother nature's failing was somehow my fault.

I was wrong, though. Before me awaited a whole tree full of peaches, plump and hanging down low, so heavy they threatened to fall to the ground.

And fall we did. I clasped my hands around his face just as he'd done to mine, and we fell to the bed. The hunger built up greater, and soon enough, we were whispering to each other about all the feelings I'd been holding in and he'd been holding in, and I could have just cried happy tears to know that every single thing I was keeping tucked in my heart—it matched what he was keeping tucked in, too. How he watched me from in front of the Masses. How he saw me and wanted me.

The confetti burst out of us both, and we did something I hadn't even really known about. We did the one thing I shouldn't be doing, and he definitely shouldn't be doing. Not with me.

Heck, not with anyone.

CHAPTER TWENTY-TWO

PRESENT DAY

Morgan Jo

Morgan shifted on the exam table. Beneath her bottom, the paper cover peeled off of the back of her naked thighs.

Emmett sat in a plastic chair along the wall, chatting about the weather and a few things he needed to do later that day. He'd cleared his schedule for this appointment, and afterward they were supposed to meet his mom for a late lunch at Casa Duardo, Mrs. Dawson's favorite Mexican food place.

A quick rap sounded at the heavy wooden door, but it opened before either Morgan or Emmett could say anything.

"H'why hello, you two!" drawled a cheery-looking man with a small, round build and small, round glasses to match. He first offered his hand to Morgan, not squeezing but simply holding it for a brief moment. "I'm Dr. Wigman. *Lamont*," he added for a down-home effect.

"Morgan." It came out cracked. She cleared her voice. "I'm Morgan Jo. Nice to meet you."

"And you must be Emmett. Your mama has told me every-thing there is to know about you, young man." Morgan watched as Emmett stood, and the two shared a visibly firm shake. Dr. Wigman squeezed Emmett's shoulder with his free hand. Then he raised both hands in surrender. "Don't sue me!" Lamont —Dr. Wigman—guffawed at his own joke. Morgan managed a smile, and Emmett laughed good-naturedly.

"We've heard about you, too, Doc. All good things." Emmett was on his best behavior, which wasn't saying much on account of the fact that it was his default attitude.

The doctor plopped heavily onto a squat rolling chair and pulled out an iPad, swiping faster than Morgan expected. "So. Seems to me we're all here today to talk about *babies*." His cheeks turned to big red apples as he flashed a smile.

Babies. Like an anchor that fell smack in the middle of the deck of a boat, rather than off to the side into the water. The word crushed through her insides, flooding her chest and her heart and sinking her back onto the exam table as a nurse entered to oversee things.

Emmett moved to the chair closer to her head, out of decency and support. He held her hand and gave her a winning smile. She imagined that instead of an exam table, she was on a birthing table. Her feet were in stirrups and instead of advising her to relax, the doctors were telling her to push. Emmett was crying. A baby was crying.

Morgan was crying.

"MoJo," Emmett whispered. His thumb rubbed a tear from her cheek. She really *was* crying. A quiet pair of tears streaked from either eye.

"All done!" the doctor announced.

Her outsides returned to insides and Emmett helped Morgan sit up. "Next, we do a scope. This happens under local anesthesia, assuming the general tests are nice and *negative*."

Negative.

Morgan knew that in medicine, negative results were positive.

Unless you were trying to get pregnant.

"Oh, *Morgan*, honey!" Mrs. Dawson rose from a white-cloth-draped table. She held Morgan's fingers and pulled her in for pretend cheek kisses, then opened her arms wide to Emmett. "My *baby*."

Mrs. Dawson was dressed as though she was going to the Derby. She wore a cream-colored silk blouse that seemed to drift like the surf around her body. Slenderizing black slacks that fell in clean lines down her long legs, stopping just above cream-colored canvas espadrilles. Her nails and toes were French-tipped, and big, bobbly, cream-colored rocks hung around her wrist and her neck.

All that was missing was a great big hat, cocked just so.

"Sit. Sit!" She pointed down at the table set for three.

Their orders were whisked away, and Mrs. Dawson wasted no time in getting down to the nitty-gritty. "Morgan, honey. *Tell* me. How did it go with *Lamont*."

"He was very kind." Morgan sipped from the white wine she'd ordered. The thought occurred to her to chug, but then again she didn't want to embarrass Emmett.

"It's a waiting game right now. Right, Mo?" He squeezed her hand on the table. "Preliminary tests. Next week, we've got an appointment for a scope." He grimaced and squeezed her hand again before moving it to grab a roll to butter. He offered the roll to Morgan.

"Preliminary tests!" Mrs. Dawson threw up her hands. "What a waste." She clicked her tongue. Her eyes turned wide and she went for a long slug of her own wine. Morgan took it as permission to do the same. If she was going to make it through dinner, then she'd better drink a little faster.

Mrs. Dawson pointed one of her perfect, white-tipped nails

at Morgan. "Although, the main goal is to make sure you're *healthy*, honey. That's the *main* thing."

Morgan wondered if this was her chance to clarify the real goal. Then again, it might be rude to announce that the real goal was to get Mrs. Dawson off her back.

Wasn't it? She took another long swig.

Their food arrived.

Mrs. Dawson pointed to Morgan's entrée, medium-rare prime rib, her favorite. "Enjoy that while you can. You'll want to stick to *well done* once baby boards that li'l belly."

Morgan pinned her eyes to the food.

"Well done?" Emmett scratched his jawline. "What's the *point*?" He moved the conversation to his dad. His uncle. The family law firm where Emmett was a partner. Lots of other boring things that gave Morgan a brief reprieve from playing along.

In the middle of dessert—crème brûlée, which Mrs. Dawson declined, Emmett encouraged, and Morgan only picked at—Mrs. Dawson turned the conversation squarely back to Morgan. "Morgan, honey, what I *really* wanted to discuss tonight was the wedding *shower*. Honey, my girlfriends are just about dyin' to meet you and spoil you and my baby rotten." With a flourish, she dipped her hand into her leather Coach tote. A day planner with a heavy-looking pen materialized. "*We* were thinkin'—my girlfriends and I—about Labor Day weekend." A false-sounding laugh bubbled out her mouth. "*Well*, truth be told, I wanted Labor Day back when I imagined a gorgeous engagement party for the both of you. But you know Emmett. He says a wedding is more than he can handle."

Morgan frowned and couldn't help but snap her head to her fiancé. He read the question in her eyes, because his features turned stern. "Mom," Emmett snapped. "That's not what I said. What I said was that *you* are more than I can handle. And if you're gonna insist on being so involved in the wedding, then that's about as much of *you* and your planning as I can take."

Still silence swept across the table.

Mrs. Dawson sucked in a sharp breath. "Well, then."

Morgan hated the tension. "I can't wait for the shower. You just ignore Emmett, Mrs. Dawson." She gave her future mother-in-law a winning smile. "Labor Day is *perfect*."

CHAPTER TWENTY-THREE

PRESENT DAY

Amber

Rain showers pelted the farm the better half of July. Not two days went by without a downpour. Some were brief, as if God saw Amber and Julia, Morgan and Emmett sweating out in the heat and decided they needed a reprieve.

Some wet spells lasted the best part of the afternoons, sending them into the barn to perfect recipes, bottle product, slap labels, and handle other tedious logistics that felt both satisfying and unending.

Morgan had them working seven days a week, twelve or more hours a day. Even the Fourth of July wasn't much of an event. Just a small family barbecue.

During those weeks, Amber and Callum hadn't managed to see much of one another. Between Amber's work—both at the farm and with a smattering of hair appointments—and Callum working as the sole clerk under Hank, they were both too busy. At least, that's what Amber was telling herself.

Maybe the real matter had nothing to do with crazy schedules. Maybe the real matter was that Amber's family was too crazy for Callum.

It wasn't just her family, though. With every passing week, something was changing inside of Amber. When she stopped to think about it, she was beginning to wonder if she had joined the ranks of her wild ancestors. Maybe she had hit that point in life where she became crazy, too.

Though the strange spells of nausea had long since vanished, Amber couldn't ignore that she was still feeling... not quite right.

Over a Saturday family cookout in the middle of August, Amber felt particularly odd.

Most of the family was there, as usual. Barb, Tiff, and Trav. Geddy—and Julia, too. Morgan and Emmett. And just Amber. She had invited Callum, but he worked until close. He wished he could make it, he said.

While the group sank their teeth into medium-cooked T-bone steaks—it was on sale at the market and Geddy scooped up a whole shelfful—Tiff poked her fork in Amber's direction. "You love steak."

Amber looked at her own plate. She'd hardly touched her meal. Only the side salad had any appeal. It had been like this for a while, Amber realized. As if she'd lost any interest in meat. Maybe this was how people became vegetarians, she suddenly thought.

When Amber looked back up, all eyes were on her. They were expecting an answer to Tiff's remark.

Amber didn't have one. "I know. I *do*. Or, I did?"

"You feelin' sick again, Amber?" Barb asked her daughter. Both her palms hit the table, urgency lighting up her face.

"No?" Amber squeezed her eyes shut and shook her head. "I don't know. I just... I don't want steak."

Trav tipped his long neck at her. "You said the same thing about burgers last Saturday."

"I've got some fried cod in the freezer," Aunt Carla offered, moving to stand.

Amber didn't realize it, but she must have made a face. "No thanks." The last time they'd fried up fish, she hadn't touched it either.

"She's tryin' to lose weight, I bet." Tiff pursed her lips, all skinny face and smug features. Amber wanted to slap her.

"No."

"You do look *good*," Barb pointed out.

Amber rolled her eyes. "*Thanks*. I'm not trying to do anything."

A car pulled up along the gravel drive, the perfect distraction.

All eyes flew to kicked-up gravel dust, billowing. It was probably another relative. Maybe Uncle Gary, who'd been invited every week but had never showed. Maybe cousin Rachel, who worked at the county library and managed to use that as an excuse to avoid the cookouts half the time.

Instead of sticking around to find out, Amber excused herself to the restroom.

Once inside the bathroom, she splashed water on her face and studied herself in the mirror. In fact, her face was the opposite of sick-looking. Even without makeup—which she didn't bother to put on if Callum wasn't coming over—her cheeks had a rosy-pink flush to them. Her lips, bee-stung.

Otherwise, though, she did look thinner—at least in the neck and face. Although she didn't feel thinner anywhere else. Amber turned and looked back at the mirror, examining her full bosom and thick waist. She ran a hand down her torso, and her stomach felt taut against her light cotton shirt.

That's when it hit her.

The headaches. Nausea. The bouts of sadness and bursts of emotion.

She counted on her fingers back to spring.

She counted again.

August. July. June. May... April? April.

April. May. June. July. *August*, now.

Five.

Heat climbed up Amber's spine, turning into ice at the base of her skull. Her hair prickled up, and goosebumps spread across her flesh.

How could it be? There was just the once. The *one* time they weren't *careful*. The time Grant persuaded her that if they wanted to get married, then they ought to be more *open* with each other.

And though she didn't feel nauseous at all, not anymore, Amber promptly bent over the sink and retched.

CHAPTER TWENTY-FOUR

1991

CarlaMay

We made it a habit. It couldn't be a relationship, after all. Not in the true sense of a relationship. What we had was more serious.

More dangerous.

More real.

Like a dandelion seed, our love had blown on an accident—a chance. It had nestled into the soil of the university, the bed of my dorm room. In the dark, when no one was watching, it grew roots.

We called each other lovers. At first, I protested. It was a crass word.

He disagreed. What we were doing wasn't having sex.

We were making love. We were in love. So, we were lovers.

I still had my old roommate's key, which I gave to him. He used it any night he wasn't working—meeting, teaching, reading, preparing for his talks.

All those nights, we learned about each other, and I think we learned about ourselves.

He was from a great big Catholic family. Grew up outside of Pittsburg. The middle child. His daddy was a miner. His mama stayed at home and brought up the kids. All the boys—he had four brothers—were expected to go to the mines once they gradu-ated high school, if not sooner.

There was only one way out of that life, and it was a long and academic journey that landed him there, in Louisville.

With me.

CHAPTER TWENTY-FIVE

PRESENT DAY

Morgan Jo

Morgan had no idea how she'd missed it. Maybe because she was too concerned with her own personal business? Or maybe because she'd always taken Amber and Grant for a pair of friends and not a romantic couple with a secret life, shielded from the family's eyes by a basement door.

Before the unexpected guest could get out of his car—one unfamiliar to Morgan—she left the table. "I'm going to check on the dessert."

"Don't forget the ice cream!" Aunt Barb called after her. "Homemade!"

Morgan was in the door, pretending to search for the apple pie that Tiff had made from scratch—her one contribution. Tiff was an exceptional baker, despite being something of a black sheep and a gossip. She argued that baking could take a while. It helped if you had someone else's drama to keep you company while you waited for the crust to set.

"Amber?" Morgan lifted her voice to a stage whisper. "Amber?"

A muffled sound came from the bathroom just off the laundry.

Morgan rapped with two knuckles. "Amber? You okay?"

The door cracked at first, then opened wide. Inside, Amber stood, one hand on the sink and one along the door's edge, like she was bracing herself.

Their eyes met. Amber's wide and worrisome. Morgan's furrowed, hesitant.

Together, the cousins' gazes fell to Amber's hands, which moved in slow motion to her belly.

"Oh my *gosh*," Morgan breathed the words.

They looked up again at each other, and matching smiles formed on each one's mouth.

Morgan hugged Amber, frantic with excitement and happiness. Then she gripped Amber's shoulders and held her arm's length away. "Are you *okay*?" she repeated.

Amber's smile widened until it broke, and tears sprang to her eyes. "Somehow... *yes*."

They hugged again, and that's when Morgan realized that she was *not*.

CHAPTER TWENTY-SIX

PRESENT DAY

Amber

They wiped their eyes—Morgan seemed just as emotional about the whole thing as Amber—then swore to keep it a secret. At least, until Amber could *confirm* what she and her cousin both suspected.

Morgan left first, murmuring something about an apple pie and ice cream.

Amber followed, several squares of toilet paper carefully folded and pressed down into her jeans pocket. Just in case.

She'd make an appointment first thing Monday, but before that, her next step was to go to the service station off of Brambleberry for the necessary kit, or whatever it was that would allow Amber to test her newfound theory.

Leaving the bathroom, a change came upon the cadence of her step. A lightness. An excitement. Of course, Amber had no right to be excited, but it was hard not to be.

Even so, she pressed down the bubbles of elation and made her way from the bathroom, through the mudroom, and onto the thick carpet of Kentucky bluegrass that spread from the back porch into eternity.

And that's when she saw him.

"Amber!" he hollered, his hand waving wildly as he left the picnic table and strode toward her. "Hi."

Amber's stomach twisted all up in knots. When he got to her, she froze, her voice caught in her throat like a too-big bite of T-bone steak. She swallowed and swallowed again, and just as soon as he was within hugging distance, she was miraculously able to breathe again. Amber whispered, "Callum."

There was only one thing to do, and that was to act normal. For now, at least.

Amber gave Callum as contactless a hug as was humanly possible, more aware than ever of her changing form. She slipped her arms from his and looked up at him. "I thought you had to work?"

"Your dad was feeling generous, I guess. He took over on my shift." Callum lifted an eyebrow. "And he says *hi*."

The message swirled through Amber's mind like a gust of wind, nearly blowing her over. "Oh." It was all she could muster.

"And," Callum went on, "he sent me along with the tapes." Callum hooked a thumb toward his car which Amber saw sat, its engine probably cooling, in the drive.

The tapes. Of everything that was now going on in Amber's life, the tapes were taking more of a back seat than ever. What with it being August, they had just two months before the vineyard opening and the wedding. And now with the secret Amber held in her heart, in her loins... even those two things seemed unimportant.

"Do you want some steak? I'm sure there's an extra T-bone," Amber started for the barbecue, but as soon as she lifted her head, she saw everyone was watching the pair of them. "Oh."

"Yeah." Callum made a playful grimace. "Seems like we're..."

"A point of interest?"

"Anyway. I'm not too hungry. I'd packed a brown bag for dinner and ate it." He shrugged.

Morgan passed Amber and Callum, her arms laden with the pie, a carton of ice cream, and teetering on top of that bowls with spoons clanging inside of them.

Callum moved to help her, but Morgan shook him off right away. "I've got this! You two go on."

Amber shot her a grateful look then waved Callum to the gravel drive, and away from the prying eyes of her family. "Let's go get the tapes."

As Amber opened the exterior door to her basement apartment, she saw her living quarters as if she were an outsider, despite the fact that Callum had visited once before.

Mint and Julep mewed themselves awake from a fluffy pile on the sofa. One of the sofa cushions sat crooked. The smell of furniture polish—Amber liked to dust on Saturdays—was strong at this point of entrance, acrid like essence of lemon and heavy as motor oil.

"Sorry about that." Amber grabbed a pile of folded laundry from the armchair and swiveled with it, hurrying off to her bedroom, where she laid it on the bed and backed out of the room, praying he wouldn't see yesterday's bra strewn carelessly at the edge of the mattress.

She closed the door and turned to Callum, who stood with the box balanced along his arms, waiting.

"Sorry. Here." She cleared a pair of complementary candles from the narrow coffee table. Pumpkin and Apple. Sally's Soaps 'n' Sundries had finally put out the autumn collection, and Amber firmly believed in transitioning to the next season as soon as possible.

"Thanks." Callum set the box down and removed a VCR from the top of it. The same VCR he'd had at the shop. A bridle of colorful cords hung from the back. He scooped them up. "Mind if I play around a bit?"

Amber indicated the TV. "Have at it."

Callum shifted the TV at an angle to access the back of it.

She peeked around. "Anything I can do?"

He pushed one of the adapters into the back of the TV, moved it back into place, and clapped his hands. "Nope." Then, he pressed the power button on the TV and then the one on the VCR. Then, he pressed play.

Grandad came to life on the screen. Not fuzzy, but crystal clear. "The quality is incredible!" Amber admired, slowly lowering herself to her sofa.

"I cleaned the tape. This one is labeled 'Blueberry Wine.'"

Callum settled back onto the sofa with Amber, who was sucking in her belly as far as she could stand it.

They watched in quasi-comfortable silence as Grandad bore on about collecting good grapes.

Ten minutes into it, Callum's hand made its way close to hers on the center cushion that spread between them. Amber's sofa was small, almost like a hybrid between a full-length and a love seat. She was certain she could feel the heat of his skin.

He cleared his throat.

Amber forced herself to keep her gaze on Grandad. The grouchy old man did little to grease the wheels of romance, but Amber's newly realized secret did even less.

And yet...

The screen went fuzzy before them.

Callum gave a small jolt. "It'll come back. There are blips on the ones I was able to save. Bits missing."

"Lost to time."

"Well, they're damaged, really," he added.

Amber's hand moved from the sofa to her waist. *Damaged.* It was fitting.

And yet, come Monday morning when the doctor returned to Amber's lonesome exam room, test results in hand, he'd congratulated her.

"Miss Amber," Dr. Maycomb said, his ruddy cheeks about to burst from his palpable joy, "You, ma'am, are *pregnant. Very* pregnant."

CHAPTER TWENTY-SEVEN

PRESENT DAY

Morgan Jo

Monday was supposed to be Branding Day for the business. Morgan had already arranged a meeting of the team for the late afternoon, but ahead of that, she wanted to put together a vision board filled with the inspirations behind Moonshine Creek Vineyard—which was only a *working* title.

That day, she even wanted to design some mock-up logos.

Morgan finished off her coffee and bid her mother farewell—it was back-to-school week at Our Lady of the Shepherd School, where CarlaMay served as school secretary. CarlaMay promised that she'd be home in time for the team meeting, and after that, she'd sit down with Morgan to talk wedding dresses.

Just as she was about to sit down at her computer, her phone buzzed.

"Amber?" Morgan answered with a sharp intake of breath. "*Well?*"

A sob came in reply.

"Oh, *Amber.*" Morgan *knew* she should have insisted on

accompanying her cousin, but Amber had been adamant. It was something she needed to attend to herself.

Even so, Morgan pushed out of her chair, ran for her purse and keys and flew to Dr. Maycomb's office in town.

Amber was just leaving the back hallway and coming into the waiting room. One hand rested protectively on her stomach, but it really didn't stick out much.

"You could have been featured in that show," Morgan joked. "What is it called? The one where women go into labor and they never even knew."

Amber laughed, though her eyes and nose were red. In her free hand was a wadded-up tissue. Dr. Maycomb led her out, hands on her shoulders.

"Miss Morgan Jo Coyle!" Dr. Maycomb cheered. "You make that follow-up yet?" He stared down his nose and over his little round glasses at her. "I got the paperwork sent down from the city. You put me as your primary." He pushed his glasses back up and smiled. "Exciting times for the both of you, girls."

Morgan blanched and managed to mumble a weak *yes*. Anyway, this wasn't about Morgan's fertility questions. It was about Amber's fertility answers.

"How far along are you?" Morgan asked, ushering her cousin out onto the street. An unspoken plan to walk Main for a bit fell into place.

Amber took a deep breath. "Four, we think, based on my crude math and HCG levels. I go in for a scan this afternoon." She looked up at Morgan. "I might be late for our meeting."

"Our meeting isn't your priority anymore," Morgan chided her. "You've got bigger fish to fry these days." A beat passed. "Maybe we all do."

"My due date could be bad timing."

Morgan frowned at her then looped her arm around

Amber's shoulders, pulling her in for a hug and planting a fat kiss on top of her head. "A baby is never bad timing."

As they walked, it became harder and harder for Morgan to keep a smile on her face and kindness in her heart. Ultimately, their tables had turned. Morgan might have Emmett and the big house and all the things Amber seemed to long for. Meanwhile, Amber now had the one thing Morgan was nearly positive she'd never have.

They came to a stop outside the diner. A milkshake sounded perfect right about now. Maybe splitting a burger would help to wash things down and make them feel more normal, too. Morgan remembered the first time she met Grant. She was home for a weekend in the summer. Amber invited her to the Dewdrop, and there he was, splayed across a whole bench. He didn't stand up when Morgan arrived.

"Have you told Grant yet?" she wondered aloud.

Amber's shoulders sagged. "I wanted to wait until I had confirmation."

"Do you need my help—"

Amber cut her off with a flash of her phone screen.

Morgan read a short text exchange. Amber had sent a message first.

Hey, Grant. This is crazy, but you should know I'm pregnant.

Morgan glanced up. "When did you send this?"

"Right after the doctor told me. I didn't want to chicken out." She pressed the screen again at Morgan to continue reading.

Grant's response made bile creep up the back of Morgan's throat. *And you think it's mine? Lol.*

"Oh, my word," Morgan whispered.

Amber lowered her phone. "Let's just say I'll be filing for sole custody."

"Do you think he'll give up his rights?"

"I don't think. I *know*." She lifted her phone up again, and Morgan read on.

> *Grant, this baby is yours, like it or not. Do you want to meet and talk?*

Grant doubled down on his derision. *No.*

Amber clicked her phone back to darkness. She sighed, but her expression wasn't devoid of all hope. "The good news is, I can probably have him sign away all of his rights."

"Sounds like it won't be a battle. But—" Morgan chewed her lower lip. "You'll want child support."

Amber shook her head sadly. "No. Grant has given me *enough*."

They entered the diner and tucked themselves into a cozy back booth. Amber still didn't have much of an appetite, but Morgan was starving. She ordered a cheeseburger and two shakes. "I'll drink yours if you can't manage."

Instead of answering her, Amber's face twisted. She asked, "What do I tell Callum?"

Morgan hadn't thought of Callum. It hadn't occurred to her that Amber might be growing real feelings for him. Maybe Morgan had been too busy with other things to take much notice. Now, though, Amber's eyes told her all she needed to know. Not only was Amber in a terrible pickle of a pregnancy with Grant out of the picture. But she might be on the brink of losing the one thing that was going to drag her away from that loser for good.

Morgan didn't know the right answer. If Amber told Callum she was pregnant with her ex's baby, it was sure to scare him away. If Amber *didn't* tell Callum, the truth would come out eventually anyway.

"Morgan Jo?"

Resolve calcified in Morgan's veins. Her gaze dropped to Amber's belly. "Once upon a time, that was me."

"What?" Amber braced both hands along her torso. "*You?*"

"I don't have a dad, you know."

"You have a dad," Amber insisted. Morgan knew her cousin wasn't trying to be dismissive, but that's how it felt.

Morgan added, "I have no idea who he is. My mom has kept his identity a secret from me."

Amber was silent a moment. Then, quietly, she said, "I don't think she's meant to keep a secret from you all these years, Morgan Jo."

"Just because you don't *mean* to do something, doesn't mean it can't happen." Morgan let out a sigh. "I've gone over every possibility in my head. Did my dad ever know about me? If so, did he want me?"

"No man knows what he wants."

"Or," Morgan went on, "did my mom even tell him? Maybe he didn't know. Maybe he *would* want me. Or maybe he wouldn't. Right? I mean, mathematically, there must be a million different ways things could have worked out for me. There must be a million different truths."

"Sometimes I feel like that about my parents. They broke up for no good reason, it seems like. But there *has* to be a good reason."

At this, Morgan shrugged. She knew as little as Amber did when it came to the elusive Hank Taylor. And Barb, like Carla-May, was tight-lipped.

Morgan studied her cousin for a moment. Amber looked helpless. And hot. Sweat broke out along her hairline. She pulled at her blouse uncomfortably. "So, you're basically saying

I should leave him well enough alone? Not wrap him up in my drama?"

"I'm not saying that. I'm saying..." What *was* Morgan saying? The answer was simple enough. "I'm saying that you and I—*we*—have a chance to break the cycle."

"The cycle?" Amber's eyes narrowed in suspicion.

"The cycle of family secrets."

CHAPTER TWENTY-EIGHT

1991

CarlaMay

After three months, our rhythm changed.

Each time I returned to the peach tree, there were fewer fruits to pick. And the ones left weren't as juicy. Slowly, almost so slowly that I didn't notice, they were shriveling up.

The seasons were changing.

I wondered if I had better change with them, and so I proposed something dangerous.

"Let's go with Barb and her boyfriend to dinner," I said one lazy night as we traced shapes onto each other's skin. I pulled a heart into its point in the center of his chest.

With his thumb, he outlined a diamond into my cheek and stared at me sleepily, uninspired, even. "You know I can't do that."

"You can go out to eat. You do anyway. What's the difference if it's with me?"

I pressed my finger into his skin, thinking of what to draw next. A house came to mind. I started on the square.

He withdrew his hand from my cheek. "The difference is that with your sister and her boyfriend, it'll look like a date."

I added a door to the house, a rectangle in the center of the square. "We can go out of the city. Somewhere no one will know you."

A shadow crossed his face. "CarlaMay," he began, taking my wrist and pulling it from his chest. I hadn't even drawn the triangle for a roof yet.

I looked at him, my bedroom eyes narrowing. "What is it?" I sat up sharp. Too sharp.

"We can't do this anymore." He said it with the gumption of a dandelion. The words floated away, and in spite of them, he pulled my face in and kissed me, softly at first. The kiss turned into more and soon enough we were back to where we began, tickling one another's skin with the tips of our fingers. I finished the house on his chest, adding a trio of stick figures, a little family.

On my head, he made the sign of the cross.

CHAPTER TWENTY-NINE

PRESENT DAY

Morgan Jo

Morgan's initial lab work came up roses. All was a go for her to schedule the scope. She made her appointment for the week before Labor Day. Morgan decided to put it off until after they'd finished packaging the product. She'd wanted her focus to remain on the opening gala.

And remain there, it had.

August arrived like a plow, pushing Morgan and her team into late summer whether they were ready or not.

Mostly, though, they were ready. Material orders had been placed in late June, and according to the vendors, everything would arrive at the crack of August, from tables to chairs down to the place settings.

Unlike with a wedding, the pieces they ordered weren't rentals. They'd stay. This had been Amber's idea, in fact. Amber, who seemed to be bubbling over with big ideas ever since her big news, declared that Morgan's colors were neutral and pretty enough to work well for tastings, should they decide to have tastings.

At the mention of it, Morgan was hooked. The idea wasn't entirely new. It had surfaced during preliminary brainstorms, but back then it felt like too much work. Now, however? It could be the perfect addition. "Tastings?" she'd pressed Amber, quickly thinking through the notion, poking it for holes. "The only thing is—*where?*"

"I'll work on it," Amber promised.

By the middle of the month, Morgan expected to receive the dishware, napkins, and table linens, including cloths and runners. Chargers, too.

The truck arrived right on time, and two efficient teenagers unloaded everything to a cleaned-out corner of the barn. While watching as box after box, chair pile after chair pile materialized before their eyes, Emmett had tugged Morgan into a hug. "It's really happening."

She'd glowed. "Yes. Just two months, and Moonshine Creek will be back in business."

Morgan felt Emmett's arm go slack. Slowly, he'd released her. "Actually, I meant that we'd be *married.*"

It wasn't the first time she became aware of a growing disconnect between them.

While Morgan trained herself to see the event through the lens of a business opening, Emmett only saw wedding bells. It was easier this way. Anyhow, she could just as soon agree that any decision for the business worked for the wedding. They went so tightly hand in hand, that she pretended not to notice his frustration.

Every time Emmett brought it up, she'd pushed it off. Vows? They'd go by the book—whatever was traditional. He was fine with traditional. Basked in it, even. However, he'd kept nagging her. Did she really *want* traditional? What about for the service? Was she certain they should skip the church ceremony?

Even Morgan had to admit that this particular detail did snag into her skin like a starved tick. For now, the plan was to exchange vows in a non-religious, vaguely spiritual, and very brief ceremony. That way they'd avoid offending some and boring others.

But, down the road—would Morgan and Emmett regret a secular ceremony? Emmett was easygoing enough... and he didn't much go to church. Similarly, Morgan wasn't practicing her Catholic faith. And yet, they were still Catholic. Plus, what about her family?

Emmett's parents were a whole other matter. His mom was as Catholic as they came, and she'd spared no hints on the matter.

"I've got a great priest," she told Morgan when they met to plan the shower. She'd said it like she had a great eyebrow waxer or a great mechanic. Like she could snap her fingers and he'd appear, holy tools in hand. All the right knowledge and words to bestow the *perfect* treatment.

It was a Saturday morning in August. CarlaMay had invited the bridal party and the mothers together to the farm for a brunch and planning session.

Mrs. Dawson again brought up her priest. Father Bartholomew. "Father Bart—that's what I call him, honey—he'll put on a High Mass. Have you ever been to a High Mass?" Mrs. Dawson looked around the farmhouse table, beginning at Carla-May, moving to Morgan, then Julia, Amber, Tiff, and Rachel. For attendants, Morgan and Emmett agreed on just one person each. Julia would stand up for Morgan. Geddy would stand up for Emmett. But Morgan still wanted her closest cousins to play a special part, and so Amber, Tiff, and Rachel each would act as usherettes.

Everyone shook her head. The Nelson–Coyle clan may be Catholic, but they weren't *that* Catholic.

"Well!" Mrs. Dawson clasped her bauble-adorned hands one in the other and her face lit up. "Let me tell you, it's *worth* it."

"I think so far as a ceremony is concerned, we'll keep things to the event," Morgan replied.

The woman's features twitched. "The *event*. Yes. Emmett tells me we're combining the opening gala with the wedding reception."

"And ceremony. Both." Morgan took a small sip of her lemonade—Mrs. Dawson wasn't one for sweet tea. Luckily, CarlaMay could make lemonade so sweet you almost didn't get that sour bite.

Mrs. Dawson gave a tight smile. Her patience was wearing thin. She looked to the rest of the table as if searching for help. For backing.

Amber, who'd regained her appetite about a week prior, tucked into her dessert—lemon meringue pie. Rachel read from a book beneath the table. Tiff kept stealing glances at her phone.

Even CarlaMay pretended to study the grandfather clock with a dumb confusion.

"Maybe *you* have a priest you'd like to officiate? As a matter of fact, I hope you've begun your marriage sessions at St. Mary's?"

Morgan frowned. Surely Mrs. Dawson knew the answer to all these questions. Emmett was honest as he was sweet. Still, correcting Mrs. Dawson felt impossible. Morgan glanced pleadingly at her mom.

CarlaMay cleared her throat. "You know, we've been *so* busy, Caroline."

Mrs. Dawson stiffened. "Mmm. After we finish here, I'll go ahead and put in a call to Father Bart."

CarlaMay pulled her fork from her lips, licking away the last of the pie cream. "That won't be necessary, Caroline. I know someone. I'll talk to him."

.   .   .

Plans for the shower tightly in place, the brunch dispersed. Mrs. Dawson back up to her sprawling Bardstown estate. Rachel to her rental cottage a block from Main. Tiff to her bunkhouse. And Amber downstairs, where she was busy nesting.

"Father David?" Morgan asked her mom, when they were alone together, washing the dishes.

CarlaMay's hand paused on a roasting pan. "Well, yes. He's our family priest."

"Not anymore." Morgan took the pan and dried it. "You told me, like a few months ago, that he retired, or whatever it is priests do when they're done."

"Right. He did. But he *was*, once upon a time, our priest. He delivered Mass when you received your First Communion. He granted your Confirmation, for goodness' sake."

Morgan waited for her mother's eyes to lift and meet Morgan's gaze. After several beats, CarlaMay looked up. Morgan said, "You lied to Emmett's mom."

"I didn't say I knew a *priest*. I said I knew *someone*."

"Anyway, how in the world are you going to get in touch with him now?"

"I already am. We never lost touch."

Father David was close to the family, there was no question of that. He'd given the eulogy at Memaw's funeral. Grandad's, too.

"Why did he retire, anyway? Don't priests, like, stay priests until they die?"

"Normally, if they are unable to continue on in all of their duties, they become emeritus priests. They continue their ministry without all the admin. But David—Father David—he stepped down from his position entirely. He's just a layperson now." CarlaMay carried on with scrubbing. "Anyway, he can help us make a plan. He knows all about Catholic marriages."

"He won't be able to marry us?" Morgan couldn't seem to let the matter drop.

"I didn't say he'd marry you. And anyway, he didn't lose his ordination. Not technically. It doesn't work that way. He's just, sort of—"

"Condemned to purgatory, probably," Morgan muttered. She knew enough about her religion to know that some sins weren't as forgivable as others. No matter what God wanted you to believe.

CHAPTER THIRTY

PRESENT DAY

Amber

Pregnancy delighted Amber. It turned out that she was well suited to motherhood, once the initial shock had worn off, that was.

It took about a week to come to terms with things. A week of nagging Grant to get on board—to no avail. He'd even gone so far as to say, "Once again, I want nothin' to do with you or any of your crazy family. If that baby is mine, I don't even want to know. You can write me off."

Easy enough.

It hadn't taken Amber all of five minutes to decide that she could and she would raise up the baby without a single dime from Grant. After all, Amber had a stable home. She had Morgan Jo and Aunt Carla upstairs. Her brother, sister, and cousin on the same grounds. She had all the support she could ever ask for.

And that was *before* Amber made the big announcement at the following Saturday barbecue.

While holding Morgan Jo's hand, Amber had stood at the

helm of the picnic table and spilled her guts—figuratively. That's when the thrill *really* descended. Barb sprang into happy sobs. Tiff rattled off a billion names she'd had stored up for the day the family would greet the first baby of the next generation. Even goofy Trav got choked up, declaring that he always wanted to be an uncle.

Aunt Dana, who'd made a rare appearance, announced that she already *knew*, which made everyone roll their eyes and laugh. Rachel, for her part, seemed confused. Once she closed her book and tuned in, she said she'd curate an infant section in the bookstore.

Geddy and Julia got all googly about the whole thing, and Julia also admitted she'd begun to wonder. Amber had caught Morgan Jo giving her a *look*, and it was then that Amber realized maybe she was kind of the last to know she was pregnant. Maybe it had been more obvious.

For her part, Morgan Jo had squeezed Amber's hand, hugged her tight, then slipped onto Emmett's lap. Amber caught him whispering into Morgan Jo's ear, and tears filled her eyes.

Amber's heart ached for her cousin. That was the only moment Amber wondered if her pregnancy was a bad thing. She wasn't next in line to have this milestone.

Morgan Jo was.

But just as soon as the thought occurred to Amber, Morgan Jo had given her a great big smile and a thumbs up. She'd mouthed, "I love you."

It was all Amber needed to hear.

From there, not a single whisper of judgment was cast. Only love and happiness. Morgan Jo hadn't cried anymore. She'd sent Amber articles about the second trimester. Name ideas. At one point, she'd even mused on about how fun it might have been if the baby was born in time for the holidays.

Morgan Jo's positivity served to carry Amber through

another week. That week was one of dodging Callum's calls and texts.

For the time being, she decided to put him off, as unfair as that might seem. Both to him, *and* to her. After all, before news of the baby, Callum had taken root as the main thing on Amber's mind. Finding space for both of them felt improbable at best. Impossible at worst.

And mostly, it felt like the wrong thing to do when a woman was expecting a baby. Unfortunately, it was also the wrong thing to do when you were nursing a heavy crush on someone who seemed to like you back.

After the brunch with the bridal party, Amber planned to get some more cleaning done. She wasn't far enough along to get the so-called nesting bug. However, she did want to steal any spare second to deep-clean her apartment before she brought in baby equipment.

Tiff, who dabbled in multilevel marketing businesses, supplied her with a haul of all-natural cleaning supplies.

Once downstairs, Amber changed out of her buttery-yellow sundress and into sweats and a tee and filled up the kitchen sink with hot soapy water. Today would be kitchen day.

Just as Amber turned off the kitchen sink tap, a knock came at the interior door upstairs. "Come on down!" she hollered.

Morgan appeared. "Hey."

"The bridal brunch was nice," Amber remarked. "I think Emmett's mom is a little uptight, but she really seems to care."

"Yeah." Morgan slumped into a chair at the small kitchen bistro set. "She cares, all right."

As soon as Morgan was seated, she popped back up and took the rag from Amber. "Here. You sit down."

Instead of sitting, Amber opened the fridge and inspected its contents. Cleaning the fridge out was a time-honored tradition in the family. That's what happened when you wasted not and wanted not. You ended up wasting anyway.

Amber removed a basket of blueberries Geddy had given her from Uncle Gary's farm. He'd had surplus and given out a whole slew of 'em. But that was three weeks ago, and Amber couldn't tell if the white edge was mold or not. She stifled a gag and tossed the basket.

"Next time I'll freeze 'em," she declared, reaching for a half-gallon carton of milk and twisting off the cap to give it a whiff. "Still good."

Behind, Morgan lifted appliances on the short, narrow kitchen counter, wiping beneath them then dunking the rag in the sink.

A wedge of iceberg lettuce sat in the crisper next to a sagging head of butter lettuce. "Lettuce always sounds so good when I'm shopping. And then for, like, the first two days. After that, it's like it grows, or something. I can't keep up." Amber clicked her tongue at her own improvidence and kept on checking expiration dates and clearing shelves.

When she turned around from the fridge to grab a spare rag and wipe the shelves, she caught sight of Morgan Jo, who was scrubbing a spot on the counter and staring out into space.

"You're going to rub a hole in the Formica." Amber peeled a fresh rag off the pile of bleached ones, but before turning back to the fridge, she noticed Morgan Jo hadn't so much as flinched. "Morgan Jo," she repeated.

The trance remained.

Amber set her arm gently on her cousin's hand, stilling the repetitive movement and unlocking Morgan Jo from her reverie. "Morgan Jo, what's wrong?"

Slowly, Morgan turned to her. "I'm having doubts."

CHAPTER THIRTY-ONE

1991

CarlaMay

A week later, I got sick.

He called and asked to meet me at the Newman Center.

My spine tingled at his request, but not out of exhilaration.

Out of fear.

The Newman Center was as neutral a location as anything. Why did he want to meet there? Would we be alone? What was happening?

He answered mildly, "To talk, CarlaMay."

That was the moment when I started feeling sick.

That same night, Whit had a birthday, and Hank, none the wiser, set up a get-together.

Barb and I discussed it over the phone beforehand. I said, "I don't really like Whit."

"But he's handsome," Barb argued.

"I think he's a creep." I debated on whether to tell Barb what had happened. But if I did, then I'd have to tell her the rest. I'd

have to tell her about him. *I'd have to tell her all my secrets. The thing in my family is, you don't tell somebody one of your secrets unless you can use it as currency. As a way to get something you want. There wasn't nothing from Barb I wanted or needed, and so I kept my trap shut.*

"He's a flirt is what he is." Barb cackled like she'd made an evil joke, but I knew she wasn't making a joke. More 'n likely, Barb had a crush on Whit. The thing about that was, Barb and Hank were full-on dating by now. They'd been on exactly five dates. They hadn't "done it" yet, though, you see. Barb, unlike me, didn't hold close to her virtue. She whipped it out and swung it around like a flag. Sure enough, Barb was the black sheep of the family for that very trait—her debauchery.

"You're a flirt, too." I said it as a warning. A threat. Not a dare.

Barb cackled at that, too, but then she said, "I don't even know if Hank and me are gonna make it. I can't tell if he likes me. He's not—"

"A real man?" I couldn't hide my annoyance. In Barb's world, sexy men had to be clichés. They had to have rough hands and dirt caked into their Wranglers. "Barb, when are you going to wise up and pick someone who's good for you?"

I should talk.

Barb told me to feel better and promptly hung up.

I thought about them. Barb and Hank. Whit. Whit and Barb. Flirting. Hank being none the wiser to his would-be girlfriend's wandering heart.

The whole thing stank of a bad night. For everyone, not least of all me, who'd be stuck in my room, going mad with boredom and worry.

I felt sicker by the minute, and soon enough, fell into a fitful, nightmare-fueled sleep.

In the middle of the night, I woke up to the sound of hammering.

At first, I thought it was my head. A wave of nausea built up in my chest and threatened my throat. A migraine must have been coming on, I figured.

I pulled my pillow tight over my eyes and took a deep breath.

The hammering continued. Harder, crisper. It sent horrible booms into my head, worsening the throb.

Whoever was at the door was going to get a piece of my mind, I decided. I'd swing that door open and raise my finger up and cite the late hour and make great big threats about calling the dorm mother and decency and this, that, and the other.

But by the time I made it to the door, my resolve softened.

What if it was him?

What if he'd come to apologize and tell me he'd gotten cold feet but now he was ready? To shirk his life for me.

To give me all of himself, even.

I was wrong, though. I opened the door, and it wasn't him.

It was a broken, scared girl. Alone. Tear-streaked. And shaking.

It was my sister.

CHAPTER THIRTY-TWO

PRESENT DAY

Morgan Jo

Morgan and Amber stopped cleaning the kitchen. Morgan wrung out her rag and draped it over the side of the sink. She followed Amber, whose little basement bachelorette pad was beginning to feel more like a small family home.

They sat on the sofa. Morgan cried.

"Maybe you're pregnant, too," Amber joked. Morgan cried harder. "Oh cuz, I'm *sorry*. I was just being dumb. Unless—"

"That's a whole other thing," Morgan wailed between sobs. "I've got that appointment coming up. What if it goes all wrong? I should have waited."

"You mean the scope?"

Morgan nodded miserably. "Mrs. Dawson is so set on steering everything about our marriage. I'm sure of it. She's, like, a control freak or something." Another sob escaped. "I love her, and I love Emmett to the moon, but the *pressure*."

"Does she know you might have a problem?"

"Of course she knows. That's why she's sent me to her

doctor to see about all this. She's scared I won't be able to carry on the Dawson family bloodlines."

Amber snorted. "Does she know you're not a derby horse?"

Morgan's sobs skidded to a stop, and she grinned through bleary tears at her cousin. "Who's gonna break it to her?"

They laughed together. Cathartic relief poured into Morgan Jo's veins in the form of a second spell of laughter. "I love you, Amber Lee."

"I love you, Morgan Jo. Don't fret on Mrs. Dawson. She means well. She cares about you."

"I don't think I can do it."

"Do you mean marry him?" Amber's face filled with worry.

Morgan frowned and shook her head. "No. *No.* Of course I can marry Emmett. Heck, I'd elope right now if he asked me."

"What did you mean about having doubts, then?"

Morgan took in a deep breath. "Maybe I don't even want children. Or maybe I do, but I'm scared. Maybe I don't want to open the winery. Or maybe I want to open the winery first, then have a wedding. Maybe combining the gala with our wedding— the whole idea of a soft opening—maybe it's crap."

"Maybe."

As if stung by a bee, Morgan felt the word like it was a pinch. "What?"

Amber reached across the sofa and grabbed Morgan's hand. "Maybe you're right. Maybe you don't want kids. Maybe you are scared. You don't want to open the winery. You do. You want a wedding first. Later. You want a combo event to ease up the pressure. You want to split the events to ease up the pressure. Maybe your ideas are all a big ol' pile of crap." She grinned.

Morgan worried her lower lip between her teeth. "Maybe all of this can just be, like, plan A. If I get another bad feeling, or something, I can just—"

"Go to plan B?" Amber asked. "And what exactly is your plan B?"

Shaking her head slowly, Morgan replied, "Give up."

"You could run away, while you're at it," Amber pointed out. "I hear Tucson has cowboys."

A smile tickled its way onto Morgan's mouth. "You're a turd, you know that?"

"Naw. I just don't believe in backup plans, remember, cuz?"

That was true. Amber had this funny value about following through on your dreams. Not settling for second-best.

Like a raincloud over her head cleared and blue skies let in the sun, something in Morgan released. Her body sank into the sofa. A niggling headache lifted. And then, resolve came. She stood. "You know what? Neither do I."

CHAPTER THIRTY-THREE

PRESENT DAY

Amber

The Tuesday following her come-to-Jesus with Morgan Jo, Amber was due at the salon for her very last appointment ever.

After doing hair at the Cutting Edge for nearly ten years, Amber was ready to hang up her shears and turn her attention fully to life at Moonshine Creek. The winery. Family. And, most importantly, her baby.

Barb and Tiff said they'd come to the salon and help Amber clean out her station once the hair appointment was over, midday. After, the three of them would have lunch at the diner then go to Clancy's and shop for maternity clothes. All in all, it was shaping up to be the perfect Tuesday.

The bell above the salon door clanged. Amber stepped through feeling fresh and full of anticipation for what was to come.

The salon manager, Marge, stood at the product shelf, organizing. "Hi, Amber Lee! Happy Last Day!" She turned and passed an ivory envelope to Amber. "This is from all of us here."

Amber tore into it. On the front, a bassinet with a tiny gray baby elephant. Inside, it read: *Babies are a blessing! Congratulations, Amber Lee. Come back anytime.* Tucked in the note was a generous gift card to Baby's World.

Amber got a little teary and gave Marge a hug. "I mean that, too." Marge pointed to the card. "If you get sick of your fancy new life, you'll always have a chair here."

Happy and teary and bursting with joy, Amber prepped her station for her last appointment. She called over her shoulder, "Who's the client, again?" All of Amber's regulars had officially transitioned to other stylists. Whoever had booked today's appointment was a one-off, as Amber called them.

"Let me look," Marge chirped from the front desk. "Henry T."

"Henry T." Amber took the information and pulled out her clippers, wiping the blade and humming a lullaby to herself. "Henry. *Henry.*" She made a point to commit client names to memory even before they appeared in her chair. It was one of the things that she'd been good at—Amber was a people person, first.

"Must be a passer-through," Marge added. "He's got an out-of-town number."

They didn't get many passers-through in Brambleberry. It wasn't a roadside town or even something of a pit stop. To get to Brambleberry, you had to drive a few minutes out of your way at least, depending on what interstate or byway you were on.

The clock slowly ticked closer and closer to ten, her appointment time. Amber checked her wristwatch at five past ten. She glanced up at the door. No sign yet.

She sent a text to her mom and Tiff. *Might be closer to eleven.*

Her mom replied, *Men's haircut, though, right?*

Tiff wrote, *We'll come at 10:30, still. Need a solid hour to clean, then lunch. YAY.*

Amber ran her hand around her belly. It still hadn't really

popped out, but there was a growing bump beneath her flowy silk blouse. She'd lately taken to moving her hand all over her torso, trying in vain to feel that first kick.

The door swung open. Amber looked at the reflection to see a familiar-looking woman step into the salon from the sidewalk. Amber swiveled at her post, narrowing her gaze, but Marge cut her off at the pass.

"Hi, Elaine! What're we doing today?"

Amber returned to her phone, tapping back to her sister and mother in the group chat. *Still not here...*

The bells above the salon door again rang to life, clattering as the aluminum-frame door pushed inward. Again, a familiar-looking person. But Marge was the only other one in the salon that morning.

The man was tall and middle-aged with a paunch but an otherwise lanky build. He looked nervous, like he wasn't used to being in salons, a common feature of their male clients—young or old, the guys were never as at home.

Marge hollered a hello and pointed with her comb in Amber's direction. Amber took the cue. "You must be my ten o'clock. Come on back. I'm Amber Lee." Instead of a hand-shake, she patted the back of her dressing chair and gave the man a great big smile before reaching back for her phone to tell Barb and Tiff he'd made it. They could keep their time frame, more or less.

But the customer hesitated near the front desk. "I won't bite. Scout's honor!" Amber promised with another winning grin and a show of two fingers.

He dipped his head and pushed his hands down into his pockets, deep, shaking his shaggy, salt-and-pepper hair into his eyes rather than out. Amber clocked him as the type who had a fear of scissors. Or maybe, in his youth, his mama had forced him to shave off his hair when he didn't want to. Even as they aged, the trauma clung to those poor boys like hair slivers clung to Amber's glossed lips. She made a preliminary spitting attempt just thinking about the pesky short hairs that would attach themselves everywhere. Luckily, it would be for the last time.

Amber patted the chair again. "Come on back. We in for a trim today? Or are you thinking something more drastic?"

But when he finally edged away from the desk and moved down the narrow slip of linoleum and back to where Amber's station was, about twenty yards from the front of the shop, Amber's cheeriness ebbed.

Like Elaine, Marge's client, this man was also vaguely familiar. Actually, no. He was *very* familiar.

With each step that drew him closer to Amber, her breath turned shorter and shallower. By the time the tall, kind-faced man arrived at her chair, Amber felt like she might faint.

"Hi, Amber Lee," he said, soft and low.

Amber's heart twitched. "Dad?"

CHAPTER THIRTY-FOUR

1991

CarlaMay

"Barb, what happened?" I peeked out into the hallway to see if she was chased here. I grabbed her by the hands and pulled her inside.

She didn't look up. She shook so hard I was worried she'd start convulsing on the dorm room floor. "Barb, shh. Shh." I lowered her onto my desk chair and smoothed her hair back from her head.

"Barb, talk to me," I urged her, squeezing her hands.

She didn't see me, though. Her dead gaze remained over my shoulder like she wasn't there. Like the Barb I knew was still back at the bar, canoodling in the dim lights against the beat of a banjo. With Hank.

"Where's Hank?" I asked. "Where is he?" Moving my hands up her trembling body, I gave her shoulders a gentle shake. "Hank? Barb?"

Her next words came out on choked sobs.

"I—he—" She sucked in a ragged breath. "It went too far."

Over the next thirty minutes, in stuttering half-sentences, Barb recounted the confusing events of the night.

She got drunk—too drunk. Hank got upset, accusing her not of being drunk but of being a drunk. He went outside. Maybe for fresh air. Maybe a cigar. She didn't know, but she was mad as a tied hog.

"Whit was so sweet to me." She hiccupped through the words. "He told me I wasn't a drunk and Hank was wrong. He told me how pretty he thought I was. He told me I deserved to have a little fun." A fresh sob racked her body.

Dread pounded in my head, worsening the already-there migraine. Luckily, though, the nausea had vanished.

"Where was Hank?"

"I don't know," Barb whispered, her voice ratcheted back up in panic. "I don't know! I never saw him after he went outside." Her chest heaved.

"What happened next?"

"I followed Whit. I was stupid to do it, but I was so mad at Hank. I was—" She swallowed down a sob. "I was out of my mind, CarlaMay. I never should have gone—"

"What happened, Barb?"

She didn't have to say what happened. The pain on her face said it all.

After that, I threw up.

It's been one week now, and I have thrown up every day since. It should be me driving Barb to the doctor. After what Whit had done.

Instead, Barb took me.

CHAPTER THIRTY-FIVE

PRESENT DAY

Morgan Jo

Tuesday morning, Morgan woke up early. The weekend hadn't been as productive as she'd have liked, what with the bridal brunch and then helping Amber clean her kitchen. But she'd needed a break from the vineyard and ended up taking a long nap on Sunday before enjoying a lazy dinner with Emmett up in Bardstown.

Dinner had gone well. Morgan dove into the spread Emmett had prepared—lemon-garlic salmon and steamed rice with broccoli. As a general rule, Morgan tried not to be too healthy, and so she'd baked an apple pie for dessert and picked up a carton of ice cream on the way over.

Once supper was over and after cleaning their plates at the sink, the pair put music on his record player, and Emmett filled two glasses with a bottle of orange Pinot, straight from the fledgling winery.

Morgan had fiddled at his record player, wondering how she'd managed to fall in love with someone like her Grandad.

Then again, Emmett and Grandad only shared the most super-
ficial of qualities. Hadn't they?

Or was there more to the similarities? Was there a core
quality that linked the two men? Maybe. Maybe there was
something that Morgan couldn't put a finger on. Something
real. Not a love for antiquated music players. Not a heart for the
farm. But what was it?

Morgan pushed the question aside and sipped her wine,
conjuring up the right taste profile. Dry? Yes. Fruity? No. Notes
of citrus. A true white wine but not without its orange blush.

She'd picked an Elvis record. Emmett had sipped his wine
and stared at her.

"What?" Morgan loved the way he looked at her, all blue
eyes and dark brows cutting across thick lashes. His lips, full
and delicious. Peachy, like the color of the dress Morgan had
worn that night. She'd wanted his lips to get lost in her dress.

"Suspicious Minds" had come on then. Emmett had asked
her what song she was thinking for their first dance.

"Well, not that one." She'd laughed. He'd set his wine down
and took hers from her hands, pulling them to his neck.

Before she had been able to muster the courage to share her
anxieties, he'd said, "Let's elope."

In some twisted way, hearing the option aloud jarred her.
Instead of snapping up the idea, she'd balked in defensiveness.
"No *way*."

"Oh, right. I wouldn't want to ruin the '*gala*.'" He clipped
the word with his fingers like air quotes. "Sorry. I didn't mean it
that way."

"I don't want to elope, because I don't want to leave our
families out of the equation."

"Eloping can be romantic. Just us. No one else's ideas. No
other worries."

It wasn't *unappealing*, she agreed.

That was when Morgan had asked him. "What if we do a *wedding* planning day this week?"

"You mean instead of a *business* planning day?"

"Exactly." She let out a sigh of relief and squeezed Emmett's hands, giving them a playful shake. "What if we devote a whole day to talking solely about the *us* part of this business." It was as cheesy a joke as she could manage, and even worse, she had to spell it out for him. "Get it? Business has an *us* in it?"

Emmett gave her a look but grinned. "You're a dork."

"I'm *your* dork. Anyway, don't you want the world to know that?"

"That you are *my* dork? Didn't strike me as a point of pride, but..." He leaned forward and kissed her on the nose. "I suppose I *do* want the world to witness us saying our vows. There are some out there who might not even believe it."

They'd set their wedding planning day for Tuesday.

Emmett cleared his schedule, and Morgan expected him for coffee and eggs promptly at eight. He was more excited about this meeting than any other, she noted with a small thrill. Perhaps there was something to be said for simply turning one's attention back where it belongs. Maybe Morgan's anxiety about the vineyard had etched a scar in everything else. It was time to fix that.

So, she woke up early on Tuesday and committed to *enjoying* her home for once. She set aside work and got ready for a walk.

Picking a pair of threadbare jeans that accentuated her curves, Morgan turned in her bathroom mirror. Every once in a while, she saw in herself what Emmett purported to see. Satisfied that her butt looked good, she pulled a white T-shirt from her bureau and pulled it over her head. Morgan added a quick pump of styling cream to her hair, scrunching and tossing around her long waves, then she slathered on sunscreen and a quick layer of mascara. Primed for a happy day, she grabbed her water bottle and set off into the cool morning air for a long walk.

Ever since Morgan's official move back to Brambleberry, the act of *walking* had transitioned from a mild chore into a joy. No one who looked at her now would have any idea that for five years she strode unevenly, more often limping than strolling. Being home meant she could make real progress toward recovery, from the help of Julia's therapy stretches, to a new medical regime downgraded from prescription painkillers to a daily dose of ibuprofen, and including Morgan's physical work on the farm. It was funny how she hadn't needed fewer steps or handicapped accessible showers to feel better. She'd needed hard work.

But Morgan wasn't too high and mighty to forget that some wounds never did get worked out like kinks.

Monday had been a productive day. Together with Amber, Morgan tallied product, materials, and did a walk-through of the vineyard. There was only one thing missing for their grand opening at this point: a name for the business.

With invitations due to go out that week, she was out of time. No one else had seemed to care as much about the naming as Morgan did, and so she decided that her one final job before Emmett arrived that Tuesday was to come up with something on her own. To do this, she wanted to take in the greater farm. See it as if from someone else's eyes.

Clean lawn lines zigzagged over the dark green carpet of the gentle hills that carried Morgan along the fence and toward the back of the property. She bypassed the gap that would take her into the vineyard—the point now was to get the bigger picture.

For the gala, they planned to erect a great big wreathen arch over that gap, ushering guests back into the secret beyond the fence.

Secret.

She continued along the fence, passing the barn. Inside that barn had been decades' worth of work, and it wasn't only tools that had ever lived in there. Once upon a time, livestock had called the barn home. A refuge from bad weather or hot sun. And now, a boutique factory for fermenting and bottling wine. Just by looking at it, with a fresh coat of cherry-red paint and snow-white trim—it looked like nothing more than a barn you might see in a pastoral jigsaw puzzle.

Another secret.

Morgan walked on, stopping to take a long pull of her ice-cold water. She mounted the gentle green slope, leaving the fence line and moving closer to the hangar, now.

Rarely did she come near the hangar. As if the tragedy within was contagious, she'd mainly preferred to keep her distance.

This morning, however, Morgan felt bold. She reached for the padlock to see it was hanging open, the metal rusting so badly it was likely teeming with tetanus.

Morgan pulled it off and dropped the lock to the grass, then opened the heavy wooden door as wide as it'd go, letting the morning sun bleach the cavernous space.

She stepped in.

Her Memaw had told Morgan that people in town didn't *really* know what had happened to Dottie, her twin. All they'd heard was rumor and gossip—great horror stories about the child hanging herself or drinking antifreeze or catching a hunter's stray shot.

No one, save for the family, knew the truth. And even the family who knew the truth didn't dare talk of it. It was too brutal. Too sad. It'd upset Memaw.

Then again, Memaw hadn't been altogether shy about sharing the full events with Morgan. Not only that, but she'd even had a plan for the building which had played shroud to that terrible family tragedy from so long ago. Tear the damn thing down, that's what.

But Grandad didn't want that. He'd had greater aspirations. He'd prayed for a rejuvenation of the tobacco industry. Or the birth of a new one, maybe. A new purpose for a well-built structure. Grandad had seen potential.

Memaw had seen nothing but a heartbreaking secret.

CHAPTER THIRTY-SIX

PRESENT DAY

Amber

Amber's chest turned hollow at the sight of him.

Her dad. Hank Taylor.

In the flesh, in the salon. In front of Amber.

It hadn't occurred to Amber that her father would look different from the last time she'd seen him, which was over twenty years before. She was only a little girl—not yet five years old—the last time Amber had been in her daddy's presence, or he in hers.

After that, having only seen one fuzzy, dated photograph hadn't been enough to give Amber a clear image of who her father had become over the years.

And yet, he was just the same.

In a way, seeing him was like seeing a long-lost love. Like a small part of Amber's heart had been pounding for him all these years. "Henry T.?"

He flushed, paled, and looked away. "I didn't want to tip you off."

Despite everything—all the years he'd been gone and, more

recently, standing her up—she wasn't mad. Confused, maybe. Not mad.

Amber grabbed a black cape from her counter and shook it out, but he held up a hand. "You don't have to cut my hair."

"It looks like it needs one," she blurted.

He ran his hand up the back of his head, scruffing his shaggy style. "Really?"

Then, as if it were the most natural thing in the world, Amber's dad sank into her chair, and she gave him a trim.

At first, heavy silence hung around them. But slowly, small talk emerged. "Today is my last appointment. *You* are my last appointment."

"You're going on vacation?"

Amber smiled. "In a way." She turned on the clippers, lifted her voice over the din. "I'm leaving the profession."

"Oh!" His eyes widened in genuine curiosity. "Moving on to greener pastures?"

"You could say that. Morgan Jo and me—you remember Morgan Jo?"

He nodded. "Sure I do."

Relief flooded Amber's chest. He still knew her. He still knew *all* of them. "We're opening a vineyard at the farm there off the creek."

"Bill's farm?"

"Grandad? Yep. Grandad and Memaw's farm. Moonshine Creek."

"I heard about Miss Essie. I'm real sorry. What's it been, a year?"

"Nearly. How'd you hear?" Amber turned off the clippers and brushed the back of his neck. It was like a map, her daddy's bare skin. Weird thoughts pushed through. Her own hands, small and grubby, clinging to that neck as her daddy swung her up onto his shoulders and carried her around like a circus act.

She pulled out shears and pinched his hair between her first two fingers, dragging it out and trimming.

"My mom."

Amber's grandmother. The one she didn't know. The one who abandoned Amber and her siblings right along with Hank. Granny Taylor had taken his side. It had made things worse, Barb had always said.

"Oh."

"How's Barb?"

"Good. I know she had to cancel on you for that, um, dinner." Months back, Amber had had grand plans of setting her parents up on a date. She'd gone so far as to book them a nice meal. But then Amber and Grant broke up, creating fresh drama and ruining the potential for a reunion. After that, Amber had slowly begun to lose interest in her mom and dad's love life. She'd instead had to recover from her own.

"I'd have canceled if she hadn't beat me to the punch," he said by way of brushing Amber off.

She frowned, stopped trimming. Looked at him in the mirror. "Why?"

He loosened a hand from the cape and tugged at where it pinched his neck. "Oh, I don't know. A little awkward, I guess? Plus, I hadn't been back in town very long at that point. Still settling in."

"Are you living here? In Brambleberry?"

"Yep. Got a place down south of town."

"A house?"

"You could call it that. The property was a farm at one point, but the owners parceled off the land, sold bits and pieces. I got a little hunting cabin at the corner. Cheap. It works."

"Why did you come back?"

She had stopped cutting his hair altogether. It wasn't done. She needed to trim up around his ears and shape the back. Even so, Amber couldn't go on. She had to watch him answer her. She had to hear everything that came from his lips.

He slid his gaze from where they'd been making eye contact in the mirror to her actual eyes. Their reflections became background noise. "I always wanted to be here."

"You were a Hollywood guy."

He laughed. "Hardly. That was a pipe dream. An escape. Not the real deal."

"You missed us." She didn't ask. She said it. Willed it, even.

Hank looked at her harder. "I've never stopped missing Barb."

A shot to her heart. Amber's entire body buzzed with invisible whiplash. "Barb," she repeated listlessly.

Of all the ways Hank Taylor could hurt her, Amber had never thought it could be through her mother. His ex. Their one uniting thing.

Abruptly, Amber stood up. She spun his chair with careful force, facing him squarely to the mirror. "You'll be glad to know, then, that she's on her way here now."

CHAPTER THIRTY-SEVEN

1991

CarlaMay

Plainly enough, I turned out to be pregnant. I didn't know where to turn or what to do. I knew I couldn't finish school, and so after that semester, I dropped out.

But I didn't quit church. I went to the Newman Center every single Sunday, praying so hard I wondered if I'd lose the baby from being a religious zealot if not from how long I lasted on my knees. It couldn't have been good for my body—all that kneeling and praying.

Of course, it was my only chance to see him, *though.*

He was there, too, like clockwork. An authority figure. A stranger.

And then, later, he returned to me as neither of those things but instead, as my lover. We kept on for some time, until he was transferred out west.

The letters came and went between the two of us. Love letters, every last one of them.

In one such letter, he promised me that one day he'd come back for me. He'd find a way to break with charity.

I wondered then if I should tell him what had happened. That I was having his baby.

But I decided not to. I figured that one day, he'd come back to me.

One day, we would raise our baby in the light of the public eye.

One day, we would do the right thing.

But until then, he was stuck doing the Lord's work.

And the last thing I wanted to do was get him in trouble. After all, he was more than the love of my life.

He was my priest, too.

CHAPTER THIRTY-EIGHT

PRESENT DAY

Morgan Jo

As she crept across the dusty, hay-strewn dirt floor to the back corner of the hangar, something caught Morgan's eye.

At the boarded-up back corner, the plywood popped out at the top left, as if it were peeling away from the hidden hollow space behind.

She stopped, her body flush against the plywood as she walked her fingers up the edge of the added sheet of wood. The nails along where it should be a flush seam had come loose, unmooring themselves one by one, perhaps from rain, perhaps from time, and then, toward the top, the whole sheet was warped away from the corner.

Another secret?

It couldn't be. There was no secret in the hangar. Not to Morgan, at least.

Sure, her family's history was a troubled one. But a great lot of good had also come to the Nelsons and the Coyles.

After all, the secrets of Moonshine Creek were just like her fruit. Some were good secrets, like CarlaMay's secret pregnancy from so long ago, all the way to Amber's surprise pregnancy today. Some secrets were rotten. Dottie's death. Morgan's incident.

Here on the sprawling tract of Kentucky bluegrass, the earth was bursting to life with these hidden truths. It only made sense that a chintzy piece of plywood couldn't possibly contain one of the foulest of them.

An innocent person could walk onto the farm and, like the Garden of Eden, find beauty and danger in equal measure. The highest of highs and lowest of lows had taken place here.

Life had grown here, and it had died here. All the death, though, it churned itself back into the earth and fed new life, like a garden.

Morgan pushed up high on the balls of her feet, pulling herself by the tips of her fingers as she tried to pry the wood fully from the wall.

The board snapped, shocking her and sending her sprawling back onto her butt. A triangular section of plywood lay next to her, its jagged edge proof of her crime. "Crap."

But then, did it really matter? If necessary, she could just nail this piece back up as if she hadn't torn it free. She stood and patted the silty hay from her butt and thighs, then picked up the board and leaned it against the wall.

Then, Morgan peered into the gap.

Cobwebs streaked in silken, symmetric patterns in the corners within the little cubby. At the floor inside, it looked near the same to the rest of the hangar. Sprays of hay lay scattered over the top of the packed dirt floor.

A spider scurried back up to the farthest corner of her web as Morgan's gaze flicked to the ladder that carried up into the loft above. Though as old as time, the ladder looked perfectly functional, like if Morgan tried to climb it now, the rungs would hold just fine. She leaned further onto the balls of her feet, pressing her chest over the craggy lip of the plywood covering.

Sharp, thick splinters pushed into her ribcage, but she was desperate to see up, up, up. To where the ladder disappeared into that square shelf above.

Morgan pushed onto her tiptoes and pulled herself, her palms screaming with the pressure of the plywood's rough-hewn teeth.

On the very brink of the ledge up above, something poked out.

At first, Morgan's breath stopped. Almost as if she was seeing a stiff, bloodied edge of her late aunt's cotton dress stuck out in a perfectly triangular point to complement the chunk of plywood Morgan had tugged free.

She narrowed her eyes, pressing herself higher still, until she was certain the sharp points of broken plywood would cut through her skin and her toenails would bruise. It wasn't fabric. It wasn't another sheet of plywood, either. It looked like... a *book?*

"MoJo!"

Morgan's hands instinctively released the rough wooden edge. It scraped up her chest, grating through her shirt and scratching her skin. She landed hard on her heels, wincing. "Ow." Her hands flew to her chest, gripping it and biting down on her lower lip.

"Whoa, whoa, *whoa.*" Emmett came up behind her, gripping her at the waist. "What's going on in here?"

Morgan let out a breath and released her chest. The burning had gone away. She looked at her white shirt to see sawdust and regular dust smeared, but no tears. It was just a scrape. Through the shirt and through her bra. She wasn't really hurt.

Her eyes flew back to the hole in the boarded-up corner. "I was just..." She lifted a hand and let it fall again. "Looking," she added wistfully.

"Looking at what?" Emmett took a step forward and poked his head more easily into the cavity she'd left.

"Nothing." She shouldn't do this. Morgan should not start a whole new secret out of nothing. No, siree. "I thought I saw something up there, on the loft, but—it's nothing."

Emmett, none the wiser, cocked his head and lifted a finger toward the gaping wound of the boarded-up corner. "Isn't this where—"

Morgan grabbed his hand and twirled him back to her. "Exactly."

"Are we still thinking of doing something with this place?"

She shrugged. "Yes. And no. I mean, right now, it feels like too much."

"In the future, it could make for a fabulous storage hangar."

Morgan shot him a look. "Storage? No. This place is going to be something better than that."

Emmett smiled and rubbed his thumb across her cheek. "Dirt. Anyway, I've got a hammer in the barn. You want me to put this back together?" He indicated the broken-off chunk.

She swallowed. "I don't think so."

Their eyes met, and Morgan could see clear as day that Emmett was thinking exactly what she was. Maybe wedding talk *could* wait. "Instead of a hammer—" she began.

But he was already heading out and toward the barn. He called over his shoulder at the door, "A pry bar."

CHAPTER THIRTY-NINE

PRESENT DAY

Amber

At the drop of Barb's name, Hank was up, out of Amber's chair, and tugging his cape from around his neck.

"You're going to leave? *Again?*" She folded her arms. Up to now, nothing had bothered Amber enough to be mad at her father. It was as though something in her snapped. Clearly, Hank still loved her mother. He still loved Trav. He'd invited Trav up to the city not too long ago—right after word had come that Hank was back in town. Tiff—it was unclear how Hank felt about her, because Tiff couldn't give two licks for the guy.

But why did Hank utterly hate Amber?

Hank cleared his throat, smoothed the sides of his head and looked in the mirror. Then he turned and looked at Amber. "Listen. I didn't only come back for Barb. I came back for all of you."

"All of us." She let out a short laugh. "It's fine. I've got other things to worry about." She refrained from moving her hands to her belly. Hank didn't deserve to know Amber's secret. Not yet, anyway. Still, she *wanted* to believe him. A smile lifted one corner of her mouth. "Anyway, we're going for lunch."

"Lunch?"

"I have to clean out my station."

"I'll help."

"My mom and Tiff are coming to help. That's what I meant when I said they were coming here first."

"Okay." He carefully folded the cape. "Amber, I'm sorry about the video shop, by the way."

"The video shop." She blinked. "Right. It's fine. Like I said, I'm so busy. I don't really have time to go back on things right now."

"You and Callum, though, you've watched the tapes. Right?"

Amber stopped in the middle of packing up her combs. She looked at Hank. "We started 'em. Lots are damaged."

"Damaged?" He made a scoffing sound. "They're good-quality."

Amber frowned. "Did you help Callum work on them?" Callum. His name stung her tongue.

Hank's face changed. "No—" Before he could say more, the front doorbell jangled.

In walked Barb and Tiff.

Barb cried out a loud, "Happy Last Day!" Tiff carried a bouquet of colorful balloons. Neither one seemed to notice Hank.

Not at first.

He looked at Amber, a promise that he had more to say to her, privately. Barb clocked him, though, and Tiff did, too. The air in the salon turned hot and dry. Amber felt a clammy layer of sweat spread over her chest and up the back of her neck. Her breath turned shallow. Thoughts of Callum and the tapes mingled with her thoughts of her father. His hair. His abandonment. Her attempt to reunite him with her mother. His ragged return to the fold, like a stray who neared only in short darts, as if to grab a morsel of food out of desperation. Not because he wanted these strangers to take him in.

The difference between Hank Taylor and a stray, though, was that strays got that way because of their circumstances, ones out of their control. Not because they *wanted* to leave.

"BarbaraJean Coyle," Hank said. "In the flesh."

Barb snorted, but Amber saw her mom's lips purse. Her cheeks went hollow, like she was sucking 'em. "I could say the same about you." She propped her hands on her hips, let out a long whistle and took him in, head to toe.

Amber flushed. Tiff gave her a look.

"Well!" Amber clapped her hands together. "I need to wipe everything down and finish here."

"We'll help," Tiff said. It wasn't a question, and yet, Barb gave her a grateful smile.

"Hank, honey, do you want to join us for lunch at the Dewdrop? I can call Trav over. He'll probably be on a break soon 'nuff—"

"Mom, we told Amber we'd help her. You're gonna stay. Right?" Tiff's voice was hard and blunt, rough.

"Actually, you two go ahead." Amber stared daggers at her sister. Tiff may not want their parents to patch things up, but Amber, even despite how Hank treated her, *did*. If Barb and Hank got back together, something told Amber that her life would be whole again. Although that goal did seem to be slipping through her fingers with each passing day. Each passing day brought something else to focus Amber's attention on.

In fact, as she stood here now, cleaning spare hairs from a round brush and watching her parents catch up, Amber wondered if she really needed her dad after all.

CHAPTER FORTY

1991

CarlaMay

While I got more pregnant by the day, Barb and Hank continued to date.

She never told him about the night at The Holler with Whit.

And that was how Whit came to keep hangin' around.

About six months on, when I was so pregnant I had to start fessin' up, Barb had a birthday party. I couldn't drink, of course, but I went along anyhow.

Barb got drunker than a pig. She was having a good ol' time of it, though, and I liked to watch her be happy. It took my mind off things. Namely, the fact that my mama was on the brink of reporting me to the Catholic church for my indecency. My mama is like that, devout. And what I'd gotten myself into was as bad as you could think of.

Even worse than Barb's carryin' on with shots and beers and doing a striptease right there on the dance floor of The Tavern.

Things between Hank and Barb looked to be goin' well, too, until that birthday party. Now that I think back on it, it was probably the beginning of the end. And now that I'm writing about it, I realize that it's liable to become the most dangerous part of this here journal. That's why I'm glad I got one with a lock and key. Just in case...

CHAPTER FORTY-ONE

PRESENT DAY

Morgan Jo

Morgan and Emmett decided to return to the hangar, with pry bars and tools, another time. She was satisfied that they were going to dig more into it, but she wasn't so anxious as to forgo breakfast. Anyway, Morgan's stomach was rumbling something awful, and Emmett worried he'd get a headache if he missed his morning caffeine.

Morgan lined bacon up on a baking sheet while he beat half a dozen eggs in a mixing bowl. The coffee percolated on the counter, and Emmett brought her up to speed on his work—the office kind. He had a handful clients at the present, and each of them mired in some interesting drama. Emmett took care not to reveal any names, but Morgan enjoyed trying to figure out who was whom. There was the landlady who'd been trying to evict her third-floor tenant. The tenant who was waging war on his farmhouse landlord. The soon-to-be divorcee with a penchant for making her ex's life a living hell.

Most interestingly to Morgan was a pro bono family and children case Emmett had taken on recently. Well, he'd taken it on initially but had ended up turning it over to a colleague, preferring instead to consult on it. In this case, a teenage girl had a baby, the baby was shuffled into foster care, and now the teenager wanted custody again. In a deviation from his normal line-up, Emmett had consulted for the state's side, rather than the families'.

Now that baby's fate hung in the air while strangers decided what would become of him.

"You don't think the family would be the best place for the baby?" she asked, after he'd given her the update that the baby was again in foster care and would hopefully stay there until the state found a permanent placement.

Emmett didn't so much as flinch. His tone turned severe. "This family thinks keeping their granddaughter would somehow save them, too."

"What do you mean?"

"The father—er, grandfather, I should say—is a poorly functioning alcoholic. The mother is a serial cheater. They had another, younger child who they lost to an O.D., already." Emmett sighed and pushed his hands through his hair. "This baby—any baby—deserves better than that."

"How old is he?" Morgan couldn't suppress her curiosity. She felt inextricably pulled to know more.

"*She*. She's three months now."

Morgan cringed. "Just a newborn."

He eyed Morgan for a minute. "Would you ever—"

"Ever what?" she studied him. "Would I ever what?"

"Nothing."

Morgan made an assumption about what Emmett was going to say. "Would I ever give my baby up for adoption? No. But that doesn't mean what the teenager did was wrong. I can't fathom being a teen mom."

Emmett cleared his throat. "Well, that's—yeah. I get that."

He shook his head. "I feel so bad for the baby. I just want the best for her."

Morgan squeezed his shoulder. "She's lucky to have you fighting for her, then, Emmett."

"The hard thing is—" Emmett said it with a heavy sadness in his voice and a pained expression. He shook his head. "The hard thing is that I've seen worse, and I wasn't always able to help them. Sometimes, I was on the other side or sometimes I just heard about the case in passing." His expression turned weary.

"How can you stand to take these cases at all?" she asked.

"How can I *not*?"

Morgan nuzzled her nose into his shoulder then pushed up on her toes and kissed him on the cheek. "You're too good for this world."

Emmett just shrugged. "Everyone has these problems. Not just my clients or my colleagues' clients."

Morgan considered this. There were a million comparisons she could make between her own family and Emmett's case-load, but not a single one seemed as bad as a sweet little newborn baby without a family to love her. A good family, who not only had the love to give but also the resources and ability. Her stomach clenched over the thought.

Emmett said, "I'm sorry. Let's talk about something else for now. You've got your final dress fitting soon, right?"

Morgan sighed. "Yes. Right." Her dress fitting felt like a speck of sand along the beaches of the Atlantic. Irrelevant at best. "You know, I've been thinking, and I want you to come. To the fitting, I mean."

He stopped in the middle of pouring the eggs into the skillet. "That's against tradition."

"I know, but aren't we already bucking tradition?"

Resuming the pour, and selecting a wooden ladle to stir with, Emmett's features returned to neutral. "True." His brows lowered, though. "But why? You've got your mom and aunts and cousins. Plus my mom. Lots of lady folk who want to help you, Mo."

"You're right, but... I guess I just want you to see it *before* the chaos. I don't want some big surprise. I want you to see me and be... *pleased*. Not horrified."

Emmett chuckled, tapped the ladle on the edge of the skillet and set it on a laid-out hand towel. He picked Morgan's hands up in his, kissed the backs of them and looked her in the eye. "No matter what dress you've picked and no matter how it fits, you will stun me, Morgan Jo Coyle. You always have." He raised an eyebrow. "You *could* always show up in a bikini. I mean, since we're bucking tradition and all."

Morgan let her head fall back as she laughed. "You're wild."

He kissed her hands again, then turned them, kissed the insides of her wrists. His gentle lips on such delicate skin made Morgan's entire body flash in goosebumps. She looked down at her palms as Emmett raised his head. Morgan wore her engagement ring every day, and it was just fine. But they'd already had to have her wedding band resized once and Emmett's resized twice. "Rings!" Her head whipped up.

He let her hands slip away before pulling her in for a quick kiss on the lips. Then, Emmett returned to the eggs, and Morgan asked, "Have you heard back from the jeweler yet?"

Emmett said, "Yep. All's good. I pick them up the first Tuesday of September. Gives us a whole month just in case."

Her body relaxed, and she picked up her mug, cradling it in her hands and sipping the strong brew. "Good. So, then, there's my final fitting. Bouquets. Speeches—*vows*?"

"Vows. Are we going non-traditional with that, too?" He pointed at her with the yellow-tipped ladle.

"That depends." Morgan frowned and gave him a look.

"Right. The priest thing. When is he coming, again?"

Morgan answered, "Tonight."

CHAPTER FORTY-TWO

PRESENT DAY

Amber

Tiffany made it clear she didn't want Hank to join them for lunch. She also made it clear she didn't want Barb and Hank to go off ahead of them, stealing away for a romantic moment.

Still, Amber insisted. "You two go on. You've got lots to catch up on, I reckon. Tiff'll help me here. We won't be long."

Once their parents left, Tiff eyed Amber. "What in the *hell* is wrong with you? I would say this is a pregnancy thing, but you been wantin' them to get back together for eons. *Why?*"

Amber shrugged, adjusted her glasses higher up her nose, and stowed the last of her tools into a large canvas tote. "Don't you want them to be together?"

"He left us high and dry when we were babies. All I need to know about Hank Taylor I learned that day."

"You don't even remember that day," Amber pointed out, but her defeat was obvious enough. She sank into her chair and rested both hands on her taut stomach. Inside of Amber, her own little baby grew. It was harder to defend Hank now, knowing that Amber was headed for parenthood. Even though she was early into her pregnancy, Amber couldn't fathom just up and leaving. Even so, she tried for some semblance of an explanation. After all, if the plain truth was that Hank didn't love them—didn't love *her*—then what did that really say about Amber? "Maybe there's a reason he left. Aren't you curious to know that?"

"If there was a reason he left, Mom would have told us." Tiff folded her arms over her chest.

"Maybe Mom didn't know the reason."

"Maybe she did and she's complicit."

"When are you going to apply for the police academy?"

Tiff shrugged, unfolded her arms, and picked up a rag. "Let's get done and get over there before they decide to remarry."

The Dewdrop rushed with lunch. As if all of Main Street were there, it was packed—from the bar to the very back booths. "Where are they?" Tiff stretched her neck to look around the place. "It's *Tuesday*. Why are people *here*?"

"It's *Tuesday*," Amber replied. "Business days are crazy here, you know. It's a retailer's lunch spot. Like, every single day." She pointed to a foursome sitting at a table in the center of the crowded floor. "The newspaper staff." In the booth just around the corner from the hostess stand, "There's the florist and her assistant. Speaking of which, Morgan asked me to check in with them today."

Tiff pointed across the diner to the bar. "Is that Mrs. Clancy?"

Amber spied the elderly woman who ran Clancy's Boutique. "Yep."

"She's still alive?"

Amber nodded.

The hostess appeared. A familiar-looking girl who'd gradu-ated from Brambleberry High just a few years after Amber. "Hi y'all. Two for lunch?" She tapped a chewed-on pencil against the hostess stand and kept her gaze on a long list of waiting customers.

"Actually, you might have seen our mom come in? Barb, you know. Curvy woman with white-blonde hair and great big blue eyes?" Tiff wasn't exaggerating, but to hear their mom described that way was almost laughable.

Amber added, "She's with Hank Taylor. Tall, dark-haired guy."

The hostess popped a big, pink gum bubble. "Oh, yeah. Miss Barb." She pressed a long pink nail onto the page and dragged it down a column of at least five uncrossed-through names. "Another ten minutes. Maybe twenty."

"They aren't seated?" Tiff glared, even though it wasn't the poor hostess's fault. Amber rested her hand on her sister's arm. "Let's go. They probably went for a little walk."

Just as the two returned to the sidewalk and glanced up and down Main, searching for their parents, Amber's phone chimed. Tiff's did, too. Their mom had sent a group text.

Long wait. Hank is giving me a tour of his shop!!!

"Three exclamation marks?" Tiff rolled her eyes. "She's as bad as *you*."

"Yeah, well." Amber twisted her fingers together, blinking and looking around for the right response to her mom. She took to her phone. *We'll wait at the diner.*

Tiff read Amber's message then snorted. "No, we won't. If we're doing this, then we're *doing* this." She grabbed Amber by the elbow and began to drag her down Main and toward Olde Towne Video. "I can't go there," Amber protested, digging her heels into the cement. "No *way*."

Tiff stopped. "Oh. That's right." Tiff knew everything.

Especially the things Amber didn't tell her. Tiff gazed at her younger sister curiously now. "Callum."

"I'm not going."

"You haven't told him?"

Amber shook her head in shame.

"Well, no time like the present." Tiff tugged at her elbow again. "Come on, Amber Lee."

"I can't."

"You have to."

"Says who?"

"Says me. We're going. You can tell him everything, and by the time you're done, then we'll have our table at the Dewdrop and we could move from one awkward conversation with one man into a whole other awkward conversation with a whole other man. 'Kay?" Tiff gave her a winning grin.

"This is a really bad idea." But even as Amber said it and felt it and *knew* it to be true, something down inside of her disagreed. Like a rag doll, she let her sister pull her down Main Street and directly into the belly of the whale.

CHAPTER FORTY-THREE

PRESENT DAY

Amber

Reluctantly, Amber followed Tiff in the door of Olde Towne Video. Though, was she *really* reluctant? Or was she waiting for this chance? This moment to be pressed up against her fate. Her past. Her future.

Probably, she was.

"There you are!" Barb's voice boomed from the back of the shop. Amber looked around, briefly thankful and disappointed to see no sign of Callum. "Did you know they still stock VHS tapes?" Barb added, once Amber and Tiff shuffled past the Romantic Comedy section and toward their parents.

The question their mom posed was awkward, not because VHS tapes were old, but because she was pretending like everything was fine. Like she wasn't chatting up the love of her life right there, in front of her two daughters. The same two that this man had left behind. *His* daughters. That's not even to mention the son he had or the wife he'd once considered Barb to be.

Amber wondered what her mother was feeling seeing Hank.

She knew what she was feeling. Weird. Her heart sank into her stomach. Her breathing turned shallow. Her skin slicked over, clammy and itchy and all kinds of uncomfortable.

Olde Towne Video, for being as small as it was, had just about everything, and everything in there had its place. Orderly rows and columns, each labeled with genre and medium. DVD spanned the front of the shop. A small offering of VHS tapes stood at the back. Walking through the crammed-but-few shelves felt a lot like walking through fire to get to her mom and... well, *dad*.

"It's for us vintage types. Old school." Hank grinned and managed to peel his eyes off of Barb and look at his daughters. He studied them both in a way that Amber figured was meant to be kind. In fact, his eyes were the *kind* type. Gentle and brown, a lot like Trav's, Amber realized. He shoved his hands deep in his pockets and sucked in a breath. "Hi."

Amber wondered if he was thinking about shaking hands, too. She gave a small wave and looked at her sister.

Hank must have figured his only safety was in the movies that lined them on either side. He proffered up a VHS. His voice wobbled as he asked, "Tiff, did you ever see *True Lies*?"

Tiff twisted her features into a look of disgust. "It's *Tiffany*."

But Hank was unfazed. "You know, it was *me* who started calling you Tiff."

Amber felt her sister melt, but only a little. Did Amber get a nickname back then? Something she couldn't remember? Something like how Morgan Jo was MoJo to her best friends. And Travis was only ever Trav. And Tiff, well, Tiff. A burning need to ask arose in her chest but she tamped it down, because the answer was an obvious no. Amber Lee was just Amber. Not even Amber Lee.

But Hank cleared his throat. "I called you Amber Berry."

"I remember that," Barb said fondly. "Brambleberry Amber Berry."

"I wanted your middle name to be Berry," Hank added.

Amber whispered, "Amber Berry," to herself, but it jogged no memory. Nothing shook loose. The nickname was wholly unfamiliar. "Amber Berry Brambleberry."

"Brambleberry Amber Berry," Hank corrected. "I guess it didn't stick."

"Well, once you left us, there was no one else to call her that," Barb pointed out, poking a finger into Hank's chest.

The little back-and-forth did nothing to charm Amber or warm her heart. Instead, she felt emptier for it. "I would have liked that."

Hank looked down and kicked at a black hump of old gum that had long ago been dropped and smudged deep into the carpet. He looked back up at Amber. "I could still call you that."

Amber felt herself grow hot. She loved the idea of a nickname and especially one bequeathed to her by her dad. But all of this was feeling like... what was the saying? Too little, too late. She shrugged and looked away.

Hank tried again. "How about this one." He returned *True Lies* to its shelf, moved his hand down from Action to Drama and selected a new cassette, passing it in Amber and Tiff's general direction.

Tiff let her arms drop and reluctantly accepted the cassette. Hank tapped a finger on it and caught Amber's eye. "You should watch it."

Amber glanced at the cover. *On Golden Pond.* She'd heard of it.

"Amber?"

Callum appeared behind them, a *Back to the Future* vintage tee hanging loose from his wiry frame and a crooked, hopeful smile lighting up his features. "You're here." He glanced at Hank as if they'd been in cahoots, maybe.

Amber sensed everyone dissolving into the backdrop of the shop except for her and Callum.

"I—my—" Amber groped her mind for the right word. *Dad* seemed wrong. "Hank, um, we were going to lunch? He got a haircut. I'm leaving the salon." The staccato mess of words tumbled out of her mouth like a cup of dice, landing in no orderly combination but rather in a scramble of random numbers. "Sorry," she whispered, feeling the most pregnant she had felt since she'd learned she was pregnant. She had to force herself *not* to rest her hands on her stomach protectively. It was no use, though, and they crept across her belly, holding her baby in as she held in her breath, too.

"Yeah, it's my fault. I'm the butthead." Hank scratched the back of his head. "When the diner had a wait, I figured we could just come here. I mean, you two know each other, right?"

Tiff clapped her hands together. "Mom, we should go."

Amber gave her sister a pleading look, but Hank was all too happy to get away from the shop, and from Amber, too, probably. "Great idea, Tiff. Let's go."

Before Amber knew it, they were gone, and it was only she and Callum standing in front of a rack of VHS tapes, asking each other how they'd been.

CHAPTER FORTY-FOUR

1991

CarlaMay

Barb's birthday party went south, to put it plain.

Hank got just as drunk as Barb this time around, and at one point, he went out for a cigar and never did come back in. Not that I saw anyway.

Of course, I had to leave early. I was tired and I hated to be in a bar while pregnant. Especially late into the night. It felt gross to me.

It was the next day that Barb told me what happened.

Hank had stayed out with his cigar for too long, I guess. Whit came onto Barb. This time, Barb said she turned him down, but he got handsy and Barb didn't have her wits about her.

One thing led to another, Barb said, and soon enough, Whit was downright taking advantage of the situation.

When Barb told me, her biggest worry was with Hank. If he knew what she'd done, he would break up with her, she was positive of it.

And the problem with that was that the very next day, on Barb's actual birthday, Hank proposed marriage.

Three years later, Barb told him everything, and he left.

And that was when I realized I would have to keep my secret, too. At least, until I could talk to David face to face.

CHAPTER FORTY-FIVE

PRESENT DAY

Amber

Amber couldn't stand to hang around the video shop making small talk with Callum, but he didn't seem to mind.

"Listen, I know you've been busy"—he started walking toward the back room, and she realized she was supposed to follow him—"but I made more progress on the tapes. I didn't get a chance to watch this one in its entirety, but the first five minutes are working real smooth. Maybe we could sit and watch it?" As soon as he turned to look at her, his anxious smile fell away. "Right, you're busy." They were in the back room now, and Callum fiddled with the VCR and a tape as if he wasn't as nervous as he looked. As Amber felt. He rambled on, filling their shared air with noise. "And Mr. Taylor—you guys are... back in touch? That's really great, Amber."

It was Amber's turn to talk now. To clarify.

To explain.

"Callum, listen," she started, as he slid the tape into the VCR and pushed a few buttons, situated a few plugs. "I *am* so busy. I mean, with the vineyard thing and now Morgan Jo's wedding and all that. I'm an usherette, and it's basically like being a bridesmaid, and we've got her shower coming up and before you know it the big day will be here—"

He turned and looked at her, his fidgetiness suddenly gone, his face placid, still. "Amber, I *heard*."

"Heard what?" She frowned and again her hands flew to her stomach. She pressed them flat against it, willing any evidence to be concealed by the fact that Amber was already curvaceous.

Shame filled up her heart. She had no reason to hide her baby. And yet, if she did have a reason, he was standing right there in front of her.

Behind Callum, the video came to life with images of Grandad Bill in overalls, a wad of chew swelling his lower lip, as he droned on about getting crocks from the A&P.

Suddenly, Amber wished she could go back in time. Back when you could follow the railroad tracks on the east side of the farm all the way north to the A&P at the farthest corner of town. You could get a soda for fifty cents. You could ask for the produce scraps and take 'em back home to make backyard wine.

And yet, Amber didn't want to change a thing. Not about her past. Not about her present.

She took in a deep breath, let it out, moved her hands to the lower part of her belly, where her jeans were fastened with the help of a hair tie. She'd threaded the small rubber band through the eyehole on the left and secured it around the button on the right, allowing her favorite jeans to grow with her tummy.

Callum took a step closer. "Amber," he said, his voice low but his features pleasant, "*congratulations*."

Amber had a choice after that. She could say thanks, leave, go back to Hank and her starry-eyed mother and teeth-gritting sister. Or, she could talk to Callum.

She reached behind him and pressed the pause button on the VCR. "Can we talk?"

"I'd love to."

They settled into the pair of metal folding chairs that sat like a mini theater in front of the AV cart with its heavy box TV. "I didn't say anything sooner because it's so uncomfortable. It wasn't expected. This, I mean." She held her tummy and looked at it as though she could see her little baby growing inside. In a way, she could. Everything Amber saw now was through the lens of having a baby, of being a mother. A parent.

"I understand." He shook his hair off his face and turned his hand over on his knee. She wasn't sure if she was supposed to take it. He reached out to her. "Here."

Amber slipped her hand into Callum's, and she wanted to cry. She wanted to kiss him. She wanted to leave. She wanted to go back in time after all.

She wanted to never have met Callum Dockerty. Maybe she *did* want to change that part of her past.

Her present.

"I really like you, Amber."

Amber's gaze lifted up to Callum's. Tears spilled over her lower eyelids, soundless tears, quiet sadness. "I liked you, too."

"Has that changed?" he whispered, genuine and soft and butter smooth as ever.

She broke eye contact and pulled her hand from his, looking away and wiping her face with the back of her hand. "Everything has changed."

"That's life."

"That's life?" Amber sniffled.

"Before I moved here, I lived with my twin. Callista."

"Callista and Callum." Amber smiled. "That's pretty cute."

"Yeah. Living with my sister was up and down, you know? Like, one day, we were best friends. The next, eh, not so much."

"Siblings." Amber immediately let her mind wander to the

distant—or not-so-distant—future. Would this baby have little brothers and sisters?

"Exactly."

"Let me guess, when you moved, she was crushed. She guilt-tripped you. That's how it is in my family. God forbid somebody follows her dream." Amber wasn't used to feeling bitter, especially toward her family. She shook her head, quietly apologizing inside, to herself, to her family. To Callum, too. She opened her mouth to say something, to explain that she didn't mean to sound nasty. She didn't mean to ghost him. She didn't mean a lot of things... but Callum cut her off at the pass.

"No. She died."

A heavy thud of a sentence.

Amber's mouth fell open. She worked to close it, worked to say something. Nothing came. Not for a long, tortured moment. Finally, she managed, "Oh, Callum. I'm sorry."

"Thanks." He pressed his full lips into a tight line. His whole face tightened, like he was holding back an avalanche. He probably was. Instead of letting loose the floodgates, he blew out a slow, long breath. "It was awful. Still is."

Amber bit her lip then grabbed Callum's hand again, squeezing. "Are you okay?"

"Some days, yeah. Some days, it's rough." He took a beat, then glanced away. "It was suicide."

Amber's body went still with the news. *Suicide.* She'd never personally known someone who'd committed suicide. The horror of it struck Amber hard. The degree of heartache and pain that led to the taking of one's own life—to Amber it felt unfathomable. And yet, it was a real thing. Torturously real.

"Oh my," she whispered. "I'm so *terribly* sorry." A million questions swirled in her head. How? Why? But none of them were appropriate. Not right now, anyway, at such an early and tender time in her budding relationship with Callum. Even if they only ever became friends and nothing more, Amber realized that this was the sort of conversation that couldn't be henpecked out of someone. But it *was* the sort of information that Amber would protect. She'd hold it in her heart for him and for his sister. A sad seed of knowledge that would grow. At least, that was the hope. That Callum and Amber would become closer and closer, and one day, he'd feel comfortable to bare his soul to her.

There was something in his dark, brooding affect that belied a yearning to talk. But Amber, a descendant of women who forced you to cough up anything from your life, knew better than to pump him for facts.

After a long moment, Callum said, "Thanks. It's... it's been hard."

"If you want to talk about it, I want to listen."

Callum looked thoughtful. "I'm getting better at that, but sometimes I don't know what to say."

"You don't have to say anything. Sometimes talking about something starts with silence." Amber had culled this up from her experience with Grant. After finding out about his affair, it was in her quietest moments that she felt she had the most to say.

"I guess the biggest thing on my mind about it is how in an *instant*, my whole world changed."

Amber frowned. Tears threatened behind her eyes, but this was not her tragedy to mourn. Not her grief. Not *now*, at least. All she could do now was keep squeezing his hand and listening. She nodded along and tried for a gentle smile.

Callum went on, "I'm not trying to be a downer or anything. I'm just pointing out that life, well, it can be shorter than you realize."

Amber met his gaze and saw in it the depths of his heart. Somehow, they'd taken their budding relationship, zipped it through time and tragedy, and wound up on the other side, in the present moment again. Maybe now was not the time, but then—if you went by that rotten ol' adage, you never did say what you needed to. "Callum?" she asked.

"Yeah?"

"I still like you."

A grin formed over his mouth. "I *still* like you, too." His gaze fell to her stomach. Amber's followed. "How are you feeling?"

She shrugged. "I'm feeling well, now. Turns out I'd been sick off and on during the first trimester, but it's died down. I'm a little more quick to tire, but, all in all, life is good."

"That's great. Do you know if it's a boy or girl?"

She shook her head. "Not yet. A couple more weeks, but I'm not sure I want to know."

"I respect that. Surprises can be fun."

Amber agreed.

"Do you need to get to the diner for lunch? I mean, your dad... that's important, right?"

"It *is* important, but—" Amber ached to stay right there. A thought occurred to her. She moved so she faced Callum, picked up both his hands and said, "So are you."

CHAPTER FORTY-SIX

PRESENT DAY

Morgan Jo

Morgan checked her watch. The second hand shuffled to the twelve. The short hand slid into the hour. Six o'clock.

"It's six!" she cried out.

CarlaMay emerged from her bedroom, curlers pulled from her head, hair sprayed into place. She held a tube of lipstick and ran it over her mouth, studying the table. "Looks perfect, Morgan Jo."

The table did look perfect. For supper, CarlaMay and Morgan had toiled over one of the family classics: Memaw's Famous Farm Table Fried Chicken. The key to the crispy, golden southern dish was to throw all the ingredients into bowls and spread 'em out along the kitchen table. It was a sittin' recipe, Memaw had always said. Not a standing-up recipe. That's what made it *real* comfort food. According to Memaw, you could only call a dish comfort food if it was made at the comfort of the kitchen table, while laughing over family gossip.

With aprons tied at the neck and waist, CarlaMay and Morgan had crumbled the crust of homemade white bread, seasoning it with salt, pepper, and a hearty shake of Lawry's. Then, they'd cracked eggs into a bowl and soaked the dry-patted meat while they'd set about the batter: a mixture of flour, breadcrumbs, and crushed Saltines. Soon enough, it'd come time to coat the meat in the batter, taking care to ensure a thick coat before lining the thighs and legs along a platter then getting up and filling a great big pot with oil, which they set to a boil ahead of frying up the chicken.

For sides, the mother–daughter duo whipped together collard greens, skillet-baked cornbread, and fried okra. For dessert, Amber had promised her famous peach cobbler, another cast-iron specialty.

All told, the spread was decadent, and Morgan had even wondered aloud if maybe this could be the wedding dinner. CarlaMay agreed readily. "Save us on the catering," she'd remarked.

Now, both women emerged into the kitchen from their respective bedrooms, ready for the special evening. If all went well, they'd come out with a plan for a wedding officiant who'd please both the Coyles as well as the Dawsons.

And that officiant would be David McRae, former priest and forever family friend.

Morgan was dressed chastely in a white linen smock that hit at her knees. Beige ballet flats and the small cross pendant she'd received for her Confirmation in eleventh grade. Morgan had often vacillated about wearing the pendant. Though she rarely attended church and generally was a non-practicing Catholic, she was still very much a believer. Tonight, she'd clasped it on not to impress Father David—*David*—but to calm her buzzing nerves.

She'd tied her hair back, taming the wild waves in a barrette at the nape of her neck. Only minimal makeup to keep her fresh-faced and pretty. Nothing distracting.

CarlaMay, on the other hand, had gone all out. A bright

red-and-white silk polka-dot blouse with fanciful ruffled sleeves at her shoulders, showing off her long, sinewy arms. Her nails were painted red to match. White skinny jeans.

"Mom." Morgan made a face. "What—?"

"We have precious few days before Labor Day, Morgan Jo. I intend to wear all the white jeans I can before it's too late."

"It's not the jeans—you look like you're going to a sock hop, but you're Rizzo, not Sandy."

CarlaMay bristled. "No. I look nice. And that's how we want to look." She crossed to Morgan and reached a hand up to her daughter's face, then tugged loose a tendril of wavy hair. "You look..."

"Devout?"

CarlaMay smiled. "Beautiful."

A knock came at the door. "I'll get it." CarlaMay strode to the front, and Morgan took in a stilling breath.

It was Emmett. "You came back," Morgan joked, taking his sport jacket—an unnecessary but welcome touch.

He chuckled. "Did I have a choice?"

"There's always a choice."

"Emmett, you look dashing." CarlaMay turned to Morgan. "Any word from Amber yet? She *is* coming, right?"

Of all the extraneous people involved in their pending nuptials, Amber had emerged as the most prominent. She lived downstairs, and proximity was nice. Plus, she'd offered to bake the cake for the wedding—a huge gift to Morgan and Emmett. And, since she'd be providing the peach cobbler for tonight, Morgan couldn't *not* invite her. Anyway, it'd be good to have an objective party present for posterity. That was Emmett's suggestion, anyway.

Morgan glanced at her phone for the umpteenth time. "Not yet."

"Did you call her? If you kids would just put a phone call through, half your problems would be solved."

"Mom, you sound like Memaw."

"A double criticism. Lovely." CarlaMay was snippety. Nervous, maybe. She flitted away, her red-tipped fingers waving in the air as she left for the depths of the kitchen to do something that needn't be done.

Morgan tapped Amber's name on her phone contacts list and held the device to her ear. It rang through to the voicemail. "Hey, girl. Emmett's here. I think the guest of honor will arrive anytime now. Just checking on you—did you say you were going to your mom's to bake?" Morgan mouthed to Emmett, "Better oven."

When Morgan ended the message, Emmett cocked his head. "She's not here?"

"No. I've banged on her door three times. I could even hear the cats meowing at me from the inside, and I got worried, used my spare to let myself in. She wasn't there."

"Were the cats okay?" Emmett's features pinched in.

"They're fine. Just curious. I let them come up while I got ready."

"She'll be here," he assured Morgan, grabbing her hand and giving it a squeeze. "It'll be fine."

David—*Father David*—arrived ten minutes late, unfashionably so. Just as his tires crunched over the gravel drive, Amber finally returned Morgan's calls, but with a text. *Something important has come up. I'll be late.*

Morgan hated to ask, but the promise of Amber's famous peach cobbler felt like it might be the only thing holding the night together. *Peach cobbler??* She thought better of it, deleted the words and wrote first: *Are you okay?*

Amber's reply came quick. *Yes. I'll be there in an hour.*

Morgan frowned. *Peach cobbler???*

Amber answered with an anxious-faced emoji.

Morgan frowned deeper.

"What is it?" Emmett asked.

Before Morgan could reply, their guest of honor knocked at the front door. Morgan silenced her phone, slid it onto the front table and waved her mom to the door.

CarlaMay teetered over on platform wedges. "Okay, everyone just... be nice."

"Why wouldn't we be nice?" Morgan looked at Emmett for an answer, but he'd already put his nice face on.

"David." CarlaMay beamed, and the former priest took her hand in his then drew his face to her cheek, kissing it.

Morgan studied him in that brief moment. He looked very much the same as she remembered. Tall with brown hair, a nice brown color, sort of like Morgan's. Chestnut-y or caramel. It was close-cropped to his head, but she could see that gray hairs were beginning to creep into the sides. His eyes, light green and piercing, belied years of keeping people's secrets. Kind and handsome, they left CarlaMay and turned themselves on Morgan, like headlights.

The man's smile slowly drifted from his mouth. "Morgan Jo," he half murmured. "Do you *remember* me?" His eyes glistened.

"I do," Morgan answered. She felt Emmett's hand slide into hers. "This is my fiancé. Emmett Dawson."

"Emmett." David stuck his hand out and Emmett shook it. "Good to meet you."

"Good to meet you, too. And thank you so much for coming to meet with us. I know this is an odd situation."

"Not at all," David replied, rubbing his hands together. "Anyway, CarlaMay has promised me a delicious supper." He winked at CarlaMay, who Morgan was certain flushed red.

"Speaking of which, shall we?" CarlaMay held a hand in the direction of the kitchen, and they wove back that way, settling at the table and making light small talk.

"Who'd like to say Grace?" CarlaMay asked.

"I'd love to. Anyway, it's a good chance for me to put my

résumé to use here." He chuckled, and Morgan and Emmett exchanged a look. There was something in the air other than the hope for a wedding officiant. Emmett could feel it, too, Morgan knew.

After he blessed the meal and everyone had crossed himself and herself, CarlaMay served the food and Morgan poured fresh-brewed sweet tea.

Emmett said, "David—should I call you Father?"

The older man cleared his throat. "I suppose now's as good a time as any for me to explain my ministry situation."

Morgan took a tentative bite of her chicken. The skin was crunchy and savory, and the meat cooked perfectly. She relished the taste and let her mind drift away to the big day. They'd arranged for a formal dinner, catered by a restaurant out of Bardstown. Chicken Piccata and a flight of white wine or filet mignon and a flight of red. It would be labor-intensive and costly to put together enough flights for every guest, but Morgan hoped that it would be a great way to showcase not only their products but also their brand and presentation.

"That's right," Emmett replied to David. "Morgan tells me you've been the family priest for ages."

"Ages. *Oof.*" David made a show of pretending to have been shot in the heart. "But you're right. Yes. I've been blessed to serve the Coyle family and the Brambleberry parish since I was in my twenties." As he said it, a kink formed in his eyebrow. "But it's been a rocky road for me."

Morgan lowered her chicken leg, eyed the priest, then her mother, who visibly tensed. "A rocky road? I know church membership is declining. Is that what you mean?"

David pressed his lips into a line. "When I began my path as a priest, there was a steep learning curve. I came from a raucous, big family. I never knew my place there. I figured I'd know my place in the church, but nothing is ever black and white."

"Our faith is, though," CarlaMay added, superciliously.

David swallowed a bite of chicken then pressed his cloth napkin to his mouth for a moment. "I'd have to agree. Faith can be a changing thing, too. Just come to Sunday Mass. The numbers dwindle, flow, dwindle, *flood*, then one week it'll be a ghost hall. Not only Mass attendance, I mean. I think we each have moments of spiritual highs and moments of spiritual lows."

"And personal lows," CarlaMay said.

"Yes, and the two are intertwined."

"Inextricable, really." Emmett took a hearty bite of fried okra. "This is divine, by the way, ladies."

"Sacrilege!" David cried, but he laughed loudly. "I kid. I *kid*." His happy face was flush but the color drained along with his smile. "Anyhow, I made mistakes as a young clergyman."

"Wine, anyone?" CarlaMay stood up abruptly.

"I haven't opened it," Morgan objected.

"I'll open two bottles. Red and white."

"We have to let them breathe," Morgan pointed out.

CarlaMay gave her a look. "It's fine."

"It's fine. I don't mind a glass of stuffy wine." David's face returned to its former cheeriness. "Anyhow, it took me a long time—three decades—of reflection before I realized my mistakes weren't fleeting." He continued to smile and held Morgan's gaze for a moment, then he looked at Emmett. "In the Catholic church, priests can appeal to the Pope for a dispensation from ministry, effectively."

"A dispensation?" Emmett propped his elbows on the table-top, laced his fingers, and leaned in. He looked every bit the lawyer.

"Right. It's not common. And it's not necessarily something to be proud of, but it happens. When a priest comes to terms with the fact that he can no longer serve the Lord in the capacity of priesthood."

"You got a divorce from the church. That's sort of what it's like, huh?" Morgan asked.

"Annulment, more like." He smiled. "All is well in my soul, though, and I maintain my ordainment as a secular officiant, which your mother tells me is what brings me here tonight."

Emmett unlaced his fingers and dove into a chicken thigh. Between bites, he said, "My mother is hoping for a High Mass, but as I understand it, that's not possible outside of the physical church."

"A High Mass would require a church ceremony," David confirmed.

"And my mom is also concerned that we can't have a Catholic ceremony at all if it's outdoors."

David leaned his head left and right as CarlaMay returned with two bottles of wine, then darted back to the kitchen for the glasses. "Any word from Amber, by the way?"

"She'll be late," Morgan replied, turning her attention back to David and Emmett. "I've heard the same thing as Emmett. I don't see how we can have a Catholic ceremony on the same day as our gala."

"Right. Well, you *do* have options. Some priests are willing to marry a couple outdoors with special arrangements through the diocese. Or, you could have a Catholic ceremony a day or so earlier."

"That would make a second ceremony on the day of the gala unnecessary, and even..." Emmett drifted off.

"It would look like an act." Morgan grabbed Emmett's hand on the table and gave it a squeeze. "Neither Emmett nor I are devout. We'd like to have our marriage blessed, but for this gala, we'd much rather host something comfortable and spiritual and *genuine*."

"I could do that for you," David said. "I could not bless your wedding, but I *could* ordain the marriage legally and offer a traditional prayer."

Morgan's face lit up. "You could?" She grinned at Emmett. "This might be perfect then."

"But I won't."

Silence stilled the table. Morgan turned, confused. She looked at her mother, then David. "Why not?"

He shifted uncomfortably in his seat, reached for the wine CarlaMay had just poured. Then pinned Morgan with a serious expression. "I—um... it's complicated." David cleared his throat.

Then, CarlaMay stood and poured the white wine into Morgan's and Emmett's glasses. "It's not *that* complicated, David," she remarked, her voice smooth as sea glass.

That's when it clicked. David's dispensation from the church. CarlaMay's loud outfit. Date nights. The tension that hung in the air over their fried chicken supper.

Morgan's hand flew to her mouth in shock. "You're dating."

CHAPTER FORTY-SEVEN

1991

CarlaMay

Just after Morgan Jo's Confirmation, St. Mary's got a new priest.

You can believe that I was just as shocked as anyone to find out it was my very own David, coming to little ol' Brambleberry, Kentucky, to serve the Lord in His house right up the street from my house.

It wasn't long before he and I found ourselves alone in the parish hall, cleaning up after Bingo Night.

The lone nun of the parish had gone to bed. No one else was around.

David asked me point blank: who was the girl I brought to Mass?

I answered him truthfully. "Your daughter."

He broke down and cried. And I did, too.

CHAPTER FORTY-EIGHT

PRESENT DAY

Amber

Stunned. Amber Lee Taylor was stunned. She'd only stuck around the video shop in order to enjoy some light reflections on a moonshiner. With Callum. Maybe they'd do something sweet like hold hands—not out of romance, seeing as she was in a delicate and complicated state—but out of a friendship that might one day become more.

Then, it all changed.

As soon as the footage and audio blared forth from the screen, Callum had turned to her, alarmed as all get-out on her behalf.

She'd sat, confused at first. After some moments, numbness had drowned her.

Logically, she might have gone to her mother or sister. She might have even called up Morgan Jo. Inexplicably, however, Amber had turned to Callum and asked if he was hungry.

He'd fumbled to reply that he was, but—he could not leave the store.

Amber hadn't cared. She'd gone to the door that opened to the rest of the shop, confirming no one was around. Then, Amber had asked for Callum's keys, grabbed the tape from the VCR player and they left. Amber twisted the sign on the shop to read CLOSED and pulled Callum by force to the back parking lot.

They'd driven, aimlessly for a while. Then, they'd passed an old hole-in-the-wall diner at the south edge of town: Bodean's. Amber had told Callum to park. He had.

Bodean Granger was a local from way back when. His tumbledown café only still existed because nobody had taken a wrecking ball to it.

Yet.

The sign was faded down so you could only really make out the "o" and the "d," which wasn't reassuring. A white clapboard structure that previously might have been a little farmhouse, the whole thing had never once been touched with a paintbrush or rollers, and therefore it wasn't exactly white anymore.

Just outside on a narrow porch sat a rocking chair and in that rocking chair a man so old that everyone just accepted he had to be Bodean Granger himself. That's what legend said, anyway. Bodean—or whoever he was—wore a yellowed, thread-bare undershirt beneath dirt-crusted overalls. His skin was sheathed over in gray-white stubble and grime. He rocked slowly with his eyes closed, a length of straw tucked into the side of his mouth.

"Is this *safe?*" Callum had whispered as they made their way in.

"It's *Bodean's,*" Amber had snapped.

A tired, aggravated waitress had hollered at the pair to take a seat wherever. No menus had been passed out. Amber had ordered for the both of them.

An hour had passed before they got their drinks or food. An

hour of utter silence. Amber had taken turns laying her head on top of the red Formica table and staring out of the window, wondering where Kentucky ended and Tennessee began.

"Praise the Lord and pass the gravy," Amber had muttered, as soon as their biscuits were delivered.

Callum had given her the space to eat and think, and she'd been grateful. But once they'd finished and balled up their napkins and dropped them on their plates, Amber had felt ready to talk.

The bill had been for a pitiful amount, which both belied and underscored the reason Bodean's was still open. Amber had pulled a twenty from her wallet, but Callum pushed it back to her and offered up his own cash.

Once outside again, Amber noted the sun had begun to sink. Somehow, she and Callum had managed to kill off half a day together, in veritable silence.

Bodean—if that was really him—continued rocking as they passed by him on their way to Callum's car. The night air was muggy, promising rain. Rain they didn't necessarily need, but that Amber might just appreciate. Maybe it'd rain hard and wash everything away, and she'd wake up the next morning and the nightmare would be over.

"Where to next?" Callum asked now, running his hand over his stomach and stretching back. Funny, how comfortable they'd become in the space of just hours together. Hours in which they'd barely said a peep to one another. There was something nice about it.

Amber looked at her watch. "Oh, Lord." She squeezed her eyes shut and doubled over. "*No.*"

"What?" Callum's face lit up in concern. "Do you feel like you're going to throw up? Is it the baby, or the food we just had?"

Amber rose up, both hands on her cheeks. "Nooo. It's the

supper with the priest. With Father David, or whatever. I was supposed to make peach cobbler for Morgan Jo. I'm supposed to be there. I *forgot*."

"I can take you there now if you want?"

Amber pulled her phone from the depths of her purse where she'd buried it upon their great, horrible discovery. Amber had never considered herself the type to run from problems, but there was not a single person she'd wanted to speak with after hearing what she'd heard on that damnable tape.

She considered what to do and where to go next. Eventually, she'd have to go home. And eventually, Callum would have to face Hank Taylor and explain why he randomly closed the shop down for his entire shift. Amber had promised him she'd make sure he didn't get in trouble, but by the time they'd driven around the whole of Brambleberry Creek, Callum didn't seem to care anymore. He seemed content to just be with Amber. Maybe even happy.

"I'm not ready to go back to the farm. I need to make a peach cobbler still. I can't show up without it."

"Do you want me to take you to your mom's house or something?" Callum was already well aware that Amber couldn't just throw together a dessert on the down-low in her basement apartment while the dinner raged upstairs. It was a comfort to realize that despite the fact they hadn't gotten much further than watching tapes together, they were beginning to know each other on a deeper, more personal level.

"No. What if Hank goes there?"

"You think they've already kissed and made up?"

Amber looked at Callum. "You know too much about us."

He shrugged. "Small—"

"—town. Yeah, I know." She took off for his car. "Maybe instead of peach cobbler, I can show up with something else. Something better."

Callum followed her and they climbed in together, buckling up at the same time. "What could be better than peach cobbler?"

"Well, maybe not *better* but quicker."

Callum didn't start the engine. He frowned at Amber. "Listen, you don't have to run back home and cook for your family right now, you know. You can take some time to digest what we just found out."

Amber stared out through the windshield, north along the road that would carry them to Moonshine Creek. She thought about her options. Pretending like everything was normal for now was the only way to go. At the very least, it'd save Morgan's special dinner.

"We could swing by the market on Main and get a tin of cookies?"

"Yes. Let's start there, but not for cookies."

"Brownies?"

Amber lifted her eyebrow at Callum. "I don't really do store-bought desserts."

He hit the gas and peeled out of Bodean's and onto Brambleberry, up into town. "You don't do store-bought desserts, but we're going to the market?"

"I have something better in mind."

They arrived at the grocer's up on Main in record time—no traffic on a Tuesday evening. Amber and Callum parted ways. He headed to the video shop to make his explanation to Hank and ensure the shop was good to go for the night.

If that worked, and if Amber found what she needed at the market, they'd reconvene at his car, parked strategically along the eastern street side.

Geddy greeted Amber as soon as she walked in. "Hey, cuzzo!" He wore a black apron with the market emblem—a wooden basket of produce spilling out. "What're you doin' in here at this hour?" Geddy knew Amber well enough to know she was a Monday-morning shopper. A swift trip every Monday to fill her modest pantry and small fridge. Just the basics, normally, plus enough to throw together one fancy meal a week and one decadent dessert.

"Hey, Ged, I need cheese and a pretty wooden cutting board."

He loaded paper grocery sacks onto the side of the check stand and then pointed, walking swiftly in the direction of the deli. "What kind of cheese we talking? What's it for?"

Amber didn't need his advice. She selected a cake of creamy Brie and said, "Cutting boards?"

"This-a-way, ma'am." Geddy scooted around a shelf of kitchen supplies and led her directly to the end cap. "We're hosting a local craftsman's goods right now. They're pricey, but good-quality. You know Mr. Jim Delacy? Miss Delacy's nephew what moved to town not long ago?"

Amber gave a short nod, grabbed a good-sized slab of finely carved and waxed wood. "I know him, and this is perfect."

"Put it on your account?" Geddy asked.

"Yep. Thanks, Ged."

And with that, she was out the door and phoning Callum from the corner where the sidewalks met.

He picked up straight away. "I'm coming back now."

She squinted into the night. Sure enough, his tall form emerged from the door of the video shop. Amber waved.

"Next stop is a little drive."

Callum swung his key ring as he opened the car door for her.

She slid inside, staring out the window up at the sky. Night was falling over Brambleberry, and Morgan was probably freaking out. Amber pulled her phone from her pocket. Sure enough, a text appeared: one of several Amber had missed along with a string of phone calls. Amber shot back a quick reply. She'd be late, but she'd be there.

"Where to?" Callum turned the engine on and pressed the heels of his hands against the wheel.

She glanced his way. "All okay with your boss?"

"He barely noticed. Figured I went to lunch and took over for me."

"Weird," she murmured. But then again, this day was shaping up to be *only* weird. She pointed north. "We're going out of town. Cross the train tracks east."

"Widow's Holler?"

"How'd you guess?"

"I had to go there for a funeral once."

"A funeral? That cemetery is defunct."

"Not totally."

She stared at him. "Your sister?"

He nodded.

"But you're from the city. Why would she be buried down here?"

"Long story short, that's where our family gets buried. Back in the day, my mammy got a deal for buying up a whole slew of plots."

"Frugal." Amber lifted an eyebrow. "I like that." But another thought clouded that one. "Are you okay to go there?"

"To Widow's Holler? Sure. I go all the time." Then he looked her way. "Why do we need to go now? What's there?"

Amber set aside all her questions for Callum, about his sister, their family plots, his visits to the nearby ghost town... and she answered. "I need to get figs and a bottle of wine from my Uncle Gary. I figure it'll be easier than peach cobbler at this point."

But there was another reason, too. While she was there, she had a right mind to ask her uncle *exactly* what he knew about

Amber's childhood. After all, in a family half as big as the small town in which they lived, she could be sure that *this* particular secret wasn't much of a secret at all. Besides, the good thing about asking Uncle Gary instead of anyone else in the family was that he wouldn't tell them what Amber now knew.

CHAPTER FORTY-NINE

PRESENT DAY

Morgan Jo

Morgan had maintained composure at the bombshell news. She took a sip of her wine to still herself for a moment, then felt Emmett's hand creep under the table and rest on her thigh. A reminder to breathe.

"Well," Morgan ran her tongue over her teeth and strained for a smile, "I say this calls for a toast." She lifted her half-finished wine, fortified by the presence of Emmett and by the knowledge that even if there might be a little bit of a scandal somewhere there, she was happy for her mom.

Emmett lifted his glass dutifully. "To Miss CarlaMay and Father David."

David half winced, and CarlaMay seemed reluctant, too. "We're not—"

"It's nothing like that," David finished for her. "We're friends."

"It's complicated," CarlaMay added. They were all but talking over each other.

Morgan wondered if there really was a scandal. Had they

begun dating while he was still ordained? Was *that* the mistake they'd made?

"Life tends to be that way," Morgan said, keeping her glass held high.

Again, David and CarlaMay looked at one another. There was something more to be said that couldn't be. Morgan had the couth to leave it be. She added, "To happiness."

"To happiness, indeed." Emmett beamed a big grin, and the high spirits of the supper were enough to buoy a toast.

"There's still the question of the officiant, however." CarlaMay clinked her glass, sipped, and lowered it. "I hate to spoil the festive and supportive mood, but that's why we're here. David, you really think this is a conflict?" Her expression was pained; she'd chewed the red lipstick clear off of her lower lip, making it seem like she was all upper lip.

He cleared his throat and lowered his voice. He spoke calmly, but there was a tinge of annoyance in his voice. "Carla-May, is *this* what we came to discuss?"

"The wedding. Well, it's partly—I mean..." CarlaMay looked at Morgan, her expression pleading and supplicating, but Morgan didn't know how to reply. She was confused.

"It's about the wedding," Morgan answered David. "We're in the predicament of pleasing Emmett's mother while having the ceremony we'd like to have."

"You know what?" Emmett said, running his napkin over his mouth and folding it back neatly into his lap. "I disagree."

All eyes turned to him.

Morgan fluttered her eyes and smirked. "Emmett?"

He smiled easily and took Morgan's hand on the table. "You know what's going to have to make my mom happy?"

No one replied. Morgan's gut clenched in anticipation of what her fiancé might say. Finally, after he didn't continue for a long moment, she shook her head. "What?"

Emmett said, "Whatever makes *us* happy."

. . .

The question of who'd officiate at the wedding remained unsolved. Father David—*David*—seemed confused about even having been asked to officiate. Like he'd been summoned for some other reason. And so, they'd dropped the matter and put a pin in that particular wedding question.

The supper carried on until there were only a couple of pieces of chicken left. Morgan checked her watch, then her phone. "I'm starting to worry about Amber."

"Wasn't she clearing out her station today? Maybe it took a while longer," CarlaMay pointed out. "Maybe she and her sister went for drinks after."

"Did you talk to Aunt Barb?" Morgan asked, fidgety over what to do next, now that they'd eaten their main course but didn't have a dessert to wrap things up.

"You know, I didn't. I called her earlier, but she didn't answer."

"Let me just check the cupboards." Morgan scootched her chair back and laid her napkin over the back of it. "I could have sworn we had a box of cookies or something."

Commotion struck behind her just as soon as she disappeared into the hollow of the kitchen.

Morgan poked her head back out.

"Amber!" Morgan felt a nagging worry dissolve inside her, and when she saw Callum follow her cousin in through the door, her heart swelled. "And a special guest?"

Amber crossed through the front room and made her way to Morgan, offering a quick hug. "Callum?" Morgan whispered into Amber's ear.

Amber hissed back. "Talk about it later, 'kay?"

Morgan reared back and raised her eyebrows at her cousin, but she didn't question it. Instead, Morgan lifted both hands to Callum. "Well, hi there! I'm terribly sorry to tell you we've finished supper, but there's plenty more food. We can all—oh!" Morgan noticed his arms were laden with goodies. "What's this?" She turned to Amber. "A peach cobbler substitute? Ohh, I *love* surprises!" He carried a cutting board in one arm and in the other, held up a bottle of one of their newer products: freshly bottled blueberry wine. "What's this?!" she cried, impressed. "Where did you do all this?"

Then she turned back to Amber, a stitch in her expression. "And *why*?"

Amber gave her a beguiling look. *Later*, she said with her eyes. Lots of information, *later*. "Right." Morgan took the bottle and gestured for Callum to follow her, where he was introduced to Father David and reintroduced to CarlaMay and Emmett and sat down with Amber to a late, but still sumptuous, supper.

In a way, the surprising interruption was just what the dinner party needed. It functioned as both a distraction and an immersion. The menfolk chatted animatedly about the wine-making process, each of them interested for different reasons. Emmett because it was becoming his business. Callum because one of his favorite movies was *Uncorked*, a recent hit about a barbecue family with a son who wanted to be a sommelier instead. And Father David, because, well, wine was the blood of Christ, after all.

The figs and cheese went as fast as the bottle of blueberry, and soon enough, all three of the girls found themselves clearing plates and alone, together, in the kitchen. "So, Amber Lee," CarlaMay started, "Callum is a *doll*. Are you two—" She poked her index fingers together in a delicate-if-gratuitous gesture.

"Ew, Mom," Morgan said. "What is *this*." She mirrored her mother's finger-poking, horrified but also delighted. Ever since Emmett had declared that they'd have their wedding/gala ceremony *their* way, it was as if the sky had opened up. Morgan felt a new-formed peace in her heart. And a new burst of love for her fiancé.

"I just mean—is there a spark there, after all?"

"You mean after I told him I'm pregnant, out of wedlock, with another guy's baby?" Amber made a face, but it softened, like something occurred to her. "I don't know about a spark, but let's just say I haven't scared him off for good. He's nice. He's... a friend."

"Friends are important," CarlaMay replied with a harrumph. "You tend to that friendship. One day, he could be your best friend."

"He could be more than that," Morgan pointed out.

"Aunt Carla, you go on and visit with Father David."

"It's just David," Morgan corrected.

"Just David?" Amber appeared to stifle a smirk. "Right. Well, go ahead. I'll help Morgan Jo in here."

CarlaMay didn't need much more prodding than that. She flashed a grateful smile, untied her apron and hung it on the hook by the pantry. "Don't be long, you two." She winked at Amber. "And especially you."

"Ignore her." Morgan scrubbed the final plate, rinsed it, and dried it. "And yes—it's just David. He left the cloth, if that's the right expression."

"Father David got excommunicated?"

"No," Morgan answered. "At least, that's not what he said, but it's confusing. I guess you can have the Pope say you're allowed to step down. And that's what he did."

"Why?"

"To date my mom, apparently."

Amber's eyes widened to the size of saucers. "Get outta town. That's your mama's boyfriend?! Our *priest*?"

Morgan clicked her tongue. "I don't know if they're boyfriend and girlfriend. I don't know *anything*. I know that it's weird and that, well, obviously they've been sneaking around."

"No wonder Father David hasn't been at Mass in a while. Do you know if he's even Catholic anymore?"

"I'm sure he is. Probably more devout than ever. Maybe he even wants to get married, who knows?"

Amber and Morgan were quiet a minute.

Morgan asked, "So, what took you? What's going on with you and Callum?" She kept her voice low.

Amber's face pinched. "It's been a day."

Morgan wiped her hands on a dry dishtowel and leaned into the kitchen counter. "I'm all ears."

Amber flashed a look through to the kitchen table. "Actually, can we... slip away?"

"From them?" Morgan shrugged. "Don't see why not. I mean—will Callum feel awkward being left?"

"No. He... he *knows* I need to talk to you."

At that, Morgan's ears perked up. Amber's teasing comments had already interested her, but now she realized there was a bigger story developing. She pushed off from the counter and lifted her voice to the others. "You-all, I'm gonna help Amber with something downstairs." She wove into the kitchen and lowered to Emmett, pecking him on the cheek. "Holler before you go, okay?"

He kissed her back. "Will do."

The pair left the kitchen through the back door, tracking around the grass and toward the driveway, where Amber said she needed to get something from Callum's car.

Amber spoke in hushed tones, and Morgan had to lean down to really hear her. "Callum and I accidentally found something. I don't know who to tell or show or whatever. I don't know *what* the hell to do." Her face was streaked in agony and puzzlement. She looked like she might break down and cry.

Morgan stopped her. "Are you okay? Is it the baby?"

Amber gave her head a shake and marched ahead. "I'm fine. It's not even—I don't even know if it's... if it's about *me*. I mean, it's not about the baby." She stopped outside of the blue Oldsmobile. "I can't even say it out loud."

"Then show me."

Amber pulled a single cassette tape from the front passenger seat. Morgan followed her down to the exterior entrance to the basement, where Amber used her key to let them in. Mint and Julep met the two with purrs and cheek rubs along their ankles. Amber collected Mint in her free hand and nuzzled the kitty. "I know. I *know*," she cooed, popping the tape into her VCR, grabbing the remote and perching on the edge of the sofa. VCRs may be outdated and antiquated in mainstream culture, but Amber was a true Coyle. Of course, she knew others in Brambleberry Creek who were also loyal to their VCRs and the old ways of doing things. And anyway, in her mind, leaving behind dependable technology was like leaving behind farming. The Average Joe wouldn't think much of it, but she knew that society only managed to function because some traditions carried on, unbeknownst to the greater public consciousness.

Julep hopped up onto Amber's lap, and while she gave both cats scritches behind the ears, she patted the spot next to her. "Please. Sit with me."

Morgan did.

Amber hit the power button and then the play button, and the television set garbled to life.

Grandad filled the screen, and Morgan had to grab her chest. She hadn't seen him since his death. She hadn't watched any of the tapes yet. She hadn't so much as stolen a glance at a photograph of him. There simply weren't many. He wasn't one for pictures.

"Oh, my *Lord*," she whispered. "He looks... the same. And *different*."

"So young," Amber whispered back.

They hushed and listened in as he described the final steps

in bottling perry. *"Once you've filled the bottle up to the neck, you're gon' wanna let it set still for a while."*

In the video, Grandad wore his regular outfit of a button-up under overalls and jeans. His hair was fuller on top but still speckled in salt and pepper. He stood straighter than Morgan recalled. Looked taller. His skin was sun-beat and flushed, and gone were any traces of heavy under-eye bags, drooping jowls, or obvious back pain. But his voice—that steep holler twang—and his affect—cranky as all get-out—were very much alive in this rendering. "Grandad," Morgan whispered. She wanted to reach through the screen and give him a great big hug. The type of hug he'd complain about. The good kind.

Amber found Morgan's hand on the space of sofa between them. Their fingers interlaced automatically.

Grandad carried on in his unmistakable style, annoyed at the world but pleased with such acute attention on himself. On something of which he was a master. *"Longer the better, but down here in the crick we jes' get right down to it."* He chuckled at himself. Morgan smiled. *"It'll give ya a kick, but it'll get the job done."*

There was a pause in the recording and Grandad looked from the lens up right, as if he was tearing his gaze from Morgan Jo and Amber Lee and looking instead at someone who'd interrupted the three of them. A bothersome interloper.

Muted words came from the distance of their makeshift movie set.

Grandad held his hand behind his hear. *"H'what?"*

"I said I have to leave in five minutes."

What commenced at first was a normal conversation between Grandad and the vaguely familiar voice.

"What for?" Grandad asked, dumbfounded-acting.

"I have the test I mentioned."

"Test?" Grandad grinned like he was about to crack another joke, but he drew his hand to his mouth and wiped the smile off.

"*Oh*, that." His frown drew down so deep Morgan wanted again to reach through the screen, this time to push his chin up and tell him to cheer up.

"Who's the other voice?" Morgan murmured quickly.

Amber released her hand. "My daddy."

"Hank?" Morgan glanced her way, but both their attention returned to the screen as Hank, off camera, replied to Grandad with a grunting response. "*I told you it's something we agreed to do. It's scheduled. There's no way around it.*"

"What test?" Morgan hissed, but Amber ignored her.

"*Hank, now jes' wait a minute, would ye. You ain't got to take a test on this. I didn't mean nothin' by what I said.*"

"*You didn't mean it when you made fun of my daughter's looks?*"

"*I wa'n't makin' no fun of nobody's looks, dammit. I was jes' talkin' like a fool. It wasn't makin' fun.*"

"*Bill, can we just go ahead and wrap this segment up?*"

"*Well, hell, Hank. We're damn near the end. Might as well finish.*"

"*Fine. Go ahead and finish without me. I'll leave this here. You can do with it what you want. I'll come back to get the camera and all after the test.*"

Shuffling sounds muted out squabbling from the pair of them, Grandad and Hank. The camera moved and the screen went blurry for a moment until it returned to its former and proper angle, facing Grandad at his workbench. He spoke at length, hemming and hawing over timelines on how long to let the perry set. After a few minutes, he ambled toward the camera and fiddled at it until the screen went black.

"That's it?" Morgan asked.

Amber's stare remained on the television. "No. Watch."

Sure enough, not a moment later, the camera whirred back to life. A grunting, cursing Grandad came around in front of the lens again. "*Hello. Well, I finished my piece earlier, but then I went in to see about supper and Essie got on my case to get to workin' on the tobacco harvest we just brung in. Well, I remembered another thing I wanted to record for ye."* He cleared his throat. *"The thing about any of this wine is to remember it's jes' backyard wine. Y'can't 'spect for ever' last bottle to taste th'exact same as th'other. So, that's jes' what I come here to—"*

A scuffling sound came up behind the camera, and not half a second later, blackness fell across the screen.

But the audio continued. *"Got the results. Things have changed, Bill."*

"What's changed? That damn test? I'll tell ya a thing or two about tests. Tests ain't ever right. It's always someone with a rod up his behind givin' the thing, and then he goes over the results and marks down something wrong or marks up something this way or that, and whatever you was tryin' to prove in the first place, it don't count no more on account of the test. It's never the test. It's what you know, Hank. What you know in your heart."

"That may well be, Bill. But Barb and *the test are pretty clear on the matter."* Clunky shuffling cut across the audio, but Hank emitted one last comment before the tape went to static. *"Amber isn't mine."*

CHAPTER FIFTY

1991

CarlaMay

A year into Father David's appointment as our priest, he and I had established a routine. I helped clean the parish hall once a week. He would join me, and we would talk. I told him everything there was to know about Morgan Jo and about me. About our little town and my big ol' family. He couldn't get enough information.

One of those nights, he asked me. CarlaMay, he said, maybe it's time.

"Time for what?" I'd asked him right back.

"Time to tell Morgan Jo the truth."

You won't want to believe this, but I thought that was as good an idea as any. I wanted them to meet, as father and daughter. I wanted my secret to be free. I wanted to breathe again, damn it.

Even so, I took it home to the one person I thought might assure me. My mother. By then, she'd known the facts. She'd known them back when it happened. You can't keep secrets from Essie May Coyle, I tell you.

Anyway, I told her that David had suggested we come clean.

And she told me never to tell a damn soul, lest Father David would be excommunicated from the church. "And what's worse, CarlaMay?" she asked. "Morgan Jo finding out her daddy lives right up the way all this time and ain't never did a thing about it? Or a good religious leader losing his position? What's worse?"

What hurt the most in her words was the truth of the matter. That Morgan Jo's daddy lived right up the way all this time and ain't never did a thing about it.

I never understood the idea of a faith crisis before then, but I sure do now. I didn't go to church for a year. And when I got back, things got more confusing than ever.

CHAPTER FIFTY-ONE

PRESENT DAY

Amber

Morgan Jo rocked back, sinking into the tufted pillows of Amber's basement sofa.

Amber knew how she felt, because she knew Morgan Jo was like her. They were empaths, the Coyle girls. Just like it had with Amber, she could tell that for Morgan Jo, the whole world seemed to change shape. Morgan Jo's hands covered her mouth as if she could hide her reaction. A pointless effort.

Amber shifted the cats from her lap onto the far side of the sofa. "When I saw it at the video shop with Callum, I barfed. He's seen me barf, like twice now."

Morgan Jo ran her hands down to her legs, tucking her linen dress alongside her thighs. The gesture was prim and proper, like Morgan might be shielding herself against what Amber was.

Then again, Amber knew that whatever *she* was, Morgan Jo was just the same. Neither one knew her daddy. Not her real one, anyway.

"Amber," Morgan whispered, her voice strained. After a

moment, she shifted on the sofa, and grabbed Amber's hands in hers. "Talk to me. Are you okay? Did you call your mom? You were going to lunch—when did you—how did you see this? What *happened*?"

Amber let out a long, shuddering sigh. Her voice wobbled as she launched into an overview of the day. How her last client turned out to be Hank himself. A veritable surprise—and what seemed like a chance to perhaps make amends. Then meeting Callum. Watching the tape. Learning the truth and going off on a wild goose chase for some semblance of understanding. Of *peace*.

Amber took a pause at the part where she realized it was more important to get dessert for Morgan Jo's supper than wallow in her sorrows.

"Bodean's?" Morgan Jo asked. "I didn't even know that place was still open."

"Only barely," Amber answered.

"And so you went to the market on Main for the cheese. But the wine and figs? I'd have heard you pull up if you'd gotten that bottle from the barn."

"Well, that's where it got interesting." Mint mewed at Amber and pushed her head into Amber's side. Ever since Amber's ultrasound, both cats had doubled down on the cuddles. Amber wasn't complaining.

"Interesting how?"

"Callum drove us to Widow's Holler."

"To see Uncle Gary?" Morgan Jo's eyebrows shot up. It wasn't that they weren't reconnected to Uncle Gary. They all had. After years of writing Gary off as a runaway uncle, a black sheep of the family, they'd gotten back in touch with him thanks to Geddy. Gary was Geddy's dad, and the pair had been in cahoots on wine distribution and fruit distribution, and the partnership wasn't pure gold for the rejuvenated father-son relationship, but also for how Uncle Gary could help Morgan Jo and

Amber and the business. Uncle Gary was now their official distributor and an official distributor to Geddy's store. But even with that crucial bond and sometimes daily correspondence, Uncle Gary was still *Uncle Gary*.

"He has a whole row of fig trees. I got a few and then picked a bottle of wine."

"It was a lovely surprise."

Amber could feel Morgan Jo chomping at the bit for the so-called interesting part.

"I asked Uncle Gary point blank. Did he know about Hank Taylor not being our dad?"

Morgan Jo narrowed her eyes on Amber. "*Our.*"

Amber felt her stomach turn hollow, even though it was very much *not* hollow. "Right." She swallowed past a lump in her throat. Even her cousin seemed to instinctively notice the error in Amber's thought process. "I guess when I saw the tape I assumed that if I wasn't my dad's, then my sister and brother couldn't be, either."

"Did Uncle Gary know anything?"

"He knew everything."

Morgan Jo's face turned to ice. "*How?*"

Amber winced as she answered. "Grandad told him, and he told him that was why he ought to be leery about any woman who ever came around saying she had his baby."

"Oh, my word. That doesn't sound like Grandad. I mean... he was grouchy, but not cruel. Not... bitter."

"I know. I guess he said some other stuff, too. It came up when Geddy's mom, Jackie, was around. Grandad got real bristly about it all. Like he didn't want to deal with another hassle-stricken grandchild drama. But then Uncle Gary said something else, too."

"What?"

"He said that when Grandad told him about Hank leaving on account of me not being *his*, Grandad condemned Hank."

"Why would he condemn Hank if he blamed Barb for hoodwinkin' him?"

"Because he said there was a difference. There was a difference between siring a baby and fathering a baby. And Hank had already made his choice. He'd been fathering me and his two real kids, and he should have seen it through, because by the time my mom got us tested, it was too late. He was already my dad."

"And he left anyway."

Amber nodded, miserable over the whole mess of her life. She felt like she belonged on a daytime talk show where the host walks around the stage with a mic and pretends to discourage the crowd from booing the trash up on stage. "He left anyway."

Morgan Jo pinned Amber with a sudden, earnest expression. "So," she said, chewing her lower lip and wincing at her own words, "Who *is* your father?"

CHAPTER FIFTY-TWO

1991

CarlaMay

When I finally came back to Mass, I was set on asking David why he'd never before come around. He'd known about Morgan Jo since he'd gotten to Brambleberry. He'd come to Brambleberry to be nearer to me, so why not make things right in the first place?

He said the answer was simple. He'd made a vow to God. How could he break that vow?

His words echoed the ones of her mama and proved just how complicated a situation things were for CarlaMay.

Anyway, how could CarlaMay blame her priest? She knew the deal. She knew it from the first day she'd laid eyes on that man in his flowing robes and enchanting sermons. She'd known exactly what she'd signed up for. This wasn't David's fault.

It was hers.

CHAPTER FIFTY-THREE

PRESENT DAY

Morgan Jo

Who is your father, Amber?

The question hung in the air between them like a drowsy housefly to be swatted away. If only they could shoo the thing out and forget about it. Then everything would be fine.

But it was Amber's parentage they were talking about. The fiber of her being. Plus, it was a secret that wasn't *really* a secret. It was a family truth tended to and preserved by a select few. The older generation.

Not only that, but it hadn't escaped Morgan that she and Amber were more alike than ever. This whole trouble with fathers didn't just belong to Morgan. It belonged to others. It belonged to her very own cousin in her very own family.

Morgan realized it would be up to her to help Amber see to it that this business became known only to whom and only when Amber wanted it to. It was up to Morgan to manage the information.

But first, they needed some more of that. "Do you have a guess? Who your dad could be?"

"Do *you*?" Amber shot back. It was fair of her to ask. She pressed her fingertips to her forehead. "I'm sorry. It's just—*no*. My mom has allowed me to believe for my whole life that Hank Taylor is my father. I don't know who I hate more right now. Him or her!" She threw her hands up. Julep mewed loudly, a chastisement. "Sorry, JuJu." She petted the cat, then picked him up and held him against her chest, rocking him like a baby. Amber looked up at Morgan. "I'm sorry."

"I'd be angry, too. Actually, I *am* angry, too. On your behalf and mine. It's not just that Aunt Barb is keeping a secret in her heart. It's our whole family who are keeping the truth of us all. What else might our moms know that they aren't telling..." Morgan let her words fade out. She already knew the answer to *that*. Morgan still didn't know who her own dad was. She didn't know who her mom was dating. She didn't know a lot, in fact, about her mother. That much was becoming more painfully clear every day.

Amber seemed to read her mind. "Maybe it's time we call a family meeting. One that can't wait for the Saturday barbecue."

Morgan nodded. She was ready. Ready to take any direction—to do anything her cousin needed of her. Especially now, when Morgan was still riding high from the knowledge that in her own little world, all was well. Her fiancé was going to stand up to his mom. They'd have the ceremony with whatever officiant they could get. And even Morgan's mom had someone special in her life. It didn't matter that he was the family's old priest. All that mattered was that Morgan's life stayed as simple as possible right now. All that mattered was that they get to the bottom of Amber's situation and get right back on track to open the winery on Morgan's wedding day.

CHAPTER FIFTY-FOUR

PRESENT DAY

Amber

The minute Amber decided to play a confrontation of her mother, she regretted it. Now was *not* the time to crack open a family-wide drama. Morgan Jo had her big medical appointment that upcoming Friday. Saturday was her wedding shower. A month later, they'd be opening the vineyard and winery.

What was Amber thinking? She was thinking that the past mattered. She was thinking that her mother owed her something deeply personal.

But this didn't involve Morgan Jo. And although Amber had initially invited Morgan Jo to be part of the whole thing, Amber realized it was something she had to do for herself. Alone.

"What happens next?" Morgan Jo asked as they sat, still numb from the strange revelation from so, so long ago.

"I mean... next? Next, I go upstairs and tell Callum that he can go home. I tell him that he doesn't have to be part of my crazy life."

"Maybe he wants to be."

"Who wants to involve himself in crazy? Not a normal

person."

"Do you *want* to date a normal person?"

"We aren't dating. Morgan Jo, I'm *pregnant*! Remember?"

"I know. I just— Okay, fine. Do you *want* to be friends with a normal person?"

"Don't you think that's what I need? I mean, if I expect to bring a healthy, adjusted child into this world, should I allow randos into his life?"

"That's what your mom did, isn't it?"

"What?" Amber asked.

"She got pregnant with you, then brought in Hank. A rando. Who had to have known he wasn't your dad."

"Let's not go there. Not yet," Amber said.

"Fair enough. But... then, when?"

"Is there a hurry?" Amber asked. "I mean, do I have to talk to my mom soon? What difference will it make?"

"Will you be able to face her?"

"When will I have to?"

"At my shower. Saturday barbecues. My wedding? And that's at *minimum*."

Amber balked. "I've faced her every day for my whole life. What's the difference now?"

"Now you *know*."

"I'll fake it. Until after all of this."

"Until you have your baby? When life gets about a million times *harder*?"

"That doesn't make me feel any better."

Morgan grabbed Amber's shoulders, squaring her up. "Listen. I'm not trying to make you feel better. I'm trying to be... I'm trying to lay it all out here. That's what I'd want for me. I'd want to face it."

"The timing is terrible, Morgan Jo. Your *wedding*. The *business*. And now here I am, on my *second* major, life-changing, massive, big ol' fat splat of news in the span of weeks. On the verge of the best moments of *your* life. I'm the worst show-stealer in the world. I'm a one-upper. I'm the *worst*." Amber couldn't hold back the tears any longer. Wet sobs burst out of her, and Morgan Jo—bless her perfect li'l heart—just hugged Amber and rocked her.

Amber cried for what felt like an hour, but was probably three minutes. When the final sobs hiccupped their way out, Morgan had relaxed her arms around Amber. "Did you hear that?" She looked toward the oak staircase that led up from the basement into the big house. Amber's main artery to the heart-beat of the family farm.

Another soft hiccup bounced out of Amber. She rested a hand protectively on her belly, inwardly shushing and soothing her baby. She listened toward the stairs. A knocking.

"It's probably Emmett. He has to work in the morning. He's coming down to say goodnight."

Amber and Morgan Jo held each other's gazes, caught like deer in headlights. Frozen. Like they were down there hiding contraband. In a way, they were.

Giggles pealed out of them, and the tension broke immediately. Mint and Julep hopped off the sofa and headed for the basement door, ready to take advantage of a possible breach.

"Hello?" A muted voice echoed through the door and down the stairs.

"I need to go up there, too. Callum's probably feeling awkward and *super* ready to get the heck out of Dodge."

"Oh yeah!" Callum cried to Emmett and Father David—*David*. The trio were in an intensive conversation, and Callum's voice was half-laughter, half-shout at the other two.

Aunt Carla gave Amber and Morgan Jo a *look* as she led them from their basement tête-à-tête. "I hated to interrupt you gals, but I was starting to worry something was wrong," the older woman stage-whispered as they crossed to the kitchen table, where the men were yucking it up, knee slaps and all.

"CarlaMay," David said, "did you know *Bodean's* is still open?"

"Why, no, I didn't. I figured it went down when Bodean's eldest passed. What was his name? Tripp? Or—or was it Jax? One of those names that's a word in disguise?" Aunt Carla replied, passing a glass of the blueberry wine to Morgan Jo.

The scene was so normal. So happy and good that Amber couldn't stand that in the middle of it all she was having this personal crisis. Part of her wanted to cry out, "Stop it! Can't you see I'm ruined?" And another part wanted to wash away the memory of watching that damnable tape. That part wanted to fall into the empty seat next to Callum and joke about Mr. Bodean and his wild bunch of weirdos south of town. She wanted somebody else's family to be the hooligans for once.

Morgan Jo might have had the same thought, because she gave Amber a look, then said, "It's late, boys! We've got a long week ahead."

"Every party has a pooper!" Emmett cried, downing the last of his glass and standing up into a stumble. "Oh, hell. What was in that wine?"

Amber tried for a laugh. "You should know, Emmett Dawson. You're the one out there growing them berries."

The men cackled and Morgan Jo nudged Amber with her elbow and gave her a look. Their plan was set. Amber would save her confrontation until after the wedding shower. That would give her a week to digest the news. A week to sit with it. To think of what to say next. Of what to do.

In the meantime, everything was okay. She took a deep breath. Everything was *okay*. It was the same. It was the same as it had always been. Amber had to remind herself that just because she learned something new, it didn't change anything.

Even if it changed everything.

CHAPTER FIFTY-FIVE

1991

CarlaMay

Time went by. Morgan Jo grew on up and left the house. David watched her from afar, and I saw the pain in his face.

Finally, after Morgan Jo was good and gone and it seemed like maybe she wouldn't ever come back, David came to me. "I made a horrible mistake," he said. "How will you ever forgive me, CarlaMay?"

Here I was, holding out for him in spite of myself, all this time. And finally, he'd said the one thing I wanted him to say. He said he loved me. He would leave the church. He would do whatever it took to make things right. He was a sinner and a horrible person for leaving us to be like that for all those years. He was a horrible father. Unworthy as a priest and even more worthless as a man.

I told him he was right.

It was too late. You were long gone.

But I was still here. And after all this time and all this secret-keeping, I still loved him.

And yet now, I hated myself. How in the world could a

mother love a man who left his child as David had done? How could I face myself if I agreed to being with someone who, once he knew about Morgan Jo, didn't act?

And that's when I realized that there is one thing more important in this world than we are ever taught in church. If we are willing to forgive others, then we must also be willing to forgive ourselves.

Morgan Jo, when you read this one day, maybe soon, maybe a long time off, I hope you know that I let your father leave us not because it was good for him or good for you or me, but because I wrongly believed that it was what I deserved. That I'd done a bad thing, and I had to pay for it.

I never meant for you to pay for it, too, Morgan Jo. And I know for a fact that David didn't want that either.

I hope you'll forgive us, but just as importantly, I will also work to forgive myself. As your mama, the most important thing I can do is to teach you by example. I don't want you to go into the world feeling you deserve something bad for making one mistake in life.

We all make mistakes, but God wants us to fix them and move on. Not dwell in the house of guilt and shame all the days of our life. Not keep secrets from one another. God wants us to be truthful and to do our best.

When I look at you now, I can see that somehow, some way, I managed to do just that—my very, very best. Because you, Morgan Jo, are the best part of me.

CHAPTER FIFTY-SIX

PRESENT DAY

Morgan Jo

Morgan clutched Emmett's hand as she lay reclined on an exam bed in the clinical, ten-story building that housed Fertility Specialists of Western Kentucky. Emmett sat in a chair he'd pulled tight up next to her. The ultrasound and scope were complete—a blank-faced doctor had spent about ten minutes total studying black-and-white images on a screen, murmuring to herself and flashing patronizing smiles at Morgan and knowing looks at Emmett with every flourish of her wand.

Emmett squeezed Morgan's hand.

The woman stowed her wand and turned off the machine, then snapped off her blue exam gloves and clasped her hands around one bony knee. "Well, I can see why you've come in. Despite great labs and generally exceptional health, we might have some issues goin' on in there, honey."

"What do you mean?" Morgan frowned and sat up straighter, preparing herself for bad news.

The doctor counted along her fingers, expedient and brutal. "Your right fallopian tube is mottled up in scar tissue. That's why it was painful for you when I tried the scope there. We can clean some of that out, but from all I can tell, it wouldn't be a safe avenue, the right one, that is." She moved to her next finger. "Your left tube looks great. It's clear inside and out—totally unaffected by the previous surgery and, um, shrapnel, for lack of a better expression."

"Okay." Morgan pushed down hope that formed in her chest. She stole a glance at Emmett, whose expression remained dull and neutral. Morgan thought of it as his lawyer face.

"If a pregnancy were to take, that would be a great little road." She pulled her iPad from the rolling desk nearby and glanced at it. "Now, the ovaries. Again, our right one—appears incapacitated, as expected. The right side of your body took the brunt of the incident."

All of this was expected. Morgan asked, "And the *left?*"

"Left ovary seems fine. Interestingly, it's all a very small area in there. The scar tissue is creeping up from your hip into the organs along the right, but the left is far less affected. That's *great*, Ms. Morgan Jo." She didn't smile. "As for your uterus." She closed her eyes for longer than a split second. "If this were a run-of-the-mill hip replacement surgery, we'd be fine. Yes, any pregnancy would be higher-risk. You'd have pain. Possible nerve issues. But, if we're talking about an injury such as yours —something more substantial than a hip problem—it changes things. The current scar and nerve damage are extensive and could be problematic."

"Problematic?" It was Emmett who leaned forward now.

"Ms. Morgan Jo," she drawled heavily, "you're a hot mess in there, honey."

On instant, Morgan burst into tears. Wracking, full-body sobs that twisted the paper beneath her body and drenched the front of her exam gown. Emmett shushed her gently, more insistent on hearing everything. More unaware just how badly Morgan was damaged inside.

But something about him turned steely. "Does this all mean she can't bear children?" He talked over Morgan, whose sobbing slowed to weeping. Her instinctive reaction was over as soon as it began, a flash flood of emotion. Almost like Morgan had planned to get the bad news, freak out, then compose herself.

"I don't like to skirt around the hard stuff," the doctor answered Emmett. "Morgan might be able to get pregnant and even carry the child. We could test our theory with intrauterine insemination. However, there are no guarantees, and in fact, I'd worry it wouldn't end well. Even in the best of circumstances, pregnancies can fail. Without a hospitable environment, I can't promise that implantation would take and even if it did—scar tissue can impact the pregnancy."

"What if I got pregnant by chance? Without insemination?" Morgan managed, rubbing the back of her hand across her nose and sniffling.

"I suppose time would tell."

"Would it be irresponsible?" Emmett asked.

Morgan shot him a sharp look. "What do you mean?"

A look passed between the doctor and her fiancé, and Morgan shifted on the tabletop, sniffling once more before she resolved to stop being dramatic. "What do you mean, irresponsible?"

"Morgan Jo, honey, if you got pregnant, it may fail. That would cause heartache, no question. It's an up-and-down journey, motherhood, beginning with baby-making, sweetheart." She glanced at Emmett. "I assume that's your question?"

"Right. I mean, maybe it's not our path."

Morgan swallowed past a lump that had formed in her throat and embedded there. If only she had control over her body. If only she could will herself to heal all the way. She studied Emmett as the doctor shuffled her iPad into its sleeve and stood, smoothing her coat down her body. Emmett didn't appear altogether too crushed. But, surely, he was. He came from this long line of put-together people with great genes. He *wanted* to preserve that. To continue it. He wanted the Dawson line to live on, and he'd picked *Morgan* to make that happen.

The doctor apologized, promised further testing or referrals for second opinions if they wanted it, but once Morgan and Emmett stepped out of the building and into the bright Kentucky sun, he turned to her and took up both her hands. "I have an idea," he said.

CHAPTER FIFTY-SEVEN

PRESENT DAY

Amber

For the bridal shower, Amber was in charge of food and beverages. She hadn't made everything, but she'd coordinated every last detail. Morgan Jo hadn't so much as sent a check-in text since the day before—Friday.

Friday had been a rough day for Morgan Jo and Emmett. They'd received news that a baby wasn't on the cards for them, and this news rocked Amber's world, too. She'd gone to bed Friday wondering if there was a reason she was pregnant and alone.

Amber would like to talk things through with her mom and her aunts, her sister and her cousins, but she'd promised Morgan Jo that the conversation would wait until *after* the shower. In the meantime, Amber thought up how she'd approach her mother about Hank. What she would tell her sister and brother. What she would tell Hank, too, if anything.

Big ideas swirled in her mind. Grand scenarios. Maybe she would invite everyone to church and brunch after, then, smack dab in the middle of a French toast extravaganza at the big house, Amber would stand up and point her finger at Hank and declare that she knew the truth. She fantasized what everyone's reactions would be. Would her mother wail in humiliation? Would Hank condemn Barb publicly? Would Barb, in turn, confess who Amber's dad was and what had happened to throw her life into such a miserable mess?

At that last thought, Amber checked herself. How could she carry hard feelings against her own mama when Amber herself was in a questionable motherhood scenario? What was it printed down in the Bible? *Let him who is without sin cast the first stone.* And had Barb shown one lick of judgment against Amber since the revelation of her pregnancy?

No.

BarbaraJean Taylor had showered Amber in baby gifts. She'd yard-saled for the perfect shabby-chic crib. She'd hoarded yellow onesies and commissioned crochet blankies and cotton burp rags from friends who crafted and sewed. She'd texted Amber baby name ideas based on family names, then based on Bible names, then based on silly things like flowers and natural geological events. Amber recalled one such text. *If it's a boy, you could name him Avalanche.*

Amber had laughed out loud and called her mama straight up, and Barb had laughed too. "Sorry," she'd said. "I'm getting carried away!"

Didn't Amber want that? A mother who got carried away in excitement rather than carried away in judgment and condemnation? Yes, of course she did. So then, who was Amber to throw her disapproval at her mother? Maybe, just *maybe*, there was a good reason Barb had kept Amber's parentage from her. Maybe, like with Amber, it was a whole drama. And maybe, instead of feeling comfortable in airing the whole drama for the world to know, Barb had made the prudent, timely choice to neatly pack away the details in a hope chest, only to open it up and take it out later. At a better time.

That's what Amber chose to believe, and that was what allowed her to focus on Morgan Jo's bridal shower today.

What's more, that belief was what reminded Amber that the little baby growing inside her was *hers*. All hers.

Yes, she'd have to think carefully about what to tell that little baby about Grant. She'd have to tread lightly on the matter of secrecy, because ultimately, Amber planned to be as open as a freshly plowed field.

But still, that baby was *hers*.

And even if Morgan Jo could never ever grow a little baby of her own, Amber had a right to her blessing. And Morgan Jo could be a wonderful, amazing cousin who lived just upstairs. She'd be the baby's family. The baby's friend. The baby's protector, just as much as Amber would be.

"Amber Lee! The shrimp and grits?" Aunt Carla sang from the kitchen where she hustled about with Emmett's mom, Mrs. Dawson. Amber had once learned the woman's name, but nobody seemed to call her by it, and so Amber just stuck with Mrs. Dawson. It was the safest bet, anyhow.

Amber had just come in from outside, where she'd tied off the last oversized white balloon to the wall of others lined up along the broadside of the barn. With Tiff and Rachel's help, they'd created a gorgeous tableau for photos. An arc of various-sized balloons in all imaginable tones of white, from eggshell to cream to ivory to pearl. Beneath the banner of balloons was a pair of haystacks, each with a white chenille blanket tossed just so, across. At either side of the set-up, Amber stationed a pair of narrow, square-top side tables. All four were different heights, making for a playful symmetry. Over each table was thrown a clean white linen cloth, and on top of each cloth, a whimsical bouquet of white roses nestled into baby's breath.

Similar bouquets anchored the long, country-dressed table

that began at the barn and spread toward the vineyard. It was one of the same tables they'd use for the wedding, but today, instead of a great big white tent, they opted for a pair of peach-colored umbrellas supplied by Emmett's Aunt Avery, who owned a backyard decor business over in Lexington. Thank goodness, too, because the shower was shaping up to cost as much as the wedding would.

"Shrimp and grits!" Amber held up a finger and strode straight to the fridge. She pulled out a platter of a dozen minia-ture dishes, each with a pool of baked grits and a fresh shrimp perched on the side. "I did them this morning."

Mrs. Dawson took the platter, spun away with it.

"Drinks—" Amber said to her aunt. "My mama is setting out the tea and lemonade, but I told her *flies*."

"The pitchers have lids." Aunt Carla stole a look at the clock. "Anyway, it's *time*. I'm going to set the wine on ice, and we'll keep it along the side table on the porch."

"Mint juleps?" asked Julia, who'd just pulled off an apron and hung it up on the cupboard.

"They're downstairs in my bedroom. I don't think we'll hear them even if they start belting out a Hank Williams song."

"I mean the drinks." Julia giggled.

"Oh, right. Yes, well, Tiff is bringing the mint juleps and whiskey. She should be here any minute."

"She'd better be!" Barb rang out from the front door, where she stamped her cowgirl boots on the welcome mat. Barb wore a lacy, country-style dress and her hair was teased up to heaven. Her arms were hung heavily with gift bags. "Tiff's, mine, and yours, Amber Lee." She set the tissue-paper-stuffed bags on the sofa in the front room. It had been Barb's job to do the wrap-ping. "I talked to Tiffany in the car, and she was walking down from her place."

Amber swung to the back window that looked out from the kitchen. Sure enough, Tiffany tottered down the hill behind the barn in high red heels. She carried a deep box, which had to have the beverages inside. Amber turned to Julia, who read her mind. "On it. I'll go help her."

Amber smoothed her dress down. It was an empire-waist pale-pink number she'd found on the clearance rack at Clancy's. A soft, supple linen blend that hid bumps and blips but draped pleasantly over her growing curves. As if her body realized it was okay to tell the world about the baby, Amber's hips had already begun to stretch out and her tummy—once a firm, wide middle— had popped out just a bit. The dress didn't draw attention to Amber's growing bump, but it didn't bother to hide it, either.

She wore sensible tan ballet flats, and had diffused her hair, drawing subtle waves from her normally stalk-straight tresses. Her glasses were bothering her, moving from dark lenses to indoor-clear, and so she'd grabbed her new prescription sunglasses and carried the last of the supplies from the kitchen out to the party area, where many of the guests had already gathered, chatting in pleasant, happy tenors in small bunches in the backyard.

Within ten minutes, everything—including the beverage table—was set. The party was ready to welcome its guest of honor, Morgan Jo. The gifts filled up the grassy spaces beneath the balloons at the little photo staging area, boxes and bags of every shape, mostly white or sweet pastel in color. Soft country classics dripped slow like honey in the background of the din. Between the decadent food, the atmosphere, and the decor, the bridal shower was setting a high bar for the wedding.

Emmett was assigned to bring her from his home, where she'd gotten ready, at five minutes past the hour, and sure enough, he delivered on his promise.

His truck crunched along the gravel drive, slowly, slowly, edging to where the drive tapered off into the grassy fields that led around the side and out back of the big house.

Amber, Julia, Mrs. Dawson, and CarlaMay took it upon themselves to walk to where Emmett let Morgan Jo out of the truck, and all five women twittered with excitement as the hostesses guided Morgan Jo from Emmett's goodbye kiss over to the rest of the waiting ladies.

Congratulations spilled around like an overfilled martini, sloshing Morgan Jo in enthusiasm and happy spirit, and Amber wondered at how she was taking it all.

When they'd spoken early that morning, Morgan Jo had seemed a shade distracted, as if she'd had something other than her big day on her mind.

Of course she did. She had the vineyard and winery on her mind. And the news from the fertility clinic, too. But she'd assured Amber that in fact, all was well. She was simply looking forward to getting the show on the road.

"How are you doing?" Amber whispered to her once the party was underway and the mothers had fluttered off to their respective cliques.

Julia repeated Amber's question. "Yes, MoJo, you hanging in there? I mean, with yesterday and everything?"

Morgan Jo grabbed each of their hands and squeezed. "Believe it or not, I'm doing *well*. Bizarrely well, even." If Amber didn't know any better, she'd think Morgan Jo had laid the rouge on heavy.

Or maybe—less tastefully—she and Emmett had had a little early-morning celebration themselves? Amber was just about to ask for the morsel of salacious gossip when other cousins descended upon the trio, stealing Morgan Jo away for selfies at the photo set.

Amber filled a glass up with lemonade from the beverage table and hung close to Julia, surveying their work from the modest distance of the back porch. "It looks great," Julia said, sipping her white peach wine. "You killed it."

"*We* killed it. You've got an eye for decorating, Jules," Amber said.

"And you—" Julia popped the rest of her deviled egg into her mouth and swallowed it down greedily. "Kill it with the food. Why don't you open a kitchen? Brambleberry could *use* one. I feel like the only options are the Dewdrop or McGowan's Steakhouse out west."

"You forgot about Bodean's, then." Amber thought back to her wild day out with Callum. She thought about Callum all the time, in fact. Nearly as much as she thought about her baby and the upcoming wedding. There was so much in her world to be grateful for, but all of it served up a portion of fear, too.

"Seriously, Amber. Have you thought of doing something for the business?"

"I mean..." Amber considered this. "Yeah, sure. But, we're not there yet."

"Really? People like to eat good food with their good wine, you know. It makes sense." She dabbed at her mouth with the napkin. "That was the best deviled egg I've ever had in my life. I didn't know there was such a thing as gourmet deviled eggs. My Lord, Amber Lee."

Amber laughed. "Thanks. But we don't have a space for it, anyhow. We'll be hard pressed to make do with just the barn as a vineyard and this place for tastings."

"You're right." Morgan Jo appeared at the porch, a white sash tied over her that read *The Future Mrs. Dawson*. She pinched it with her manicured fingernails.

"Right about what?"

"We don't have a place for tastings. Not indoor, anyway. It's an issue. We need to put it on our to-do list. A tasting room."

"A tasting room. So, you're serious about doing tastings, after all?" Julia asked, a playful smirk over her pert pink pout. "You said you *only* wanted to sell the wine."

"We can't only sell wine. Especially not as a new vineyard and winery. People will want tastings. Real ones."

Morgan Jo looked for Amber to agree, and Amber offered an enthusiastic nod. "That's true," she added.

"Have you thought about a space?" Julia asked, tapping a pink-tipped finger on her mouth. "What if you convert one of the bunkhouses?"

"We can't do that. Each is rented. Trav, Tiff, and Geddy."

"Well, one of them might want to move," Julia pointed out.

Amber and Morgan Jo looked at one another and grinned mischievously. It was Morgan Jo who said, "Oh *really?*"

Julia flushed bright red. Her hands flew to her face and she fell forward in a peal of nervous giggles. "You *two!*" she cried when she launched upright again. "You-all are *bad.*"

"You and Geddy are bad. What would your mama say if you played house with a Coyle, anyway?" Amber pointed out.

Julia made a wistful sigh.

"Girls!" Mrs. Dawson came up to the porch with a glass of Amber's favorite taste, the perry. "Are you-all talking *work?*" she cried out and held her hands up, bedazzled fingers and painted nails glimmering in the late-morning sun. "You-all girls hush, hush. It's time for presents and cake!"

CHAPTER FIFTY-EIGHT

PRESENT DAY

Morgan Jo

Morgan had opened no fewer than twenty generous, lovely gifts from friends and family, and women who'd soon become friends and family to her. Emmett's Aunt Avery saved every last ribbon and bow, creating a gift-tie bouquet by tying each one onto a small wreath that CarlaMay had woven out of grapevines from the vineyard.

She looked around her now, at boxes of precious mementos and clever home goods—who'd ever heard of a salad serving bowl molded and carved and painted to look like a great big sheaf of lettuce? Emmett's female relatives had gifted her the lion share of kitchen gadgets and linens—pretty, frilly bed sheets with eyelet edging and brand-name labels.

From her own family, Morgan Jo was duly embarrassed to open lingerie by the bagfuls. Skimpy negligees of every color in the rainbow. Tasteless bras and panties that were more gag than gifts—those had come from Aunt DanaSue and Tiff, naturally. Also, though, her family had been the ones to find and wrap heirlooms. Memaw's best cotton bed sheets, sturdy farmhouse ones that had lasted the past fifty years and would last another two hundred and fifty. Which was good news, as Emmett and Morgan planned to stay on and live at the farmhouse after the wedding. Aprons and dishtowels from great-aunts and Morgan's great-grandmother. She'd add these to her growing collection of foundlings, such as the one Memaw loved best. *If Mama ain't happy, ain't nobody happy.*

Amber gave Morgan a crystal flask. Etched into the thick glass was the year 1949. Beneath the date read the words *Nelson Family Moonshine.*

Hesitantly, Morgan unscrewed the pewter cap and took a tentative sip. A normal person would probably never dare to imbibe a decade's old, homemade concoction. But Morgan was a hillbilly at her core, and so she did. The scent and taste were overpowering and immediately familiar.

"It's Grandad's moonshine." She breathed the words as she stared at her cousin. "Oh, my word, *Amber*. This flask is gorgeous. What a beautiful gift."

Amber looked bashful. "That's not all. Here." She passed Morgan a second, larger gift bag.

In it, Morgan found a framed, handwritten note. It was Memaw's letter to Morgan. The one she'd discovered not so long ago. The one that gave her permission to forgive. To move on. To *live* and to love. It reminded Morgan of a conversation the pair had had years ago. It was the conversation that taught Morgan how to pick her husband. On how to pick a man who was good and fun and who would love Morgan and push her and catch her when she fell. Someone like Emmett. "Amber Lee Taylor. *Thank you.*"

She hugged Amber hard and whispered in her ear, "This means the world."

Amber whispered back, "It meant something to me, too." When they pulled away from each other, Morgan saw in her cousin's eyes that Amber was dealing with her recent discovery in much the same way as Morgan had dealt with the blow she'd received years back.

"Here, MoJo." Julia thrust a set of two cream-colored boxes tied up in rustic string.

The first revealed a pink PJ set monogrammed with *MJD*. "Not to spoil anything, but I got ol' Em a pair to match."

"Jules," Morgan squeezed her before moving to the second gift. "This is all *too* much."

"Yeah, well. I figure you're worth the hassle." Julia gave her a small, playful shove.

Morgan loosened the strings and peeled back the paper to find a treasured remembrance from their childhood: a book they'd passed back and forth in secret all through junior high. The copy they'd shared back then was tattered and dog-eared, crusty and greasy with unknown traces of food and drink. This copy wasn't brand new—the book itself was out of print—but it was a clean, crisp edition. *Where Babies Come From.*

Morgan got teary-eyed as she flipped through the pages and her audience of friends and family laughed at the silly but special present. Julia had inscribed a note on the inside of the front cover.

MoJo, we didn't know it then, but babies don't only come from a hoo-ha. Turns out you can get them other ways, too. Love you always. Your best friend for life, Jules.

Morgan swallowed and looked up at Julia. She didn't have to say anything. Instead, she just smiled and shook her head and pushed a single tear from her cheek. Julia winked at her.

"Morgan Jo," her mama CarlaMay said, ever so slightly missing the beat, "what's *wrong*, baby?"

"Nothing," Morgan said through a partial sob. She smiled harder, but her face cracked into full-blown tears. "It's *nothing*."

Julia slid across the haystack and snuggled up against

Morgan, kissing her on the cheek and answering CarlaMay on Morgan's behalf. "Happy tears. *Hopeful* tears."

Satisfied, CarlaMay pressed her hands together. "Well, in *that* case, I think it's time for the big one."

"Big one?"

"Oh, yes. Your aunts and I went in together on this, but it was Barb's idea. We took some liberties, Morgan Jo, but we *did* get permission from Amber and Julia, i'n't that right, girls?"

Amber and Julia nodded eagerly, then got up from their positions flanking Morgan to make room.

Aunt Barb and Aunt Dana appeared from around the corner of the barn, each gripping a rope that disappeared strangely into a sweeping white sheet that hung over whatever spanned their distance—four or five feet long and probably four feet high.

"What's this?" Morgan raised her hands to her mouth and stood from the haystack, her ivory silk cocktail dress clinging to her thighs as she moved nearer to her aunts and mother.

Morgan dropped her hands to her stomach and smoothed the fabric around her waist and down around her bottom before lacing her fingers behind her body and bracing herself for the big reveal.

Her mom pulled the sheet away in one big flourish, and there, over a gorgeous, glazed cherrywood board, read the words *A Taste of Moonshine Creek.*

Morgan sucked in a breath and her hands again flew to her face, which she covered briefly before peeking again at the gift. "A Taste of Moonshine Creek," she read, the words bouncing from her tongue to her teeth and through her lips. She looked at her mom, then her aunts, then Julia and Amber and the rest of the group of party guests before looking back at the sign again and murmuring, "It's *perfect.*"

"Will it work? For the name of our vineyard?" Amber asked,

biting her lower lip expectantly. "We thought it sounded good, but we can have it redone."

Aunt Barb added, "Travis and Geddy made this, Morgan Jo. We commissioned them, thinking that what you-all are gon' have here is more than a vineyard. More than a winery. It's a sample of all that this farm has to offer, from start to finish."

"Aunt Barb, it's *perfect.*"

The crowd of women oohed and ahhed at the happy present and everyone joined in tidying up the space, toting the gifts into the big house, and winding down the party.

As Morgan started inside with her ribbon wreath filled with a promise of blessings, her mom tugged her away. "Morgan Jo, I didn't give you *my* gift." She slipped a small bag into Morgan's hands. "Open it now."

Morgan took a moment to herself, lifted an ivory-colored tag hanging slip-tied around one handle. Morgan read her mother's careful, slanted handwriting.

Something old
Something new
Something borrowed
Something blue

Morgan looked up, searching the grounds for her mother, for an explanation.

She reread the words, then lowered herself back onto the haystack where she'd sat to open the other gifts. After pulling two neatly fanned pieces of tissue from the bag, she reached a hand inside to find three tissue-wrapped boxes. The first was labeled in fine black pen: *Blue.* She unwrapped the tissue to find within a blue velvet jewelry box. In the box, a set of sapphire earrings. They matched the small blue gemstones that framed the diamond on Morgan's engagement ring. She smiled.

The next box was labeled *New.* Inside, a bracelet. White

gold with a miniature set of charms dangling. One, a cross. Another, a bunch of grapes. The last one, a silver heart.

The third box read *Borrowed*. Morgan opened the paper. Another box. This one wooden, plain. Morgan opened the lid. Inside lay a silver necklace. She lifted the delicate chain out to see a pendant dangling at the end. Morgan frowned.

A key.

Morgan looked at her mother for answers, but CarlaMay smirked and drew a finger to her lips before whispering, "*Later*."

"You really like the name?" Julia begged Morgan as she, Morgan, and Amber wandered away from the party together and toward the hangar.

Morgan and Julia were tipsy on their backyard wine, tottering into each other. Amber led the way, insisting they check out the hangar as a potential space for a tasting room.

Once the party had come to a close and the outdoor space was cleaned up, Morgan had stowed most of her gifts in her bedroom. One, however, she put on: the necklace with the key. She was anxious to talk about it with her mom, but her best friend had stayed after, convincing Amber that she'd make an excellent restaurateur. Morgan was interested enough to play along.

"I *love* it. *A Taste of Moonshine Creek*." Morgan framed her hands in the air and giggled. "That's why Julia is right, and *you* —" she poked Amber in the ribs, "have to run the tasting room part."

"Once the baby comes," Julia added. "You certainly don't need one more thing on your plate right now."

"Yeah, well. Baby or no baby, I don't have a job anymore, remember? So if your vineyard and winery don't take off, then you can bet your bottom dollar I'll sell something, and I need a place to sell it from, so—"

The three of them stopped in front of the broad-sided hangar. It looked more ancient than ever now.

Morgan frowned. A recent memory hit her like a ton of bricks. "Oh my." She peeled away from Amber and Julia and tugged open the door. "I forgot something in here."

"What?" Amber asked, following close behind as Julia stumbled around for a moment before ducking into the dark structure.

Morgan headed directly into the back right corner, where she and Emmett had explored just days before. Where she had planned to come back and dig even deeper. "There's something in there." She pulled at the jagged plywood that remained, tugging with all her might until Julia joined her, ripping it away in one great heave.

Morgan stepped into the space. Dust particles floated in the sun-washed rafters above them.

Julia asked, "Why was this boarded up?" She was still woozy from the wine, her tongue loose with frank curiosity.

Amber and Morgan looked at one another, then at Julia, expectantly.

"Oh right," Julia gasped, her memory slow to form but sharp once it gathered itself up. "Miss Dottie."

CHAPTER FIFTY-NINE

PRESENT DAY

Morgan Jo

Julia was horrified to recall the history of the hangar. It was Amber, however, who'd come up with a way to soften the blow.

"You know what this place could be?"

"A tasting room," Morgan answered. "I agree with the two of you. It's big. We can store product here. Amber, you can make up a menu. Charcuterie boards and desserts."

"Right, sure. But it could be, I don't know—sort of like a monument to the women who came before us. Memaw, but also Aunt Dottie."

"You still call her Aunt Dottie?" Julia asked. She stood, arms folded over her chest, staring up at the high rafters. The hooks that once held tobacco leaves, hanging long and sweet.

"Yeah. That's what Memaw called her to us and what our moms called her."

"I'm getting a headache comin' on," Julia complained. "But let's move forward with the tasting room thing. I swear I'm gon' get a migraine if I don't chug an ice water and lie down."

"I'll take you home," Amber offered. "Unless you've got

Geddy waiting in the wings out there to take you wherever you two run off to."

Morgan laughed at that, but Julia just groaned. "You two go on. I'm gonna try and finish pulling these boards down."

The other two left, and Morgan started after them, intent to go and grab a crowbar, but she stopped and turned back, slipped into the space that was now only boarded along just one side.

Morgan hooked her hand around the ladder rung that hit her at eye level, pulled it, hiked up her left foot and pushed it down on a lower rung, testing. She looked up into the loft space above. The object she'd seen before, whatever it was, remained sticking out over the opening where the ladder disappeared.

She stepped up onto the next rung. The ladder held. She lifted her hand again, and again, one foot carefully after the other, putting more of her weight on her left than on her right leg and more of her weight on her right hand than her left hand, until she was at the top of the ladder and her head emerged into the little loft where little girls and little boys used to play. A long time ago.

The loft was clear of anything other than dusty, aged hay and the object Morgan had spied before.

A little leather-bound diary. Complete with a lock.

CHAPTER SIXTY

PRESENT DAY

Amber

Amber returned to the farm after taking Julia home. Normally, she'd let herself in at her exterior door down below. But when she pulled her car into the gravel drive, she saw her mother's was still there, too.

Interested to get in and find out what they were gossiping about, Amber made for the front door of the big house, letting herself into the front room to find what looked like yet another family intervention.

This one much smaller.

Morgan Jo, Aunt Carla, Amber's mom, Aunt Dana, *and* Tiff and Trav sat quietly. Amber moved inside, confused. "What's going on?" she asked, turning her gaze first on Morgan Jo, who lifted a book. Amber squinted at it. "What's that?"

"Amber Lee," Barb said, and patted the sofa seat beside her. "Come sit down. There's somethin' needs talkin' 'bout."

CHAPTER SIXTY-ONE

PRESENT DAY

Morgan Jo

The diary answered everything. And *then* some.

Morgan had read it with a ferocious hunger, moving from the opening entry all the way to the last one. In total, there were just eighteen, each one heart-wrenchingly brief.

She hadn't had to so much as go into the big house to track down her mother. CarlaMay had crept out into the hangar and met Morgan there.

"Something borrowed, and something old," she said.

"You got them out of order."

"I was never much for poetry."

Morgan had passed the key and diary back to her mother, but CarlaMay had held up her hands. "This is your history. They're yours now."

"I understand, you know," Morgan had said. "I understand why he didn't... claim me. How could he? It went against his beliefs. It would have ruined his life."

"It would have saved his life," CarlaMay had said. "And it would have saved mine, too. I waited too long."

"No, you didn't. You're telling me now. Did you know I had been out here?"

"Of course. I keep tabs on you. But even so, I always planned to share this. I wrote it for you. I'd have kept writing in it, too, if the story was to go on."

"What's that supposed to mean?" Morgan had been confused. Was her mother finally ending things with David?

She'd answered, "At the supper we had, David thought we were going to come clean then. He thought I was going to share everything, but I couldn't."

"We were talking about his officiating the wedding," Morgan had said.

"Right. That was the start, but I just— I've had a hard time getting over this. It's been sealed into my heart, your truth. His. *Mine*." She'd taken a pause. "I thought so hard about what to give you for your bridal shower. I liked the idea of jewelry, of course. And you needed all those things—old, new, borrowed, blue. And then it occurred to me. Maybe it was time you knew. Ahead of the wedding. Maybe it would change things for you. *Help* you."

"Help me?"

"I've seen you struggle, Morgan Jo. I've seen your stress. With the fertility stuff. The vineyard. Even the wedding. You're fearing something. And I started to wonder if this had to do with it."

Morgan had broken down. Her mother was right. Of course she was. There was a piece missing in the puzzle of Morgan's life, and this was *it*.

"I forgive you, Mom," she'd whispered. "And I forgive him, too."

CarlaMay had broken down, as well.

They'd hugged. They'd cried.

Morgan went on and asked if David really was coming back

into their lives now, so many years later. If CarlaMay had decided to follow her heart after all.

CarlaMay had replied that ultimately, that was up to Morgan. Yes, they still had feelings for each other, David and CarlaMay. But whether the relationship could go anywhere relied upon how Morgan felt, too.

Morgan had said simply, "Okay." And they'd agreed to leave it at that. For now.

CHAPTER SIXTY-TWO

PRESENT DAY

Amber

Equally shocking wasn't that Morgan's childhood priest was her father, but that her Uncle Hank really wasn't Amber's dad either. Amber's dad was, in fact, a bad person. Someone who'd taken advantage of Barb in a moment of vulnerability.

The thing to do now was to bring everyone onto the same page. To face their haunted history together, as a family.

To make things right.

Amber closed the diary and looked up, her eyes filled to the brim with fresh tears. She looked at her mom. "Is this *true*?" She looked at Tiff and Trav. "Did you know?"

Tiff was crying. Trav was holding her against him, shaking his head, sad as a hound dog after a hunt was over.

Barb answered Amber. "I never knew what to say. Not while Hank was still around, and certainly not after."

"But you knew all along, Mama?" Amber pled. "You knew? And you never said anything about it? You never said anything when I tried to get you-all back together—you and Dad—I mean, Hank." Amber frowned. "How did he find out?"

"I told him. Back then."

"And he just left you? Left *us*?"

"I didn't tell him everything, Amber. I didn't—I didn't *know* everything. Times were different then. To me, it was my fault that it happened because I'd had a drink."

"Your fault that someone took advantage of you? And got you pregnant?"

"I didn't think Hank would understand. I didn't think anyone would understand."

Aunt Carla broke in. "What people understood was cheating. And Hank took it for cheating. So did Barb. I mean, we all just figured it was a whole big mess."

"A mess." Amber dropped her face to her hands and cried. "A *mess*."

Barb scooted closer and wrapped her arms around Amber. "A *blessed* mess."

Amber choked a sob out and sat up straighter. "Does he know *now*?"

"Who? Hank?" Barb asked.

"Does he know that you were assaulted? Did you ever tell him?"

"I told him after lunch the other day."

Amber frowned. She did some quick math in her head. "*After* lunch? After he came into the salon for a haircut?"

"Yes. I took his appearance for a... a sign, I guess."

"You mean, he didn't know that you didn't technically cheat on him before he made an appointment and came to see me? At the salon?"

"That's right, Amber Lee. It wasn't until after we ate, couldn't reach you, Tiff left. Saw you were still at the shop. Hank and I went for a long walk. I told him everything. He was devastated." Barb looked at her lap. "He's been trying to set up a family meeting, but I told him not until I talked to you."

"He doesn't know that I knew."

"You knew?" Barb asked.

Amber nodded and caught Morgan Jo's gaze. Morgan Jo gave a slight nod. An affirmation. Permission. Support. Amber nodded. "That's what we were watching, Callum and me. In the video shop. Grandad's tapes—on one of them, Hank comes out with it."

Morgan made a grunting noise. "He sounded so angry."

"This was on a *tape?*" Aunt Carla asked.

Amber nodded again. "Yes, ma'am."

Tiff asked, "What did Daddy tell Grandad?"

"He told Grandad that Mom was having them get tested."

"Tested? Why? Why not just pretend, Mom?" Trav asked. All eyes turned on Trav, who doubled down. "For all it mattered, Hank was Amber's daddy just the same as he was ours. Maybe he wouldn't have left. You could have fixed things, Mom."

But Barb was fierce in her answer. "I know the cost of lies and secrets. I saw it in my family all growing up, Travis David Taylor. I wasn't about to carry on with that particular tradition. I wanted everyone to know what was what. So yes, I told Hank there'd been another man. I told him we should find out who belonged to who. I thought it was the right thing to do."

There was a brief silence, then Aunt Dana joined in with a question of her own. "What did Dad say back to Hank?"

Amber looked at Morgan, who cleared her throat. "He said it's not about the test. It's about what you know. What you know in your heart."

Tiff's voice turned to ice. "I guess he didn't know a damn thing."

CHAPTER SIXTY-THREE

PRESENT DAY

Amber

September turned her leaves over and October swept into Brambleberry. Summer was over, and the farm welcomed autumn with open arms.

The wedding/gala was just eight days away, and there were still a couple of important details to attend to.

Three of the four—Morgan Jo, Amber, and Julia—got together for one final business meeting ahead of the big day. Emmett had an important meeting with a client in Louisville. He'd be at court until the afternoon.

They sat at the picnic table, each with an apple cider in hand. Amber didn't believe in drinking cold beverages in October, and therefore she'd insisted on brewing a spicy batch of her favorite warm drink.

Morgan Jo showed them her notepad and pointed to each item with the butt of her pen. "Flowers, *check*. Music, *check*. Decorations, including tables, linens, dishware, chairs, so forth, *check*." She moved her pen down further. "Wedding dress, groom's tux, usherette's dresses and usher's suits, *check*."

Julia reached across the table and pointed to an item mid-page. "Product? Do we have all the bottles labeled now that we've got the name and logo?"

"Yep." Morgan Jo swiveled the notepad back to herself and gave that one a big, fat check. "And yes, we should have more than enough."

"Do we have the charcuterie boards ready? Trav and Geddy were supposed to make two per table," Julia pointed out.

"I had them do four per table, and they're all ready to go. I checked yesterday," Amber assured.

"Okay, the seating chart," Morgan Jo said, scratching a line across her page then flipping it to a series of mock-up seating plans, all rectangles and squares and names. "I'm worried about plus-ones. We have a couple of people who didn't indicate a plus-one but whom I'd expected to bring a date, all the same."

"Like who?" Amber asked.

"Julia, I take it you and Geddy are officially a *thang*?" Morgan Jo smirked. "It's safe to say that neither one of you is bringing a plus-one, correct? You're not going to surprise me at the last minute?"

Julia didn't blush even half a shade. "Oh, he's my date, all right. And if he turns up with someone else on his arm, well, I'll be sure to take her out for you. Wouldn't want our numbers off." She winked and cackled, and Amber and Morgan Jo laughed, too.

Amber cleared her throat and turned serious. "Morgan Jo, your mama. Is she... do we know if David is coming?"

After some back-and-forth, Morgan Jo and Emmett had decided to have her bookish and most articulate cousin, Rachel, officiate the wedding. She'd taken the job seriously, completing her online course like she'd just gotten her doctorate and written out a beautiful set of vows certain to make even the snootiest of wine snobs dab their eyes. And there were some snooty wine snobs coming, that was for sure.

Morgan Jo sucked in a breath and set her pen down, then rubbed her hands together and returned Amber's look. "Yes. He's coming. He's gon' sit in the back, though. Doesn't want to draw attention, I guess."

Amber nodded. "Right. That's good, then."

"Amber, what about Hank?"

Since the big blowout diary/tape come-to-Jesus the month prior, Amber had spoken to Hank three times. First was with her mom and brother and sister. They sat around a table at Bodean's, where they counted on a certain degree of privacy. They cried together. Hank apologized. He promised to make it up to Amber and Trav and Tiff, and to Barb. Barb apologized, too.

The second meeting, Hank and Amber went for ice cream on Main Street. That one was like a father–daughter date, in a way. They made small talk and ventured into the parts of one another's lives they didn't really know about. It was interesting to get to know the man Amber had always assumed was her father. In a way, he'd come to feel less of a dad more than ever. In another way, though, they grew closer from it.

The third meeting, Amber told Hank she was pregnant. He already knew—how could he not? But she wanted to have a face-to-face with him about it. She wanted to be the one to tell Hank her big news, partly with the hope that he'd turn out to be a better grandfather than he'd been a father. He hadn't had much advice except to be honest, not only with Grant but with herself. Hank had offered to approach Grant and ensure he'd be around for the baby, but Amber didn't want that, Grant didn't want that, and it turned out the greater Maycomb family didn't much want that. Just a couple weeks before, they'd helped Grant give up his parental rights to the baby and Grant, along with his mom, dad, and sister, ended up moving down south into Tennessee.

But Amber didn't wish shame on anyone. What was done

was done, and she was just happy to have her little baby growing and kicking inside of her. Hank was excited, too. He'd even gone so far as to offer Amber a place to rent out of town, if she ever wanted to leave the big house and strike out on her own. He'd help her with rent. But Amber wasn't interested. She had everything she wanted at the farm. Her cousins, brother and sister, her aunt, and soon enough she'd have Emmett Dawson up there, too, setting an example for any suitor that ever came to pick Amber up for a date.

Namely, Callum.

Presently, Morgan Jo repeated, "Amber, is your daddy coming to the wedding?"

Amber swallowed. "Go on ahead and put me down for a plus-one, yes."

Morgan Jo gave her a funny look but scribbled something onto the pad.

Tires crunched over the gravel, and Amber glanced that way to see Emmett pull up in his truck.

Julia asked. "Ring bearer? Flower girl?"

Morgan Jo said, "I had a right mind to make Trav the ring bearer, but he might throw a fit. I've decided to settle on Mint and Julep, so long as they won't run off on us with the rings. Amber? Can we manage that, you think?"

Amber turned back. "We can put them on little white lace leashes. It'll be cute."

"And a flower girl?" Julia asked.

Morgan Jo looked beyond them toward Emmett's truck, now, too. He was shuffling around in the back seat for a spell, but Morgan Jo didn't take her eyes off of him. In fact, she put down her pen and stood up from the table, walking smoothly and quickly over the grass and to her fiancé and whatever it was he was pulling out of his truck.

CHAPTER SIXTY-FOUR

PRESENT DAY

Morgan Jo

Morgan's heart pounded in her chest with every step she took toward Emmett. Toward the truck.

Toward their future.

His body was folded into the back seat of the truck, and he remained there another moment before emerging with their surprise snuggled up against his chest.

Morgan reached, immediately and instinctively, into Emmett's arms and collected the little bundle. She lowered her face down and tears filled her eyes. She looked up at Emmett. "Is this for real?"

He nodded, his eyes glistening, too.

From the other side of the truck appeared a simply dressed woman. Familiar and official-looking. Emmett's co-worker, who was a registered social worker and court-appointed guardian.

For now.

"Hi, Morgan Jo," the woman greeted her.

Morgan waved, weakly, then looked again at Emmett. "What's happening right now?"

"Our paperwork is in place, which is a relief, given the hoops we had to jump through to get there. The judge looked at my handling of the case and there was no conflict of interest. We had to jump through some hoops to get the paperwork in place so quickly, and we've got a way to go... but they've granted her another visit." He glanced at the social worker, who gave him an encouraging nod and offered Morgan as sweet and assuring a smile as ever she'd seen.

"It's a start," Emmett whispered. "Right?"

She agreed and stared in wonderment down at the little one. Breathless, speechless, and yet filled with warmth and life and *hope*, Morgan hugged the precious delivery against herself and then looked down into her arms again, her eyes dazzled by the tiny little thing that lay there. "Come on," she whispered. "I think it's time we shared our news."

They walked back across the grass to the picnic table, where Amber and Julia waited, sipping cider and studying Morgan with deep suspicion.

Amber's and Julia's jaws dropped when Morgan and Emmett neared. Emmett, whose hand remained at Morgan's back, used his other hand to move the pink blanket down just a bit.

Morgan beamed at her best friend and her best cousin. "You-all, meet our little flower girl. This is Pearl. Our future foster daughter."

CHAPTER SIXTY-FIVE

EIGHT DAYS LATER

Amber

I'm here.

The text message jolted Amber from the kitchen, where she'd been waiting, outside and into the romantic environment of her cousin's wedding and the opening gala for the business.

Fresh, farm air enveloped Amber as she stepped out of the big house and smoothed her dark blonde hair. Cut fresh, it hit just below her chin and swung cleanly around her face, but she wasn't used to the tips of it sticking to her lips.

She tucked an errant strand of hair behind her ears. Her toes caught her eye.

On her feet, Amber wore sensible, strappy tan sandals, her toenails painted yellow to match the flowers she'd hold—sunflowers, naturally.

Today was the day.

Soft banjo music drifted over the crops, greeting her pleasantly. Could it be? Was that a rendition of her favorite song? "Run For The Roses?" She was certain it was. Perhaps Morgan

Jo was looking down at Amber from her window, watching her cousin recognize the heartwarming beat and smile. She looked up to the second floor windows just in time to see a cream-colored, white-lace trimmed curtain swish over Morgan Jo's bedroom window.

Squeezing her eyes shut for a moment, Amber then took a careful, labored series of steps across the lawn that sloped up gently, and leveled her gaze on the scene before her.

Beyond the porch and just through the fence, the family farm gave way to a brand-new world.

Glancing toward the gravel drive in the hopes of spying the man behind the text messages, she pinched the edges of her sleeves again, twisting the distressed fabric and chewing her bottom lip.

"Amber Lee Taylor. *Stop!*"

Amber turned left to see Julia Miles, who also wore a denim dress—and who did *not* look like a pincushion. Amber's cousin, Geddy, followed Julia. It wasn't the first they'd seen of each other that day. But it was the first they were seeing of each other after leaving the vineyard to go and shower and dress.

Julia cupped a hand beneath Amber's elbow and widened her eyes as they trailed about the stout girl's body. "You look *amazing.*"

"I *feel* fat."

Julia snorted. "Don't be silly." She pulled Amber into a careful hug, then asked, "Have you seen Morgan Jo?"

"I think she's upstairs with Aunt Carla? Getting ready."

"Probably. That *girl.*" Julia smiled big and turned to Geddy. "We'd better get out there. Where's—?"

Amber cut her off. "He just got here." She turned again to look toward the drive. "I'm going to get him."

Julia grabbed up Amber's hand and gave it a big squeeze. "Good luck."

"Thanks." Amber's breath turned shallow.

Geddy asked, "Do you want me to walk you out there?"

"No," Amber replied on a pant. "I've got this."

She turned to go, and Julia and Geddy left up toward the back of the property. Amber took another three steps just around the house, and that's when she saw him.

Tall and clad in blue jeans and a button-down and every bit the father she'd hoped for.

He saw her, too; shoved his hands into his pockets and looked sheepishly left then right, then dipped his head at her.

Before she could take another step toward him, though, Amber's stomach cramped hard, nearly doubling her over.

In a beat he was there, at her side, one hand on her back and the other holding her hand. "Are you okay?" he asked, concern filling his voice.

She looked up at him. The pain, just as sudden and strangely as it had come, had gone. And everything in that moment was more than okay.

It was everything Amber Lee Taylor had ever wanted in her life.

"I'm okay, Hank," she whispered, as he wrapped her into a hug so sweet that Amber was certain she'd never want to leave it. Not for a wedding. Or a business gala thingy. Not for nothing. But maybe... for some*one*.

"I have a surprise for you," Hank said, speaking to Amber as they pulled apart from each other, fresh with the excitement that they were building something together. Perhaps not a father-daughter bond, not yet. But something.

"A surprise?" she asked. "For *me*?"

"I brought someone else."

Amber frowned up at Hank. It was any wonder he was here at all. But Hank Taylor had accepted Barb's invitation to the wedding/gala on one condition: that he get to sit with his family.

The request was granted on instant, and now here was Amber Lee Taylor, looking up at the man she was named for, as if he was supposed to be her whole world. In a way, he was.

"You brought someone?" she asked, glad her cramp had passed but feeling hot and sticky and full of nerves.

Hank pointed his hand out toward where he'd parked and then waved someone over.

Amber squinted to see a second tall form emerge from Hank's car. Familiar. Handsome. Dressed bizarrely in a shirt and tie, rather than a movie T-shirt and jeans.

"Callum," she breathed his name.

"Miss CarlaMay gave me permission to bring him along, saying you-all had an extra seat at our table."

Amber smiled gratefully at Hank, then took a step toward Callum. When he arrived where she stood, he first put out his hand, awkwardly. "Oh," she said, offering up hers. "Right." They were still in a funny little in-between phase, where it was pretty dang clear they liked one another but pretty dang confusing on what to do with that liking, all things considered.

Callum laughed nervously and pulled his hand back before bending and wrapping Amber in a warm, gentle hug. "Hi, Amber. How you been doin'?"

"Been doin' real good. I'm so glad you came along."

"Me too. Was hoping to see what all the fuss was about. *A Taste of Moonshine Creek*, huh?"

"I didn't realize you liked wine."

"You forgot my favorite movie already?"

Amber laughed. "Oh, right. Well, I think you're in for a real treat tonight."

Callum offered his arm to Amber, and she took it. Hank followed them, and the nervous, happy trio made their way from the grassy rolling hills of the backyard of the big house, through the fence gap, and into the enchanted orchards and vineyards of Moonshine Creek.

Tall, sinewy, vine-wrapped archways gave way to stunning bouquets of sunflowers and roses, baby's breath and eucalyptus. Inside the fence, deep into the vineyard, other guests milled about. Ten minutes or so remained before the ceremony would start.

Amber spotted a nervous Rachel at the altar, reading through her talking points. She watched as Hank made his way to Barb, joining his two *other* children near the front of the bride's section.

She saw Geddy and Julia emerge from a thicket of cherry trees, Julia's face pink and dress mussed and Geddy looking like he'd hit the jackpot.

Amber felt Callum's arm drop and she glanced at him. "Is this okay?" he asked, slipping his hand down to hers and taking it up, lacing their fingers.

Amber looked down. Her heart pounded. Her skin prickled in goosebumps.

The baby kicked.

All sorts of different feels bubbled up in her chest. Fear. Anxiety. Shame, still. But mostly, she felt hope. Hope that whatever her past was, it didn't matter. Whatever her future held, she'd do right by her baby. By herself, too. And maybe, just maybe, one day, it would be her and Callum getting gussied up in whites and blacks, preparing to walk down some aisle somewhere together. Maybe one day, Amber would have a baby, a bustling family business complete with wine *and* yummy treats. Maybe one day, Amber would have all of that *and* true love.

Maybe that day was even today.

. . .

Morgan Jo Coyle stood in front of the full-length mirror in her mother's bedroom. It used to be Memaw's room, and it was the only room in the house with a full-length mirror.

It was just her and CarlaMay.

Her mother stood behind her, zipping up her dress. It was an Emmett-approved dress. A body-skimming silk bodice with thin straps and a modest neckline. Not too tight. Easy to walk in. Easier yet to get undone and off for *after* the wedding. She snorted at the thought of Emmett being so concerned with managing to get Morgan undressed later that night. She wondered how in the world they'd have any energy for lovemaking, what with the gala, the wedding, *and* a baby.

Just a week before, Emmett had also revealed that, the day after he'd proposed to Morgan, he'd begun the grueling process of earning his foster license. All along, he'd wanted her to have every opportunity. But without the pressure. His gesture wasn't only smart but it was also kind. He'd predicted that launching such a monumental task on her during the business and wedding planning... she'd struggle.

Of course, since the baby was to live with both of them, Morgan worked hard to push through all that she could. With Emmett's help (and that of a judge friend of his) she petitioned for emergency foster approval, and after just one week of online trainings, fingerprint clearances, background checks, home visits, and more—miraculously, they were approved.

Morgan and Emmett were now the temporary placement parents to little baby Pearl.

In all the madness of the ensuing week, Morgan had long forgotten the results of her medical work-up. She'd nearly forgotten her parentage troubles and her business woes and the stresses of planning a wedding. All that seemed to matter was the potential that Baby Pearl had represented.

Even Morgan's family agreed, Pearl was nothing short of a miracle in their lives. A glimmer of something new.

The surprise of motherhood wasn't lost on Morgan. In the first days, she and Emmett had talked long and hard about what their future would look like. Maybe Pearl would one day return to her family. Maybe Morgan would find herself pregnant by some incredible stroke of good fortune.

Maybe the world would end.

Maybe everything would work out just how it was meant to. That's what CarlaMay, Amber, and Julia reminded Morgan of, anyway.

Now Pearl cooed in her ivory-silk-draped baby carrier. She'd sit in that inside of a little wooden wagon, and CarlaMay would pull her up the aisle along with Mint and Julep, a motley bunch who would no doubt upstage Morgan and everything else that night. Just as it should be.

Morgan knelt down and fussed over the baby, tickling her chin and returning her binky to her little pink lips. "Mama, you be careful with her. If it's too bumpy, just pick her up. Okay?" Morgan made her mom swear.

"What about you, Morgan Jo? I'm still worried about you walking down the aisle on your own. What if you trip?" CarlaMay never stopped thinking about Morgan's bum hip, even though it wasn't too bum anymore.

Morgan assured her mother she'd be fine, checked the clock, then declared it was time to go.

But once CarlaMay and Pearl went outside to where Barb awaited with the cats and the wagon, Morgan hung back. In fact, though she'd planned to walk that aisle alone, she'd agreed with her mother.

She wasn't so worried about tripping, though. More than that, she was worried about something—or someone-else.

And so, she'd come up with an idea. After weeks of talking and getting to know each other better, Morgan had gone out on a limb and planned one last surprise. With any luck, Morgan's grand entrance would be less about her as a bride and more about something else—something *bigger* than her. Bigger than a wedding.

Bigger than the soft opening of a family vineyard.

Morgan watched from just inside the kitchen door of the big house as her mother and Aunt Barb pulled the cats on one side —a silly little stunt—and Baby Pearl in the wagon. They cleared the fence line, and that was Morgan's cue to start her walk.

"Are you ready?" he asked, appearing from the mudroom where he'd waited.

Morgan nodded and picked up her bouquet from the kitchen table. He offered his arm. She took it.

And away they went, over the grass, through the fence gap, and into an audience of family, friends, and acquaintances.

Most of the latter were blurs in the crowd, but important blurs. Various wine buffs from the area. The editor-in-chief of *Kentucky Fixin'*, a great foodie magazine. The editor of *Aged*, a wine blog out of Frankfurt. She saw just about every shop and restaurant owner in town, all of whom were anxious to carry the wine they'd be tasting tonight.

Then there were friends and family. Julia and Geddy, not-so-secretly holding hands. Jules's eyes watered. Morgan mouthed an *I love you* to her.

Tiff and Trav sat together whispering, conspiring, and smiling like a pair of goofs. With them sat Uncle Gary, who looked both out of place and utterly comfortable there, among the hodgepodge collection of wedding-goers. All three of them dipped their heads to Morgan and her escort—the cause for the whispering, no doubt.

Amber, glowing in her own right, sat with her mom and Hank on one side of her and Callum on the other. Gone was any sign of anxiety or sadness or envy. Amber looked at Morgan like she was watching an underdog win the Derby by a landslide. Joy, pride, and something akin to astonishment filled her face in the form of an ear-to-ear smile.

At the front row, Morgan glimpsed her mother, whose full attention was trained on Morgan Jo. She was crying, of course she was. Happy tears. Tears of relief. Tears that reminded Morgan that this wedding was bigger than just the union of two people. It was the reunion of many, in fact.

At the heart of the aisle awaited Emmett. His eyes were wet, too. He glanced to his left, and Morgan followed his gaze to where Baby Pearl cooed in his mother's arms. Mrs. Dawson might just be the happiest person at the wedding. Okay, well, *third or fourth* happiest, at least. Emmett looked back at Morgan, and she watched his smile ebb, his Adam's apple slide up and down, and his arm extend to Morgan's escort.

But Emmett's eyes moved back to Morgan, as though he couldn't stand to look elsewhere, even for a moment. There was a funny shuffle, where Morgan went to move aside to allow her escort to exchange a brief word with Emmett, but Emmett first pulled her up, kissing her, chastely, on the cheek and centering her in front of him.

Then, once Emmett was sure that Morgan wasn't going anywhere—that she wasn't about to run—Emmett turned to the man who'd stood, rigid and nervous and earnest, and said, "I'm glad you could make it, Father David."

The former priest smiled wryly and gave Emmett a handshake and a hug, but before he left to join CarlaMay, he reached for Morgan's hand first. "I love you," he whispered, "Morgan Jo. I always loved you." And then, he turned to Emmett. "And I know you will take good care of each other. That the two of you will do better."

"Better?" Morgan asked, smiling at her old pastor, her mother's date—her *father*. "I don't think we can do much better than *this.*" Morgan looked out at the rows of the people in her life. In them, she saw what she felt deep down inside. She saw love. Hope. Wonderment. *Secrets,* too.

And she saw that as far as any one of those wedding guests knew, hers was a nice, normal family.

A LETTER FROM ELIZABETH

Dear reader,

Thank you sincerely for reading *Secrets at the House by the Creek*. If you enjoyed my story, and want to keep up to date with all my latest releases, just sign up at the following link. Your email address will never be shared and you can unsubscribe at any time.

www.bookouture.com/elizabeth-bromke

I hope you've loved reading the Brambleberry series as much as I loved writing it. In fact, as you may know, reviews can be a huge help to writers and readers alike. I'd be very grateful if you would consider writing and posting a review if you liked my book! I'd love to hear what you think, and it makes such a difference helping new readers to discover one of my books for the first time.

One more thing: I love hearing from my readers! You can always get in touch with me on my Facebook, Twitter, or Instagram pages, or through my website.

Sincerely,

Elizabeth Bromke

KEEP IN TOUCH WITH ELIZABETH

www.elizabethbromke.com

facebook.com/elizabethbromke
twitter.com/elizabethbromke
instagram.com/authorelizabethbromke

ACKNOWLEDGMENTS

I owe so much to a great many people for the creation and fine-tuning of this story. A huge thanks, firstly, to my editor at Bookouture, Natasha Harding. Natasha, thank you for helping me figure out what goes where, when, and how. You are such a master editor! I'm forever lucky to have you on my team.

Additionally, the whole of Bookouture—thank ALL of you! Mandy Kullar, Ruth Tross, Jess Readett, Kim Nash, Emily Boyce, Alexandra Holmes, and so many more. Your belief in my work and your enthusiasm in bringing it out to the world both humble me and lift me up. Thank you!

Jenny Page and Shirley Khan, thank you both for your careful eyes on this manuscript. Your work on smoothing out the rough spots is so critical. Thank you!

Ronda Clutts: thank you for being my boots on the ground with this series. Your incredible knowledge of the region coupled with your kind and encouraging words in early editions were absolutely fabulous—thank you so, so much!

My family has always been the foundation for any successes I've managed in life. If Brambleberry is a success, then it's surely because of the love and support I've been so lucky to enjoy all of my life. My grandparents, aunts, uncles, cousins, in-laws, brother, sisters, nieces, and nephews: thank you all for being treasures in my life. Dad, thank you for always listening to me lament my plot holes. Mom, thank you for being there on my rough days and celebrating with me on my best days. Your critical eye and generous praise have gotten me to where I am. I love you so much! All of you!

Every single book I write, I start with my purpose. My intention. It always boils down to two special guys: Ed and Eddie. I love writing stories, because I love to write stories. And that I get to do this for a living? A dream come true. But at the end of the day, I started this journey only because of you two. Everything I do is for you boys. You are my world. Thank you for also being my *reason*.

Made in the USA
Las Vegas, NV
23 March 2023